Patricia Angadi, who published her first novel at the age of seventy, has had a varied and interesting career. She abandoned her conservative English lifestyle to marry Ayana Angadi, an Indian writer and lecturer, Trotskyite and intellectual. Together they founded the Asian Music Circle in the late 1940s, organising an almost continuous programme of concerts and lectures on Asian music and dance in Britain and on the continent for many years. Throughout this time, Patricia Angadi was establishing herself as a talented portrait painter. At the age of fifty she took a teacher training course and subsequently taught at a primary school for thirteen years. On retiring, she started to write full time, and is now at work on her fourth novel.

Her first two novels, *The Governess* and *The Done Thing*, are also available from Black Swan.

Author photograph by Shankara Angadi

Also by Patricia Angadi

THE GOVERNESS
THE DONE THING

and published by Black Swan

The Highly-Flavoured Ladies

Patricia Angadi

BLACK SWAN

THE HIGHLY-FLAVOURED LADIES

A BLACK SWAN BOOK 0 552 99322 0

Originally published in Great Britain
by Victor Gollancz Ltd.

PRINTING HISTORY
Victor Gollancz edition published 1987
Black Swan edition published 1989

ACKNOWLEDGEMENTS
My thanks to Father Philip Dyson, Peter
Gruner, Canon Eric James, John Lawton,
Christopher Wade and Paul Webb for their
help in building up the background to the
book.

P.A.

This book is set in 11/12 pt Mallard
by Colset Private Limited, Singapore.

Black Swan Books are published by
Transworld Publishers Ltd., 61–63 Uxbridge
Road, Ealing, London W5 5SA, in Australia
by Transworld Publishers (Australia) Pty.
Ltd., 15–23 Helles Avenue, Moorebank,
NSW 2170, and in New Zealand by
Transworld Publishers (N.Z.) Ltd., Cnr.
Moselle and Waipareira Avenues,
Henderson, Auckland.

Made and printed in Great Britain by
The Guernsey Press Co. Ltd.,
Guernsey, Channel Islands.

For Shankara and Dominic
with love

1

It was on a Sunday in May 1870 that Aaron Abrahams finally decided he could no longer live with his wife, Annie, nor put up with the inscrutable gaze of his daughter Mary. Although it was not really Mary's fault, she, of course, had to go too, much as he would have liked to have kept her away from the pervading influence of his impossible wife. To say that it was not Mary's fault is perhaps not strictly true, because the situation had always revolved round her; she was actually at the bottom of it all. The phenomenon of her unspeakable 'goodness' was the intractable kernel of the whole affair. You see it was not that Aaron Abrahams did not love his daughter, not at all. He loved her with a completeness that he found disturbing and penetrating, and which he was constantly trying to suppress. He had never meant to produce her in the first place, but having done so, he felt bound to marry her mother; unfortunately, these two women, between them, were now patently destroying his life.

Not only had his inspiration for painting gradually withered and died over the past few years, but there was lately a new and dangerous state of affairs becoming apparent. In the illustrative work he had had to fall back on while inspiration for the more fundamental side of his art escaped him, the face, and more particularly the steadfast and solemn gaze, of Mary stared out from every figure, male or female, that he drew. It was disturbing because he was unable to control it, though the emotive intensity of the intrusive expression was never in keeping with the type of humorous or light-hearted illustrations upon which he was now dependent for his living. Even in the large and elaborate compositions he still managed, laboriously, to paint for the Royal Academy Summer Exhibitions, every character in the Eastern market scenes he had always enjoyed doing seemed to swing its gaze directly out of the canvas with the same unfathomable scrutiny. It was uncanny and it unnerved him.

Jessie Stranks, his favourite model, had noticed and resented it. 'What's the good of me posing here,' she said, 'if you're just going to paint in that high and mighty daughter of yours? Unnatural I call it.' But Aaron silenced her sharply. To hear her speak so of Mary seemed almost blasphemous, and gave him a sense of shock. His totally innocent and beloved child could not be remotely connected with any suspicion of the supernatural. He felt his scalp tingle. Not that he believed in such things of course, but Annie's religious fanaticism was dangerously contagious, one of the reasons things came to an explosive head on that Sunday in May.

He had been feeling uncomfortably guilty himself, and unsure that he was not becoming, perhaps, unnaturally obsessed with his own daughter. Was it that he was so engrossed in the contemplation of one of his own creations that he had become, unwittingly, engrossed in himself? He likened the possibility to his habit of sitting long hours in gratified admiration of the painting upon which he was currently working. A sort of satisfaction in his own handiwork that lacked humility. He found it difficult to understand how he had ever brought about such a masterpiece as Mary, and equally difficult to credit Annie with any share in that achievement. Was the unequivocal gaze that stared at him out of his pictures censure for his own self-satisfaction?

Sunday was always a dangerous day in any case because of Annie's religious fervour, made more fervent,

Aaron realised, because of the tainted Jewish blood that flowed, willy nilly, in their daughter's veins. Annie never ceased to practise the ritual washing away of sins in the blood of the lamb. Aaron found that he, himself, was a constant reminder to his wife of her own perfidy in having allowed herself to marry him. The moralities had become mixed; he had imagined that he was doing the right thing in marrying his daughter's mother, and yet he had somehow ended up as the guilty party. It incensed him, though he could have dismissed the whole thing as inconsequential if it had not been for Mary. That Sunday Aaron suddenly decided that he was not going to allow himself to continue living under the constant disapprobation of his wife, nor in the gentle, but disconcerting sympathy, if that's what it was, of their enigmatic daughter.

They had been to Chapel together, Annie and Mary; Annie dressed in the brown taffeta with the ruched bonnet, and Mary in her sprigged blue voile, the tiny straw hat decorated with daisies balanced serenely on the smooth fair hair, with the blue ribbons in a bow under the chin. How extraordinarily beautiful that child was. Again he experienced difficulty in believing that either he or Annie could have been responsible for her looks or her character.

He glanced at the sour expression on Annie's face as she peeled off one of her tight kid gloves. Why did he always visualise Annie either taking off or putting on her gloves? Always in his mind the meticulous fitting of long, sharp fingers into tight skin sheaths, and then the interminable smoothing out of wrinkles down the fingers until the gloves became a second skin, a mask for what was underneath. A kind of decency cloak. And the taking off? Well, that was no more and no less than the skinning of a rabbit. A revealing of white, clean flesh beneath the outer layer. He twitched nervously as he considered the indecency of her being nakedly exposed by such a skinning process.

9

Annie reached for the pins in her bonnet, and drew them out, gleaming, elongated weapons, which she placed sideways in her mouth, clamped between her teeth, while she removed the bonnet. The hatpins were then thrust sharply through the hat again. Annie's mouth twisted as she did this, Mary noticed, and she felt sympathy for the pain that the hat might feel. She took her mother's discarded bonnet and waited for the gloves, the second of which Annie now peeled off, blew into it, flipped the air from the bloated object, and folded it compactly with its partner.

Everyone in the room was waiting for her to speak. The silence lengthened awkwardly. Jessie, the model, still held the stiff, unlikely pose of someone in the act of putting up her long hair, but her eyes were wide with anticipation, and her mouth had dropped slightly open. She was afraid of Annie Abrahams and her constant scoldings, and did not care to confront her, face to face.

'I see my warnings are not heeded,' Annie snapped. 'Working on the Sabbath, Aaron Abrahams? So you break this commandment too?'

Retaliation trembled dangerously in Aaron's thoughts, but where was the use of telling her that he was behind in the time allotted to this painting? That if it were not finished within the next day or two it would miss the exhibition?

'Look at me please Jessie,' he said, trying to wrest her startled eyes back from the alarm of the confrontation. But of course the previous moment had passed. There was no carrying on as before; the concentration had gone. Jessie was no longer a voluptuous woman, merely a frightened child. He dabbed at the background disconsolately.

'And to bring this ill-educated child down to your own level of sin,' Annie continued. 'This is monstrous. Do you not know, Jessie Stranks, that you will go to Hell if you break the commandments?' Jessie kept the pose, but her eyes swivelled again to Annie and then back to Aaron. 'It is really no concern to me, should you choose to sin yourself into Hell, except that the sin of tempting you so to do is my husband's sin, which is of some concern to my daughter, who I try vainly to protect, that she may not be influenced by her father's wicked ways.'

Aaron had stopped listening some few moments earlier, in a mute rage against the silliness of this woman who happened to be his wife. How did this monster manage to snatch from him his life, his livelihood and all that he held dear? It was unendurable and unforgivable. Jessie's eyes stared at him blindly, but when he compared them with the eyes in his painting, they were not Jessie's eyes at all, but Mary's that gazed back at him, blandly, pityingly, critically.

He glanced at his daughter across the room, where she stood beside his gabbling, jabbering witch of a wife. She appeared, to Aaron, to be isolated in a blue pool of unworldliness; gentle, meek and somehow untouched, looking down at the prayerbook she held in her hands. A feeling of love for her momentarily stifled his rage, but when she raised her eyes to his, the compassion that was in them had a very strange effect. Instead of restoring the stoic calm which gave him the strength to suffer Annie's tirades, the very opposite happened. He felt a seething explosion begin within his head. Specks, stars, splinters, flew outwards from behind his eyes and sounds split his ears.

'God damn you to Hell, you diabolical witches!' Aaron screamed. It was a completely new experience for him, but his rage was so enveloping that he could not relish the sensation. He strode forward and struck Annie's vituperative mouth with all the strength of his frustrated emotions. 'Get out of my house,' he roared, 'and take your sanctimonious, stinking, bloody daughter with you!'

Jessie started to scream hysterically as Aaron opened the front door, grasped the arms of his wife and daughter, and propelled them, with extreme force, out of his house and into the street. As he leaned back inside the slammed

11

door, a great wave of pleasurable ecstasy flooded through him.

'Stow that yelping,' he shouted at Jessie, 'and go and make us a cup of strong, hot tea with a great deal of sugar.'

So that was how Annie Abrahams found herself outraged and homeless on a Sunday afternoon in May 1870. The shock of the physical as well as the emotional blow stunned her at first into a void of mindlessness. She allowed Mary to lead her away and up towards the village.

'Mrs Grimsby will take us in,' Mary said. 'She has a spare room, I know.'

'The shame of it,' Annie kept repeating, as though in a trance. She held a handkerchief to her mouth. 'The shame of it all.'

Millicent Grimsby was a widow whose children had grown and moved on. She let their rooms to respectable elderly people for reasonable rents, and thus made a decent living for herself.

Mary explained at the door that her mother had been taken poorly in the street, and might they beg a glass of water.

'She felt faint, you see,' Mary said, 'and she bruised her mouth quite badly while falling against – against . . . If you had a little witch hazel, perhaps, or boracic water . . .'

'But of course, of course.' Millicent Grimsby hurried into the kitchen in a state of shock caused by seeing Annie so stricken and silent. Though a member of her own Chapel, Annie was not a popular woman, being known for her sharp tongue, and her high and mighty ways. If it wasn't for that dear child, Mary, there would have been few who would have bothered to pass the time of day with her. And with the strange situation of the good, devout Methodist with the Jewish, artist husband, it was difficult to keep compassionate Christian

12

thoughts uppermost at all times. There was something so very shocking about Annie's unlikely marriage. One found oneself for ever asking why. So many conflicting thoughts nagged at one. The whole thing was somehow so unacceptable. Millicent Grimsby hoped that she was a charitable woman, but there was a great deal to accept if one accepted Annie Abrahams.

She stopped her thoughts running on, remembering instead the unrecognisably grey, bruised face in her front parlour, and attempted to banish any consideration that was not charitable.

'My father is not quite himself either,' Mary said, hesitantly, as she bathed her mother's swollen cheek, holding the cloth rather firmly over the mouth, as though, perhaps, to stem any arguments. 'He needs to be left quite alone to finish a big painting he is working on. He felt that he was putting my mother under a great deal of strain, and wanted her to have a complete rest and a holiday ...' The words kept pouring out, and Mary's eyes grew wide with the monstrous lies that seemed to keep forming themselves in her agitated mind. God forgive me, she thought, and she fixed Millicent Grimsby with her wide eyes. But something had to be done to relieve all this numbing distress. The true story was too near and too shattering to be dealt with at the moment. These lies were white and cushion-like, acting as buffers between herself and the stark shock that had overtaken her.

'We were going to visit my aunt in Havering when Mama was taken poorly, but now ... I am not sure ...' It had seemed an easy thing to suggest, fifteen minutes ago, that Millicent Grimsby would surely take them in. But that was in the agitated first few moments of finding themselves ejected into the hostilities of the outside world. Then it had seemed certain that friend and neighbour Mrs Grimsby would help them in their predicament. A member of their own Chapel? Of course she would take them in. But how to explain without

13

telling? Mary opened her mouth, but no words came out, and perhaps because Millicent Grimsby was at heart a more charitable Christian than she herself knew, she had a sudden and immediate understanding of the situation. Almost like a revelation it was, she thought afterwards.

'Why don't you stay here with me?' she said. 'I have a very nice room free just now. I see your dear mother would profit from a good rest from household duties and she is certainly not in a fit state to travel to Havering. The room is quite ready, just needs a bed warmer to air the sheets, and then she can go and lie down and recover herself.'

Unaccustomed tears formed themselves in Annie's eyes. 'Very kind,' she found herself saying through clamped and painful jaws. But the shame of it all, could they hide the truth? She doubted it, but given a little rest, she would no doubt be able to think up some plausible explanation. What humiliation! That he should dare to do such a thing!

'Perhaps you will take a cup of tea with me?' Mrs Grimsby said. What's the old heathen done to her? she wondered. No respect for women, that race. There's no knowing what he's been up to with those Bohemian ways of his. She felt the need to absent herself from the disquieting confrontation of such blatant distress. It was like spying on something you should not see. She had to collect herself and her reactions to the situation.

She hurried again into the kitchen, where the servant girl scoured a saucepan slowly and deliberately. 'For pity's sake,' Millicent Grimsby shouted to relieve the tension of the moment, 'haven't you finished that washing up yet? We need tea for three in the parlour. Quickly now, get on with it, and let's hope you have the kettle on the hob and not let it get cold like you usually do. Best cups and the seed cake. Come along, come along, girl.' Tutting angrily, she swished the hem of her skirt off the floor. 'This floor does not look as though the Saturday scrub was thorough either.'

Her steps were quick and sharp along the basement

stone flags, but she made the effort to return to tranquillity as she climbed back up the stairs into the gentility of Sunday's parlour day. She was unused to such goings on in her own environment, and was unsure whether the constrained excitement she felt was altogether seemly. Was she being involved in a domestic scandal? Could she afford to be so involved? Perish the thought, Millicent Grimsby. A neighbour in need? What about the good Samaritan? Mortified, she re-entered the parlour, smiling.

'I shall be honoured to have you here for as long as you wish,' she said. 'The room will be two shillings and sixpence for the week, with breakfast and a midday meal, if that will suit?'

Mary felt a flood of relief at the temporary easing of the situation. At least time to think and to plan. She, too, felt the overpowering desire to distance herself from the preceding few hours of her life. To withdraw from living for a short time, into a state where her thoughts could float, unhampered.

In the few improbable days that followed, Annie balked at accepting what had happened and launched herself, instead, upon attempting to invent a more acceptable story. What fortitude she had shown in staying with that monster for so long! This final incident had proved, once and for all, his depravity and beastly ways.

Annie Abrahams was not a woman of great imagination, so that when she had an extraordinary dream the day after the incident, she did not doubt that it was of special significance. She was, in any case, convinced that she was wide awake at the time. She heard what she took to be the voice of John the Baptist talking to her as though he were actually in the room.

'Prepare ye the way of the Lord, make his paths straight,' she heard.

'Mark chapter one verse three,' she mouthed to herself.

'There cometh one mightier than me,' the voice went

on, but Annie came to herself before he had time to finish the quotation, and heard no more.

She was profoundly impressed with this revelation, and had no doubt that it came directly from Heaven. The following day she succumbed to her deep need to discuss her troubles with Mrs Grimsby.

'Goodness knows what immorality my husband got up to with that hussy Jessie Stranks,' she said. 'But for me, marriage vows are marriage vows, and no matter what the other party may do, I still feel it my right and bounden duty to do everything in my power to keep to those vows. Those whom God hath joined together, let no man put asunder is what I say.'

'You are indeed a good woman for having been so tolerant, Mrs Abrahams.'

'I try, Mrs Grimsby. I do my best, because you see I feel I must be prepared for that most blessed event of which I am honoured by having an inner knowledge.'

'Blessed event Mrs Abrahams?'

Annie Abrahams looked round the room, with an air of mystery, and then dropped her voice dramatically. 'Ah yes, Mrs Grimsby, I am preparing for the Second Coming.' She mouthed the last words soundlessly.

'The Second Coming, Mrs Abrahams?'

'Yes.' Scarcely more than a whisper. 'It's been revealed to me you see. The Lord Jesus is about to reappear in this wicked world to save souls and punish sinners. Oh yes.'

'Really Mrs Abrahams?' Millicent Grimsby felt uncomfortable. Had the fall affected her reason?

'True as I stand here, Mrs Grimsby. So you see why I have to insist that Mary, my innocent lamb, should not be allowed to grow up among such goings on, don't you agree Mrs Grimsby? I was going to stay with my sister in Havering in order to think things out. This unfortunate fall has indeed upset my plans.'

'I perfectly understand, Mrs Abrahams, and I venture to suggest that you should stay here some few days longer in order that you may feel quite yourself again before you undertake the journey to Havering.'

The unburdening gave Annie some relief, but then came the sudden blank fear of the future. How should she live? The little money she had in her purse would not last for long. It was here that her mind refused to deal with reality, and drew, instead, a curtain across her thoughts, including a blankness that left her grimly uncommunicative with those around her. She could find no glib story to deal with this eventuality.

Mary, who had no such confidante with whom to share her troubles, took them instead to God. She had often done this through her rather isolated childhood, and had come to look on Him as a second father who had far more time to spare than her own father. It was impossible to kneel down without everyone looking askance, so she took herself off to the highest part of the Heath, sat herself down among the tall grasses, and shut her eyes. 'Our father which art in heaven,' she said, because she had never discovered a better way to address Him, 'please help me in my distress. I have lost my family and my home and I feel desolated and alone and I don't know what to do.' She allowed a tear to seep down her cheek. She was able to hear God's answer quite clearly. It was an ability she had always possessed.

'Mary,' the voice of God said, seeming to emanate from the bushes and the hum of flies and bees and the chirping of the May birds. 'Stop crying over spilt milk. Your life is just beginning and you should get off your ass and grasp the opportunity with both hands.'

She found this expression a little strange as she was not sitting on a donkey, though there was one cropping the grass a little further down the hill. 'I have arranged something very particular for you, my girl,' the voice went on. 'But you have to take things into your own hands from now on, and incidentally deal with your mother and father as well. Go and see your father, and find out what I have arranged for you.'

'But . . .' Mary said.

'But me no buts,' said God. 'Get up and go.' So she did.

She made her way back from the top of the hill, down the High Street, and beyond towards the comfortable gentility of Downshire Hill. She imagined she was removing herself from the quiet, but lonely anonymity of childhood with every step she took. One step further and one step nearer – nearer what? There was no way of telling, but Mary became more and more sure as she covered the ground that something outstanding was in store. Hadn't God said so? Was not last Sunday to be an opening, rather than a closing of her life?

She remembered, with a slight shock, that she was about to remeet her earthly father who had called her both sanctimonious and stinking, and the memory brought a sudden flush of blood to her face. The further epithet was too shocking to dwell upon. Of course he had not meant it. He had been overpowered by the rage of the moment. His rages had always been quick and all-embracing; always uncontrollable. They took reason away from him. He did not know what he was saying. But all the same, she hesitated, and slowed her steps as the fears and doubts began to hammer back into her head.

'Get on with it,' said God.

The door of her father's studio was shut fast. She stood for a few moments in the sunshine on the path where she had so often played. This was where she had first held her new kitten in her arms. It stalked now, ten years later, from under the laurel bush and pushed itself against the hem of her skirt. The tears were uncontrollable. This was her home. These were her parents. This was her whole life. She dabbed at her eyes with her pocket handkerchief and gave a quick sniff. So this was an end, but it was also a beginning, that was the part she must remember.

She tiptoed past the windows of the drawing room, grey-blinded against the sun, and stood, irresolute, before the front door. On what followed the rap on that door could rest her future life, one way or another. Take life into her own hands, He had said. 'The future lies with God in whom we trust,' she murmured to herself to build up courage, but added, 'I do not presume oh Lord . . .' and knocked apologetically on the door. God would tell her what to say, she fervently hoped.

As she stood on the step, waiting, the familiar surroundings of the door, the garden and the cat removed her from the less familiar feel of the Millicent Grimsby neighbourhood. She thought of her mother, who was at that moment resting, behind closed curtains, in her new and estranged life. Would this time also signify her beginning, Mary wondered. Standing there upon the familiar doorstep, Mary began to flow back gratefully into the old existence, but was immediately wrenched out of it again by the sight of Jessie Stranks beside the open front door. They stared at each other in silence, startled and hostile, until Aaron appeared in the hall.

'Mary –'

'Yes Papa.'

The silence was awkward and apprehensive.

'What –? Go into the morning room.'

Mary moved obediently past him and heard him say to Jessie, 'Leave us alone. Go on, leave us. Stay in the kitchen until I send for you.'

She heard a stifled mutter from Jessie, and a door banged. Mary sat on the edge of the chair she generally sat in. Last week she was leaning back in this same chair doing her embroidery. The embroidery frame and work box still lay beside the chair. Should she remove her hat? Gloves, yes, but hat? She was unsure because this was, presumably, no longer her home and therefore she must term herself a visitor. She kept her hat on.

Aaron came in and shut the door behind him. 'I meant what I said.' He said it defensively. 'I am sorry, my dear, and more particularly for the way it happened. You are of course too young to understand these things, and I

19

know it must be very painful for you, but there can be no going back for your mother and myself.'

Why did he imagine that she was too young to understand? What was there to understand? Other than that two people, who happened to be her father and mother, were violently opposed to each other? Hated each other even, and no longer could live in peace together. Mary understood that perfectly, but realised at the same time that she had never actually considered it before, that she had, in fact, lived her whole childhood within her own isolated self. So it was a new beginning; from now on she was going to have to look outwards. A large, unexplored vista spread itself out in her mind, full of a great expanse of nothing, but with a gigantic sun just out of sight, beneath the horizon. She knew it to be gigantic because of the light it engendered, and she considered the scene with a great deal of calm and an equal amount of suppressed excitement. This was what God had promised her. She was unaware that her eyes had been fixed, steadfastly and broodingly, on Aaron's face as she dreamed up her horizon.

'Don't *look* at me like that!' Aaron banged his fist on the table, and Mary jumped in her chair, back into reality.

'I wasn't looking at you, Papa.' But how to explain that she was seeing this wide, empty plain with the sun coming up?

'You were *looking* at me Mary. How can you say that you were not? You are always looking at me in that censorious way. It is scandalous. No child should look at her father with recrimination in the regard. You disobey the simplest of the commandments by not honouring your father.' He turned his back in fury.

'But Papa, I do not mean – I had no intention. I am sorry, Papa.' Because there was no way to explain.

Aaron still stood with his back to her, his hands clasped behind him. So many mixed emotions seethed within. He had not imagined parting from Annie would be emotionally difficult. He had been toying with the idea for so long now that it had moved into the realms of fantasy. Something he could dream about. No emotions were involved, just a distant vision of release, with Mary, the bright star, flitting endlessly and happily between them. This, though, was reality, and had to be dealt with here and now. He kept his back to her.

'I think you must realise that it is impossible for your mother and me to live amicably together. I very much regret it, you must understand, but I cannot work under such strain. I fall, it seems, far below the standard that your mother has set, added to which I have a temper which at times I am unable to control. I do not trust myself to control it. It is therefore far wiser for you and your mother to live separately, away from me.'

Mary felt the tears dribbling down her cheeks, but did not like to dab at them in case the movement might interrupt his flow of words. He had not been able to talk to her for a considerable time. She remembered the childish years, when she and he had talked, discussed and laughed together. They had been such friends then, whenever he could spare the time. There had been so much love between them. Hers was still there, but had to be battened down and held sharply in control, because to show it made her mother angry and bitter with her.

'But how and where shall we live, Papa?' she asked, in an attempt to bring her own emotions under control. Bring things down to the practical. 'I will gladly look after Mama of course but . . .'

He did not turn round, but straightened his back, and raised his head to look out of the window at the tops of the trees in the garden beyond. 'I have already arranged for this,' he said. 'Though the catastrophe of a few days ago came upon me before I was prepared, I had already foreseen a parting, and was waiting only for courage and determination to set the whole affair in motion.'

Mary was taken by surprise. In the silent years of adolescence, had she so misjudged her father to imagine

21

him sullen, unfeeling and unable to stand up to her mother's dominance? And all the while he had been aware, caring and planning for the future?

'Papa, I did not mean to seem sanctimonious, truly I did not,' she said suddenly, with explosive intensity at the discomfort of having so misjudged him.

He turned then, and they flew together in a rush of reconciliation and pleasure.

'I know, Mary, I know that. And you must forgive me for saying such things that I did not really mean. The reason for my outburst was that I recognised you today as my own conscience, and could not bear to come face to face with the way my conscience was looking at me.'

It was a blissful moment for Mary, this sudden understanding of her father after so many barren years.

The emotional embrace dissolved, but the charged atmosphere persisted, and they sat down, facing each other, their hands still joined.

'You know I own two adjacent cottages off the High Street do you not?' he said. 'And that the rooms are let out to bring in a small income?'

'Of course, I have been there several times with Mama to oversee the running of it.' Mary remembered the slight anxiety she had felt at entering the narrow precincts of the crowded street, even though Annie had never allowed an approach from any but the lower end, where the bigger houses were situated. Mary had wondered sometimes what dangers lurked up at the further end where it joined the High Street. The house at the end was built over the entrance to the street in the form of an arch, which looked rather inviting she thought. Her father's cottages teetered on the brink of respectability, being near to Gardnor House and Burgh House and the big white house on the corner that belonged to a rich wine merchant. She remembered the occasions that she and her mother had been on their tours of inspection, and the sleazy air of gentility that seemed to emanate from the rather prim exterior of the

22

cottages, the too neat front gardens with the large lavender bushes and the pink roses round the door.

'These cottages I am about to make over to you and your mother, equally between you, to do with them what you will. Your mother will doubtless want all the lodgers out. I can supply you with a small income, but it may be irregular, so it would be better if you could at least retain some of the paying guests, or perhaps open a small shop of some kind. I have noted in the past, Mary, that you have some good, practical qualities. It will need a deal of common sense and managing ability to make a success of any such venture, particularly in the face of probable opposition from your mother.' He smiled ruefully, and raised her hand to kiss it. 'Do you think you can take on this task? Are you up to sharing your father's responsibilities?'

Mary clasped his hand in both of hers. She was pink with excitement. 'Oh yes, dear Papa, of course, of course I can. I should be most proud and honoured to be of some worth in our family at last.'

Aaron stood up rather abruptly, not wishing to see any note of censure in his daughter's eyes for the admittedly shameful shirking of duties that were rightly his. He felt that he was taking advantage of her innocence and inexperience. How could a child of her gentle nature ever be expected to stand up to the vituperative Annie? He was condemning her to a life of misery. It was unforgivable.

But Mary was exuberant. Had she not been chosen by God to fulfil a herculean task? She looked at her father as he turned towards her, but then looked down at his feet in case the glance should be misinterpreted. She felt a little ashamed of the exhilaration that kept welling up within her, and the feeling of relief that now, at least, she could shelve the anxiety that had left her mother and herself penniless and homeless.

The sun was actually showing itself above the horizon. Her gaze crept up to Aaron's face as she relaxed her control, and she looked without seeing, and contemplated without thinking on the fact that she had, within the last few days, changed her position from a useless, unimportant appendage to her parents' lives to becoming the central pivot of the family. It fairly took her breath away. Such responsibility God had given her. She offered up a quick word of thanks in awe and gratitude. That He should have chosen her for this honour! 'My cup runneth over,' she said to Him for want of a better expression.

'You're welcome,' He said, 'But mind you don't waste the opportunity, because I have a bigger, better task for you later.'

Mary flushed with pleasure and said, 'Behold the handmaid of the Lord, let it be unto me according to thy word.'

'What did you say?' said Aaron, but without waiting for an answer, he started towards her with his fist raised, symbolically against her. 'Do I have to tell you yet again?' he roared. 'It is both dishonourable and impolite to stare so!'

This time, Mary did not shift her gaze, because her thoughts were elsewhere, at the centre of the family trinity. There was no real threat in him, and she felt a warm rush of love.

'I love you, Papa,' she said. 'And I will look after Mama to the best of my ability. We shall not be a burden upon you.'

Aaron turned again from her in fury. The presumption of this child was beyond belief. But his anger dissipated and became tempered by other sentiments. Love was paramount, of course, but he had this belief in her. Was it just that he wanted to believe in her ability to resolve these present adversities? How could so young a child have such capability?

'Bring us some tea, Jessie,' he called out of the door.

2

Annie Abrahams remained mortified by the violent change in her circumstances. She had not seen it coming, could not have imagined any such thing in fact, and the shock left her frozen, inside a brooding bitterness, for the rest of her life. Mary had returned from the visit to her father a changed personality. This was something else Annie was never able to come to terms with. At one stroke Mary had turned from the submissive, silent child who was a credit to her mother's wise and god-fearing upbringing, into a self-reliant, confident young woman, who knew exactly what she was about and where she was going. This irreparable damage that Aaron had managed to inflict upon her daughter in the course of a single afternoon was the final insult for which Annie could never forgive him. Naturally she could not imagine that it might not have been the earthly father who was to blame.

The news that they were to be installed in the lodging house owned by her husband, and that they would be expected to run it for their own profit, was yet a further bitter pill.

'A common lodging house keeper,' she repeated endlessly. 'The wicked shame of it all.'

Finding herself confronted with sudden responsibility, Mary sailed serenely into her new role. It was a remarkable transformation, but she was not perturbed, because she had half known that it would happen all along. The idea had often come back to her in her dreams; disturbing dreams, with herself always at the eye of a storm. Strange that the inferno never seemed to touch her. Possibly this was because she was conscious that God was there too, watching her. Testing her? Was He really the benign, all-caring father figure, or the malevolent tyrant? In Heaven as it is on earth, she thought.

'It will not be a common lodging house, Mama,' she said. 'It will be a haven for the family that we will gather around us. We will only take in special people so that it will become a special family home.'

Annie's lips straightened in a thin, unforgiving line. 'Family? The word has no meaning any more. Our family has been broken and destroyed by the whim of one, wicked man. The shame of it all. A common lodging house.'

'I am going to make preliminary arrangements, dear Mama.' Mary placed the smelling salts upon the table beside her mother's chair. 'You rest yourself here and I will arrange everything for our removal to our new home.'

The excitement she felt at the thought of what there was to be done was out of all proportion. This was surely the beginning of a great adventure, one for which she had been waiting – the great adventure of her life. She was being propelled towards it with an all-impelling force.

'This time,' she declared to herself as she walked up the High Street, 'I shall approach the street from this end.' It was important to tackle the task from every angle. To start at the beginning.

The close proximity of the connected shops on either side gave the access an air of cosiness rather than the disreputable ambience she had always imagined. The tradesmen and their houses enclosed rather than threatened, and there were smiles and chatter. As the lane widened out, the terraces became more private, though seemingly poorer. Most doors were open to the street, with the old and the young spilling out of them. They watched Mary's every step with an unhurried lack

26

of indifference, a staring consideration which was not hostile. She dispensed guarded smiles, which were occasionally returned.

Approached from this end, their own cottages were quite a way down, and were detached from the more usual terraces; two joined together, with two front doors and each one different, one being much smaller than the other. They seemed to lean, with a slightly genteel air, towards the more prosperous end of the street.

The door of the smaller cottage was opened to her, and she was at once swallowed up in the crammed, rather stifling, living, bed, all-purpose room. But in spite of the over-crowded and overwhelming density of the small space, Mary became unexpectedly conscious of a gust of explosive laughter welling up inside her. And she could hear it all round her. What a strange thing, she thought, because all the surface surroundings were uncommonly sad. She decided that the house was welcoming her in some inexplicable way, and she smiled down at the cross little woman who had opened the door to her and who had been in charge of the cottages for the past few years.

The smile was not returned. Resentment flared, instead, from every movement, and it was clear that being beholden to this slip of a girl was degrading. The curt note of dismissal from Mr Abrahams was humiliating enough; it would have been only decent to send his wife to make arrangements – unpleasant as the woman was – but an eighteen-year-old girl with enough airs and graces to fill the Crystal Palace – it was nothing short of shocking.

'It's most upsetting,' Mrs Darke said as she sat down on the edge of the chair. 'What with nowhere to go, and the money being that tight. We did our best to please. To be dismissed so sudden, it's a great shock.'

Mary's heart lurched in the middle of its new-found exhilaration. She had not thought of the side effects. 'Oh Mrs Darke, please do not think that my father was displeased with the performance of your duties. This is

27

not at all in his mind, I do most earnestly assure you. It's just – just a change in our family circumstances. I beg you to believe me. And as for accommodation, I am sure that we could assist you until you found something suitable.' But this cross little lady was no part of the loving family, her mind insisted, that she would gather around her in this affectionate home. No part at all. 'Until you found something suitable, we should be happy to offer you hospitality.'

Mrs Darke was angrily mollified. But there was no need to show gratitude to this chit of a girl. It was the least they could do for the faithful service they had been given.

The slight hesitation in the rush of Mary's excited anticipation was submerged quickly. 'If I might look round quietly in order to give my mother some idea . . .'

Mrs Darke jangled the keys at her waistband. 'I will escort you to ensure that my ladies and gentlemen are ready to receive you. Though I have already warned them of the changed circumstances that will ensue. These two ground floor rooms is where myself and Mr Darke were wont to reside, the better to oversee our guests whenever they entered the other house.'

Gaolers, Mary thought. Keys and bolts and watching eyes through chinks and curtains. The room smelt odious. She turned to Mrs Darke, and held out her hand for the keys. 'I am most grateful for your help, but I have many things to note down and consider. I do not wish to take up your time, Mrs Darke.'

'I assure you, I am quite prepared . . .'

'No, I do insist. Perhaps we might take a cup of tea in some little time before I go?'

Mrs Darke gave an explosive, barely controlled expression of exasperation. 'Most irregular,' she complained, but Mary's hand remained outstretched until the keys were handed over. 'All numbered,' said Mrs Darke sharply, and she swung, frowningly, away towards the back room.

Though now two separated cottages, the house had obviously been built as one. Mary stood back as she emerged from Mrs Darke's rather humble front door, and surveyed the house with a proprietorial air. How satisfactory to have a house of one's own. She checked herself; not her own of course, half belonged to Mama, and there was a group of people inside who still looked upon it as their home. But never mind, she held the key in her hand and felt every inch an owner. The key was very large, and turned rather laboriously in the oversized keyhole. She wondered to herself at the idiosyncracy of keeping the front door locked in the daytime, when most other people's doors in the street stood wide open, but realised that Mrs Darke probably enjoyed power of custodianship as much as she herself enjoyed the sense of the ownership. Shame on you, Mary Abrahams, she muttered to herself as she pushed the door back on its unwilling hinges, that you should be so ungenerous in your thoughts.

The hallway was narrow, and ran from front to back. The back door at the end of the passage was open, and she saw sunlight dappled on the wall beyond, at the back of the yard. It looked inviting, and to Mary, at that moment, quite beautiful. The small, spiralling staircase, with its curving handrail, wound upwards next to the back door, climbing past a window that silhouetted the neat, white bannisters. The whole scene was inviting her in; polished, expectant, waiting to be brought to life.

A door on her left was unexpectedly open, and she knocked, rather hesitantly, before looking into the room. It was quite empty of furniture, and ran through into the back room, from which two girls emerged, talking loudly and heatedly. Mary recognised them as her sisters.

But I have no sisters.

Her mind was blocked with confusion.

'Hi Mary, love, what's with you? You look as though you've seen a ghost.'

'I still want the room across the hall, Mags, whatever you say. It's just me. I felt it right at the start. Absolutely must have it.'

29

'And you think I don't know exactly why? Just so that you can let your men in and out of your own front door without people knowing. Not that I mind that, but you choose such awful types, don't you? And they scrounge so.'

'God, Mag, you're hopeless. I can't believe it. When we're going to have somewhere that we can share with friends, you make remarks like that, I mean what is this if we don't share? It's just so great that Ma and Pa have finally made the split. Just so great.'

'You can't say that,' Mary heard herself saying as her eyes filled up with tears. 'It's all so sad.'

'Why don't you shut up Mim.' Mary had arms wrapped round her and felt a kiss on her cheek. 'Of course it's sad, Em, in lots of ways. But you have to admit they were pretty impossible together, weren't they? Their marriage had become a bit of a farce really, they've actually been separated for years, haven't they?'

Mary's tears overflowed. 'But families should stay together, however difficult it is. They plighted their troth and everything.'

'Plighted, plit, plought,' said Mim. 'And thereto I plought thee my troth, that's nice.'

'It's wrong to split up when they've been married so long,' Mary insisted. 'And how are we going to manage alone?'

Maggie tightened her hold round Mary's waist in a hug. 'Don't you worry, love. Haven't I always looked after you? Let's face it, Ma was never much good with kids, was she? Couldn't help it, poor thing, but she just wasn't the motherly type. I think this is a fantastic solution, I really do. Thank God for Pa's money and the fact that they've finally decided to do the right and proper thing.'

'Ma and Pa really are something, aren't they?' Mim said. 'I mean how many parents would set up their kids in a house of their own, just tell me that, how many would?'

'Not many could afford to,' Maggie reminded her.

'Possibly, but even so, it's pretty progressive to hand out the money now instead of waiting till they're dead isn't it?'

'Might be interpreted as shelving responsibility and paying to get us off their backs.'

Mary looked from one to the other of these protagonists and felt that she could not align herself with either. 'No, no,' she said, tears still at the ready. 'You are wrong, I know you are, they could never want to get rid of us, it's wicked to say that. They are just being wonderfully generous.'

Mim laughed. 'Trust Em to ferret out the positive and Mag to settle for the negative. And me? I'll go for the opportune and make the most of it.'

'I still think it's wrong,' Mary moaned, and Mim flung her hands in the air.

'Oh belt up, darling. For God's sake, stop being so pious.' She lit a cigarette. 'We're actually going to *be* one great big happy family from now on, unlike the small, split, unhappy family we have been all our lives. Don't you see that? It's the family of man, man.'

'Family of men, more like,' Maggie said. 'Mim's men. But let's look at the rest of the house again and decide who's going where.'

Both girls moved past Mary into the hall and turned towards the back of the house. Mary followed them out and found the hall empty. Where was she? For a moment her mind was clouded and unsure. The empty hall was full of voices. She walked to the end and climbed the small, winding stair, with its curved bannister, and wondered where everyone had gone. But who was she looking for? At the top of the stairs there was a closed door. Maggie's room? But who was Maggie? She knocked, and the door was opened by a frail-looking woman with a baby; two other children sat on the floor. The window curtains were torn and dirty, and there was a smell of paraffin oil and cooking.

Certainty came back. 'I am Miss Stein,' she said, and

31

froze with shock. *Stein*? There was a fractional silence while her mind tried to reason, failed and instead, wiped the inexplicable from her memory. 'I am Miss Abrahams,' she said, 'and my mother and I will be taking over the cottages, I believe Mrs Darke may have told you of the change?'

'We do pay regular,' the woman said, her eyes widening.

'Oh I know, I know. I was just making a preliminary visit to see that everyone knew of the new arrangement, that's all. What a dear baby!'

Mary had a further moment of uncertainty as to whether she had been optimistic in imagining that she could stimulate a family atmosphere in this sort of surrounding with this sort of people. They seemed to shrink away from her very regard. I will overcome, she found her mind repeating, and at the same moment she looked over her shoulder because she felt the presence of two beings standing close beside her. But there was nothing. It was all a big game. She could hear laughter everywhere as she explored the house.

It was much bigger than she had imagined. She and her mother had been entertained in Mrs Darke's front room whenever they had visited before, and she had only glimpsed the rest of the house when Annie had once insisted on inspecting the front room of the letting house. Mary remembered it as very crowded with both people and furniture. She recollected several adults and several children in a dark, evil-smelling room that struck her as hostile and frightening. Today it had been full of sun and emptiness and smelling of patchouli. Whatever was patchouli? She could not recall ever hearing the word before. And weren't her sisters there? The memory clouded and erased as soon as the thought emerged, leaving her with the unsatisfactory half recall of something that she wished to remember but could not.

There were so many rooms that she had not expected. Because of the elevation of the site, the back of the house

32

became three storied, with the lavatory and outhouses in the yard at the back of an extended L-shape, and the bakery and wash house buried under part of the rest of the building. There were also many cell-like rooms, some with windows and some without, in this semi-basement area. A ladder up to a trap door came out under the white staircase in the hall. Her mother would have said she was behaving in an unladylike manner, scrabbling about below stairs like this. Her hat had been knocked a little askew, and there was a smear of dirt on her cheek. Her hands were dirty, but it was essential to explore and discover the place completely. Find out where that laughter was coming from.

Something about being three sisters – it kept flashing in and out of her mind as she made her way back along the hall. When she reached the door she had opened when she first started to look over the house, everything became momentarily clear. Of course, the three of them had been talking in this room, the other two must still be in there.

She turned the handle, but found the door locked. There being no reply to her knock, she took out the bundle of keys and opened the door. The room was full of furniture. Two beds, a wardrobe, a cupboard, a chest of drawers, a big fireplace with ashes in the grate, and a wall where there had not been one before. Heavy, red curtains were drawn across the window, and there was an unpleasant, fusty smell. But what had she expected to find? This was just as the room had been when she viewed it last with her mother. All quite normal.

She relocked the door, trying to sort out her half-memories. Must be that she was getting flashes of dream memories. That must be it. All part of those strange dreams of hers. But enough of all that nonsense; a task lay ahead, this at least was a reality. And she stepped briskly out of the front door and went to take a cup of afternoon tea with Mrs Darke.

33

3

Mary Stein had always felt herself to be a most inadequate character, in whom something was unaccountably missing. Away from her sisters she was incomplete and unhappy, like a lost soul, drifting. She was fifteen when Maggie went to University and this was the first tearing apart of herself that she had experienced. The following year Mim got into RADA, and Mary retreated into a limbo of despair. Mim, with her optimism, was forever expecting tomorrow to be better, while Maggie, because of her practicality, appeared to be confidently adequate and quite complete.

The explosion of grief that drowned Mary's final days at school lingered on at home in a blank and fearful apathy. She resisted her mother's attempts to dispatch her to a smart, residential school to learn domestic science, but agreed to continue lessons on the Irish harp, and to start private singing lessons. She did not feel in the least fulfilled by either of these activities, but agreed with Maggie when she said that it was better to be doing something other than sitting around moaning herself into an early grave.

'I'm so strengthless and crummy,' she said. 'I wish I knew what makes me like this. You and Mim aren't, and here am I, undecided, unsure, unclever, uneverything.'

'It's your genes,' Maggie said.

'My jeans?' Mary looked down at her legs. 'What's wrong with them?'

Maggie fell back against the wall, laughing. 'God!

Who but you would get the wrong meaning of *that* remark!'

Mary worked it out sheepishly and joined in the laughter. 'Yes, I suppose – that's just what I mean though. I never seem to get the point of anything. Why is everybody so much cleverer than me?'

'It's probably the bomb,' Mim said, 'or the lead in the air or aerosols not stopping ultra violet or because we eat too much meat or don't eat enough roughage or beans. And anyway, who says you're not clever?'

'I do,' Mary said. 'It's all so depressing.'

'You're not as clever as Maggie,' Mim said, 'but then neither am I, and you're far, far nicer than either of us. That's your thing. Maggie's clever, I'm sexy and you're nice. You're the only one of us three that'll get to Heaven, just think of that, Miss Em Stein, us two peering through the pearly gates at you, sitting smug on a cloud and twanging at your old harp.'

So Mary did her best to overcome her misgivings, or at any rate, keep them hidden from the world. She found this difficult to achieve, but persevered. If something is unpleasant, then don't think about it, look around for the good things. Don't question things you don't understand. Accept that there is much that is not understood and, perhaps, not understandable. The suspicion that she was not entirely within the world in which she found herself, was altogether too difficult and too insubstantial to be thought about at all. Thought only caused more confusion and more doubt. Best leave it alone.

Mim had never had much trouble with sweeping things under carpets, convincing herself, while ignoring the more unpleasant aspects of every day, that in all probability they weren't really there; she had been mistaken in ever thinking that they were. A failure could be looked on as an achievement if seen from another angle. If you did not expect too much, then you would not be disappointed. All men, for instance, were possible lovers – not necessarily good lovers, mind, nor was it necessary

35

to consider them as permanent, or the type one would want to shack up with, but everyone was worth a try, after all. She did not, in any case, feel completely at ease with any man unless there had been a modicum of love-making, or at least flirtation; more, really because she liked to reveal the whole of herself at once, so that there could be no mistaking what sort of a person she was. It was a kind of confession before you did anything rather than after. No one should have any illusions, then they could not be shattered.

'But you waste so much *time*,' Maggie complained. 'Hopping in and out of bed like that, when you could be doing something far more interesting and worthwhile.'

'Like attending a political meeting or being dragged off the road by the fuzz?'

'Exactly. At least that's not opting out. It's trying to take part in life.'

'I just can't believe in that taking part business. It's all going to happen anyway. I mean how *can* you believe the bomb isn't going to do us all in before we're very much older?'

'It's people like you who make it possible, isn't it? You just sit back and let it happen.'

'Lie back and enjoy it you mean? Whoaho – get 'em off darling!'

Maggie gave an irritated snort of laughter. 'You're a hopeless, licentious libertine.'

'A libertine's a man.'

'Don't be so sexist. Where's your pride? If men can be libertines, so can women.'

Laughter took over as suggested appellations were mulled over: Don Joan; lecheress; Cassanovi; dirty old woman; or on the other hand, easy layer; homme fatal; nymphoman.

Mim immersed herself in drama school and its continual perturbation. The constant change in the home venue only added to the drama of general living. The intensity was heightened, and therefore became a further experience from which to draw acting proficiency. She gave blow by blow accounts of her own imaginative interpretations of the family dilemmas to her friends.

'I feel desperately sorry for poor Ma, I mean, Pa is so impossible, really he is, much as I love him, and there's Clare, that's my mother, really and truly in love with this gorgeous man – I actually fancy him myself – he's just wonderful and he *needs* me, I know it. But it's all so romantic with them, and it must be the absolute pits to love someone like that and have to feel guilty about it because he's so much younger, for one thing, and of course he's married too and got an angelic baby. And Pa really is being a bit of a stinker; you know, sort of needling her the whole time and poking fun at her. And he really can't talk because some of his girl friends are the absolute end. And then they are for ever blaming themselves and each other about us, because I suppose we are rather in the way after all. Not that I mind in the least, but I have this *sweet* little sister, who is out of this world – not knowing about things I mean. You absolutely must meet her because she's a total innocent, sort of. She gives you a real insight into how innocent people think and feel and everything. I would say she's pretty unique somehow in this day and age. I based Desdemona *entirely* on her the last time I played it.'

Mim was fond of stating that relationships were an important part of her life. 'I feel so incomplete without a partner. I just have to share things you see. I mean, what is life if you can't share it with someone?' It was difficult for her to admit, even to herself, that the partners she had tested out so far had never lived up to expectations, and had left her with a sense of humiliation, mortification and disillusion. She could never quite rid herself of the suspicion that she was, herself, somehow to blame for this situation, though for the life of her she could not imagine why.

Maggie had always had a very different outlook on life

from her sisters. She was fanatically tidy and well ordered, and enjoyed the logic of a place for everything. The Convent, where they had all spent their school years, had certainly appealed to that side of her character, with its regularity and its methodical consistency.

The home intervals were disturbing, because all values were at once up-ended. The chaos of the home environment had no apparent goal. The element of chance as to where it was all leading could not be worked out in advance, even mathematically, and she was uneasy at the accepted underpinning of the seemingly purposeless life; at, for instance, the leaving of her own clutter to be cleared up by paid hands. Clothes were cleaned, mended and looked after, and food was thought out, prepared and cleared away by clockwork, unseen elements. She felt her life was being lived for her, both at home and at school, and she became enclosed and remote.

Once at Essex, her world changed immediately. The first few weeks were hectic and exhilarating. What she imagined might be termed her soul felt freed and brimful of energy. For the first time, the way ahead seemed to belong to her, rather than to the world in general. She saw it as a new file, with endless clean pages to be organised, titled and filled in with incidents of her own choice, but with each successive term she found it increasingly difficult to keep her preliminary aims clear.

The main cause for the uncertainty could perhaps be said to have stemmed from her meeting, within the first week of the first term, Matthew Sharpe, a sociology student. He was tall, lank and bent, with long, stringy brown hair to his shoulders which he sometimes tied back with a shoe lace. He wore steel-rimmed glasses and a large, unkempt moustache.

'Can we presume you chose Essex for its promised student participation and freedom from unwarranted authority?'

They sat in the coffee bar, which seemed to be the general meeting place; a sort of parade ground or common market where one paraded oneself and one's outlook on life. Maggie had expected the more formal 'What are you reading?' or 'What's your scene?' His question took her a little by surprise.

'Er, no, not really. It was just my third choice.'

He was obviously disappointed, and slouched back in his chair in a glum silence. She searched round for something to say in order to redeem herself. She remembered the nuns had not been at all keen on her putting Essex as a third choice, but she had not thought to ask why. 'You put it first?' she asked.

'Yeah.' He began to roll a cigarette. 'Just have to see if it lives up to its brochure.'

She wondered if the cigarette was marijuana, and felt embarrassed that she would not even be able to tell by the smell.

Those first weeks were an isolated period, when all the certainties of the final year as a prefect at school collapsed into a welter of self-doubt and insecurity. She seemed to meet Matthew Sharpe more often than probability might reasonably allow, and wondered whether his possible interest stemmed from a corresponding sense of inadequacy, or whether he was attracted to her. She did not feel that she could reciprocate; he looked too scruffy, it offended her sense of order. But towards the end of the first week, she began to look for him in the coffee bar, and to feel slightly outraged and disappointed if he were not there.

She found herself plunged into left-wing politics because it was all so rational and the right thing to do. There were no arguments against it, only instincts, and these, as Matthew so rightly pointed out, were the result of the sort of upbringing she had had. The sort of upbringing that had taught her to accept the inferior state of women and the inevitability of atomic warfare, he said. It was a time of exhilaration, exasperation and undoubted enjoyment.

Looking back on the whole experience of those three extraordinary years, she marvelled that such a tightly packed period could have passed so instantaneously.

'Altogether quite a concentrated piece of living,' she told her sisters. 'It's made me want to go into banking because money's the only way to wield power you know, as Marx so rightly pointed out. But unlike him, I intend to make use of the present system rather than attempt to overthrow it.'

'I think it's easier to make use of men, rather than the systems they preside over,' Mim said, 'because then you don't have to make yourself unpopular to succeed.'

Mary felt uncomfortable and upset. 'I don't want to make use of anybody or anything,' she said, 'so I suppose I shan't succeed.'

'You will,' said Maggie glumly, 'because you're just so good and gentle and sweet that everyone will rush to your aid and defence and you'll come off better than any of us. It's women like you that encourage men to remain the chauvinistic pigs they are.'

Mim laughed. 'Take no notice of her, lovey. It's the ultra left-wing Essex-type influence making itself felt, she's not being personal. She just wishes she had some of your goodness and a bit of my fatal attraction, so that she wouldn't have to work so hard at living.'

'I don't have to work hard,' Maggie said. 'It's just that when there does seem to be a glimmer of hope that the young of the world are about to get a bit of power into their hands, then I think we ought to see to it that we don't waste the opportunity.'

Mary brightened. 'Oh I do agree,' she said, 'and people are changing all the time aren't they? I mean they are beginning to talk about the power of love and the need for peace.'

Mim and Maggie both groaned. 'Love is all you need in fact,' said Mim. 'So let's join the flower children and pick flowers to put in the soldiers' rifles.'

Mary put her head on her knees to hide her distress.

She hated the cynicism. But why did she have to get upset? It was stupid. 'You're so negative,' she said.

'I'm just realistic,' Maggie said and wished that she wasn't.

'It would be neat if everyone really thought love was all you needed, wouldn't it?' said Mim. 'You'd be so busy going to bed with everyone that there wouldn't be time for bombs.'

'I suppose the best thing about being at Essex,' Maggie said, 'was that I met up with Matt. Even though I often think he's just a weak-kneed drip and he thinks I'm a hard-headed, calculating, rationalist type female, we're really quite good for each other.'

Mary wondered why she felt no interest in anyone outside her immediate family. Probably something lacking in her character she decided.

4

Clare Stein, the mother of Margaret, Miriam and Mary, was born Clare D'Arcy in 1920. She was brought up in a small castle in Herefordshire, which became more dilapidated each successive year of her childhood, because her father and mother were unwilling to change their lavish style of living to meet the diminished family fortune. She recognised, quite early on, that her parents, her brother and herself were really caricatures of the English aristocracy, and she broke free from the hunting, shooting and debts as soon as she was able.

The opportunity, in the shape of Sam Stein, came her way in 1939, a few weeks before the outbreak of war. Clare found herself overwhelmed by both his practicality and his brazenness, two characteristics she had not really met up with before. They were married within three weeks of having met, and the novelty of the situation had not had time to wear off before war was declared, and Sam had enlisted to fight for the cause of European Jews. It was all so quick and desperate, that Clare was in the WAAFs with the tears of parting still in her eyes, before any of the frothy ferment of the occasion had subsided.

After those first few weeks, they were separated for nearly the whole of the six years of war: Sam for the most part as a prisoner of war, and Clare enjoying a socially jolly, faintly hazardous, time stationed at various airfields round Britain.

They met again, as complete strangers, in 1944, when

they opened up Sam's substantial house in Sunningdale, and cautiously settled themselves down as a prosperous, post-war couple. Sam slipped back easily into his pre-war business career, and Clare adjusted herself yet again, from aristocratic caricature, through RAF wartime camaraderie, to comfortable, if commonplace, suburbia. At least it was different, and for the first few years she enjoyed the novelty of the socialising which accompanied Sam's business successes. It was not actually so far removed from the pre-war, country house gregariousness, or from the frenzied, wartime parties. The same surface tension prevailed, which she did nothing to disturb, in case she should drown in the reality beneath.

She became pregnant in 1948, and had her three daughters within five years. She was acutely conscious of her failure to produce the boy Sam had wanted, and felt, for many years, that she should somehow try to make it up to him. The girls' names were part of this intention. Margaret was an attempted amalgamation of the names of Sam's mother, Martha, and Clare's mother, Margot; a compromise that pleased neither of them. Clare then felt constrained to leave the second daughter's naming entirely to Sam, who wilted under family pressure for a biblical name. She was called Miriam, which Clare quietly detested. On the arrival of the third daughter, Sam gave up hope and any interest in the name. As the letter M seemed to have taken hold, Clare decided that the most ordinary and uncontroversial of the Ms was undoubtedly Mary; which choice Sam silently found obnoxious. It was possibly the mutual dislike of their daughter's names that led to the immediate abbreviation of them. Margaret became Maggie within moments of being born, Miriam was Mim, and Mary, though occasionally given the benefit of the whole name, was known as the last of the Ms, and thus Em.

Whether it was the choice of names that started off the slide, or whether the discrepancy between their characters and outlooks was merely intensified by the complex naming process was hard to discern, but after Mary's birth, Clare and Sam's relationship began to disintegrate slowly and relentlessly. Both partners were surprised and sad that such a thing should be happening, and yet increasingly unable to do anything about it. They clung to the alliance some ten years after the eventual break was obvious to all around them, and after both had found other partners with whom they spent most of their time. They argued endlessly with each other, agreeing only that they must on no account upset the girls and that the other had to make only a slight adjustment for the marriage to be absolutely compatible. Finally, they reluctantly wrenched themselves apart and agreed to go their own separate ways. 'You'd be so wonderful, baby,' Sam said, 'if only you could love me and trust me that little bit more than you do.'

'But it's not that I don't love you, darling,' Clare would reply. 'It's just that life is so utterly boring for me when you're not here, and you hardly ever are here, so I have to seek amusements elsewhere and with others. It's not that you don't do the same.'

Sam shrugged his bear-like shoulders. 'Women seem to crop up everywhere in my work, and you know I can't stand on ceremony. I mean, where's the sense in entertaining a female client and stopping short of going to bed?'

'Where indeed?' said Clare, so they looked for their own establishments, while remaining good friends on the whole.

'Such a shame,' Sam told his friends. 'She's a wonderful woman, you know. Just this bloody inferiority complex that stops her from achieving her real potential.'

'If only he could realise the depth of his truly loving and affectionate self,' Clare said. 'He would be perfect.'

Thus both drifted towards other lives with a sense of bewilderment and disbelief at how things could have gone so wrong. There was renewed discussion and argument about the girls, then aged between sixteen and twenty-one, who had been away to a private convent school for most of their growing lives.

'We felt it important that they should be taught some sort of belief,' Clare explained to friends. 'We did think of the Jewish Free School, but it would have been so difficult to cope at home. I mean what do either of us know about Jewish customs? Supposing they'd come home every night and refused to eat bacon or wanted to wear hats all the time – oh that's only men, isn't it? Anyway, we haven't got two fridges. But we both knew that professionals just had to know more about bringing up children than we did, so boarding school it had to be. This convent was in such a fearfully nice place, and the nuns looked so clean and sure of themselves. It was a tremendously good choice, they were all madly happy.'

Confronted, later, with three adult, alien beings, who were more than guests, Clare was thrown into confusion at the idea of being somehow responsible for them.

'Now that we have decided to split up,' she said to Sam, 'they should obviously be with you. They are totally devoted to you, as you well know, and I am not a mother in any sense of the word. Merely a receptacle I have always thought. But I could have them for some of the time of course.' Though Clare allowed herself to admit to loving and being very proud of these three beautiful beings, she could not really imagine having had any part in their creation.

'Balderdash,' Sam said amiably. 'They should be with you – that's obvious.'

'Not obvious at all darling, if I may say so. Just because I happen to be female doesn't mean that I understand adult children at all. You get on with them far better and they need a father figure at this age. Though I am not sure if they will relate well to Fanny or Mirabelle, or whoever you're going to live with.'

'Sweetheart, they will relate as well to my partners as they will to yours, so this cancels itself out.'

Clare would have liked to point out that her present

45

lover at least had children of his own, so should therefore be a better substitute parent than any of Sam's young and glamorous women, but realised that this would work against her own argument, so she remained angrily silent.

But in the awkward hiatus period between the school years and life in the real sense, things became even more difficult for Maggie, Mim and Mary, because when they had been at boarding school, the holidays had just been a small break in the dependable security of school rules and regulations. A period which you accepted as Holiday; that is, a hectic, enjoyable few weeks of rushed excitement. Real life was different; it seemed to need a base from where to start, and when this base was divided and shuffled about from one parent to the other, with little organisation and often much resentment, it was disturbing and unhappy.

'You must take them, Sam, because I'm going to Glyndebourne tomorrow and then Wiggs and I are spending the weekend with the Devines.'

Conversations between Sam and Clare often started thus during that strained, interim period before the idea of total family dispersal had surfaced.

'For God's sake, why can't you leave them alone? They're practically grown women.'

'If only they were. As soon as my back's turned Mag will have that dreadful Matt creature with the long greasy hair around, plus all his communist friends, and Mim will be in bed with all of them, and Mary will be devastated by the immorality of it all and not know how to cope. And anyway I refuse to allow any flat of mine to be cluttered up with drug addicts and anarchists. For one thing it's far too small, and you have plenty of room in that great presumptuous apartment of yours.'

Sam refused to rise and laughed instead. 'Oh all right, I'll have them for the weekend, but they've got to come back by Tuesday because I'm going to New York, and I don't want my place turned into an opium parlour or a hotbed of political intrigue any more than you do.'

Mim was the only one who did not particularly care how insubstantial the base might be. Mary was deeply disturbed by the lack of solidity and security, and Maggie was irritated at having no personal room in which she could set up her world. The true possibilities of muscling her way into a man's world were more remote than she had imagined, but she was anxious to earn and be financially independent quickly.

'I shall take a teaching post for now,' she said, 'so that I can look round and see the best sort of banks or businesses to get into.'

'Famous last words,' Matt said. 'Once in teaching you'll have no time to stand, stare or, more particularly, think.'

'Rubbish. I shall. It's just a matter of organisation. I've worked out how to gain at least eight hours to myself in a working week. I shall insist on my legitimate free time, and not hurl myself into voluntary out of school activities. Can't think why teachers do that anyway when they don't get paid extra for it. There shouldn't be any difficulty if I keep to the things I'm paid for. Shouldn't take me more than a year to find a decent job somewhere.'

But for Mary, of course, the dividing up of the home was almost unbearable. She had managed, during the school years, to transfer her original reliance on her family as the pivotal centre of her being, to the Mother Superior as the pivotal centre of the Convent, but when she was eventually removed from that environment, she found nothing left to replace it.

Sam and Clare sat opposite each other in the white leather armchairs of Clare's flat, Sam picking his teeth and Clare smoking a king size cigarette and seething inwardly. What to do with them? No way could she see herself being saddled with three adult daughters just when freedom from ties seemed to be looming. And anyway, no one really believed that she was old enough to have three adult daughters. It might be a shock to some.

'I think,' Sam said suddenly, after a considerable

period of silence, and with the new idea fresh in his mind, 'that we have fulfilled our obligations as parents, and that we should now launch our daughters on a life of their own. Push them out of the nest, in fact.'

Clare brightened. 'How?'

Sam lit a cigar, and reclined in the armchair as he thought the suggestion through. 'Well – we could buy them a flat.'

'But what would they do? I mean Maggie's only just out of university and talking nonsense about taking some business job in the city which probably means she'll be in a state of abject poverty and overwork for years to come, so that she won't be able to look after the other two, and she's the only capable one of the three. Mary's such a baby, how can we possibly push her out into a hostile world?'

Sam considered for a few moments. 'We might buy them a little house with extra rooms so that they could take in lodgers to help pay for the running of it. That would make them independent. Splendid idea. I had to start from scratch, didn't I? They will have to learn to make their own way.'

'But could they? They'd probably make a complete hash of the whole thing.'

'Nonsense, my dear.' Sam was quite carried away with his brilliant idea. It gave him the same sort of stimulation as the consideration of a new business undertaking, which, of course, it was. The investing of money into his daughters' future, he could still be a sleeping partner, to keep an eye on the progress. It was as good as done.

'It might work, I suppose,' Clare said doubtfully. Just as long as they didn't expect her to deal with it all. She doubted if they were really capable. Of course Maggie was, but the others? Mary was hopelessly immature and childish, and Mim – well Mim was scatty and sexy and hardly dependable, but it would keep them occupied at least. 'We'll have to keep an eye on them,' she said.

'Of course we'll have to keep an eye on them, but only

now and then, because it's good for them to learn by their mistakes. Maggie's got her head screwed on the right way, she won't make too many mistakes, I'll guarantee you that.'

'Well it's got to be a decent area – somewhere like Hampstead.'

'What the blazes is decent about Hampstead? Not only is it bloody expensive but it's also bloody chi-chi, and full of drug-crazed hippies. We should start them much lower down the scale and let them work their way up. Somewhere like Bow or Bethnal Green where I could expect to see a decent return on my money.'

But Clare had once had a very romantic affair with someone she had met in the bar of Jack Straw's. His flat had overlooked the Heath over which they had walked often during that whole idyllic summer, and she liked the idea of keeping alive her connection with the district.

'I will not allow you to condemn our daughters to a slum just so that you can see a good return on your money.'

'I was thinking of them as well. It's not good to start at the top and work your way down. But have it your own way, nothing is worth further hassle.' Silly bitch, he thought fondly.

The three girls were in various stages of excitement, anxiety and shock. For Maggie, the challenge infused her with a sense of purpose and exhilaration. The only reservation she had was the possibility that the accounts might not balance out. 'We shall have to be absolutely sure that our p.g.s can afford to pay,' she said. 'They'll have to be vouched for by whoever recommends them I mean.'

'But we couldn't turn people away if they're desperate and destitute,' Mary said.

'Yes we could,' Maggie insisted. 'There's always Dr Barnardo's.'

'They could pay in kind,' Mim said.

49

Maggie laughed, 'I can just imagine what your kind would be,' she said. 'But if we're not careful, the whole enterprise might collapse, and old father Sam is unlikely to give us a second chance. We've got to make a go of it.'

Clare was with them when they first looked at Lavender Cottage.

'It's such a wonderfully corny name,' Mim said. 'And there isn't even any lavender near it.'

'Unthinkable,' Clare said, 'The rooms are much too small and there are too many stairs. Three recep. and five bed indeed! All lies, of course.'

'But there's this wonderful basement,' Maggie said. 'We could easily make another room down there, and the loft is enormous.'

'It's fabulous,' Mim said. 'And what a position, right in the middle of everything! And that fantastic bow window, and it's so *sweet*.'

'But all those trees, they make it dark.' Clare was horrified that they could even consider it.

'So dark it's almost wicked.'

'And it's green dark, all those lovely leaves. Makes it compact and cosy inside.'

Mary stood in the front room and looked out at the lime trees. She wondered why they were discussing the merits of the house as though they saw it for the first time. Just as though it were not their home, but some new house they were viewing. She was confused, but not really worried, because she knew it was already theirs.

'What do you think, little Em? Do you think you could live here?'

Mary laughed out loud at the strangeness of the question. 'But I already do live here,' she said. 'What a funny question.'

She ran upstairs to her room, and saw the sun shinning through the window on to her dressing chest, with its china candlesticks and the candles, short and misshapen with wax drippings. Her sprigged muslin gown hung on the back of the door, and her straw hat with the blue streamers lay upon the bed where she had tossed it earlier. This was indeed home to her now. More so than ever the Downshire Hill studio had been. This was where she would be living her life. Where, in fact, she had already started living it.

She shed a small portion of the certainty as she swung herself downstairs again on the tiny white bannister, but the happiness still shone out as she found herself waltzed down the hallway by Mim.

'Isn't it just great? I can see by your face that you feel it's absolutely right for us all.'

They collided with Maggie by the front door, and clung in a bubbling trio of excitement and positive conviction. 'There's no other place possible.'

'It's just fabulous.'

'I've never been so sure about anything in my life.'

Maggie was startled by her own certainty. How could she be so sure when she had not gone into the economics, nor worked out a plan? It would be madness to decide before she had worked out the possibilities.

Clare peered round a corner at the excited, jogging group. 'For God's sake, calm down,' she said in irritated exasperation. 'You look like a mangled version of Botticelli's three graces. Untangle yourselves and stop behaving like the inmates of a disorderly infants' school.'

The three ceased their gyrating, but their hands still linked them in a circle, and their faces glowed with the moment.

'Yes, yes.' Maggie's broad smile belied her tone of voice. 'Ma's absolutely right. We must be serious and not let ourselves be carried away. We may love it, but it is possibly totally unsuitable.' She gave a barely suppressed giggle, and Clare and the other two all spoke at the same moment.

'Of course it's unsuitable,' said Clare.

'It's divinely suitable,' said Mim.

'But it's ours,' said Mary.

51

'The price is far too high for what it is,' Clare added. 'And you know what your father's like over a bad bargain.'

'But it's less money than some of the ones we've looked at.'

'And it's so different from all the others.'

'So mad and sort of silly, and so *sweet*.'

'It couldn't possibly belong to anyone else,' Mary said. 'It belongs to us.'

There was a great deal of argument, both then and later. Sam was aghast at the stupidity of the idea. 'I'm not going to pour money into a little mayhem. The place looks more like a chaotic labyrinth than a house. And all on a niggardly scale. It's madness.'

But it was also useless. Sam and Clare realised quite soon that this was a decision that had somehow been made for them, and was mysteriously beyond their control.

'Why am I acting against my better judgement?' Sam asked Clare as he made arrangements to transfer money into his daughters' bank accounts. 'I suppose your boring powers of persuasion still affect me, in a nauseous sort of way.'

'My powers of persuasion?' Clare's voice rose perceptibly from its everyday husky drawl. 'I can't stand the place, and think we are probably condemning them to hellfire and damnation. But as long as they *know* that's what I feel, then I can do no more.'

'And as long as they know they won't get any more money out of me, then I wash my hands of the matter.'

Clare sniffed. 'OK Pilate. Bring on the Imperial Leather. I suppose we could be said to have done our best.' And because she suddenly found herself to be in need of some material demonstration of ridding herself of the responsibility, rather than the spitting out of ineffectual little sallies of inadequate words, she moved in a sudden rush to the door of her sitting room.

'Let yourself out, darling,' she said. 'I'm going to have a bath.'

5

The move to Hampstead solved a multitude of problems for the Steins. Life in the years immediately before had not been easy for any of them because it was a kind of perpetuum mobile between Clare and Sam, and their various companions.

The new house, and the new beginning, were a great release for all three, particularly Mary, who saw at once the possibility of collecting together, round the nucleus of the three of them, the family she continued to hanker after. In a kind of stupified delight, she sat at the desk in the window of her room with its flowered bed-spread matching the curtains. The morning sun sent shafts of light directly on to the top of her head as she wrote, slowly and carefully, in her interminable diary. She felt intensely happy and contented.

'My own place,' she wrote, and then said it over and over again to herself. This was her house, her place, and her new beginning. Outside the window, a passion flower creeper crawled up the wall, and she leaned out to pick a flower. It would be a perfect illustration to this page of her diary, if she could draw it well enough. Amazingly precise it was in its symmetry. She had never really looked at a flower as perfect as this, and she stared in absorbed fascination.

Mim put her head round the door. 'Must say the sun makes your room look *great*,' she said. 'If I didn't love the mysterious murk of my private cave downstairs, I might almost be jealous.'

She came in and stretched herself out on the bed. 'It's so odd how we immediately made our own centres as soon as we moved in. This room couldn't be anyone's but yours – even without the flowers on the bedspread and wallpaper and everything. I mean even the way the sun comes in and positively floods the room, even that's absolutely you.' She squinted through the sun at Mary's silhouetted form against the window. 'You look amazing from here,' she said, forming her hands into a rectangle to frame the prospect. 'Like a sort of Rossetti Beata Beatrix, with the sun making a kind of halo all round.'

Mary was not listening. 'This flower,' she said, 'I've never really looked at one before. It's magic, look' – she held it out for Mim to see – 'look, it's just like us, don't you see? Those three things in the middle, stigmas, or whatever they're called, with all the other things all round them, sort of like people, and they're all set in that fabulously beautiful bed of petals, and that's the house.'

'Oh Em, you're such a baby, all this heavy symbolism, it's so sweet.'

'It's important,' Mary said. 'I'm sure it's important. Everything means something if only you can see it.'

'Of course it does, Birdie,' Mim's thoughts had strayed off again into whether she should ring her agent now or later. Waiting for the phone to ring was deadly and soul-destroying, but hearing the expected reply was sometimes worse. 'Nothing new, darling, I'm afraid. Yes of course I tried for that one, rang him particularly about you in fact.' But of course he didn't. She was just another file on his desk, covered with other files. Just chance if he remembered her at all. Better keep phoning to remind him. She heaved herself off the bed, wrapped in her own anxieties, and made for the telephone in the hall downstairs.

Mary sat on in the window, staring at the passion flower. She felt it was very significant, and she took a finely sharpened pencil out of the pencil jar. In her mind, she saw the delicate intricacies of the illustrated manu-

54

script her diary had for her, at that moment, become. She would wind the tendrils and leaves round the letter M that started 'My own place'.

She continued to write: 'Today I sat at the window of my new room – my own room; my home. It is so much mine that I seem to have known it for ever. When I first saw it, I recognised it, I really did. I think I have lived here for centuries.

'We believe that the house was built about 1810, at least Maggie said she thought so. She says I could probably find out if I went up and looked up the old rate books and the censuses and maps and things. I wonder if I really could, I've never done anything like that before, but I so want to know. I must know who has lived here before. We found this historic newspaper under the floor boards – at least the workmen did when they were putting in the central heating – it was dated 1872 and it was so interesting. I think I SHALL go and look things up somewhere, and see what I can find out.'

The research became an absorbing interest with her, though it took a considerable time to gain enough confidence to do anything at all. Maggie encouraged her with much enthusiasm. At last, here was something that Mary took a real interest in. Great! Fabulous! Just what she needed.

'I think it's all terribly interesting,' she said to encourage her, and in a distracted sort of way, she did. It was just that there was so little time even to be interested in things these days. Just impossible to keep up with everything. You had to sort out the most important in order to keep your thinking organised in any way. She found that the dissipation of her energies was something that threw her into a depression, and therefore she enforced the strictest control over her thoughts and actions. She made time to listen to Mary's discoveries while correcting the interminable homework.

'What have you found out? Tell me all,' while her red

biro went tick, tick, cross, exclamation mark, WHAT? NO! Not two *hundred*! Good work Melanie, and Disgracefully untidy, as automatically as her mind took in the odd sentences of Mary's long and excited accounts.

'I really think I've got somewhere today, Mags. Of course I can't be sure, because it's so difficult to know which house is ours in the rate books because they changed all the numbers once or twice, so I can't be sure about anything, but I feel certain I found something today. There's this house that *might* be ours, which was owned in the 1860s by an artist called Aaron Abrahams who lived in Downshire Hill. Isn't that a lovely name? Aaron Abrahams.' She paused to consider the sound. 'But then, suddenly one year – 1870 I think it was – it belongs to Mrs Annie Abrahams and Miss Mary Abrahams. Now isn't that odd? Someone called Mary – and exactly a hundred years ago! Isn't that a coincidence?'

Maggie's mind concentrated for a moment on the fact. 'But you don't really know if it *is* this house, do you?'

'Well no, but I'm sure it is. I just feel it somehow. I've always felt there's something special for me about this house.'

'It's not really so special that two girls called Mary might possibly have lived here . . . is it?' Maggie tried to suppress the smile that she felt. Unwise to crush the enthusiasm, but Em should be made to see the thing rationally, and to consider realities. No good letting imagination take over completely.

Mary's conviction shrivelled at once. Of course it was only speculation. There was no reason to suppose – no certainty, that is. 'I know,' she said, 'of course it's only guesswork.' Was it worth going on? 'Even so, I think it's fun to imagine why he suddenly gave them the house. Do you think it was something like us being given it? This house I mean.'

Maggie put down her pen, folded her arms, and gave her sister the full benefit of her concentration. 'I think you're a genius of inventiveness,' she said. 'And I think you

56

should let your imagination run riot, and that you should write a really good story about it. You could, you know.'

'Do you think so? I suppose I do imagine a lot, but it doesn't always seem like imagining. It seems so real when I think about it.'

'That's what would make it into a good story. What do you think happened next?'

'I'm not sure, because they go on owning it for a bit together, and then Miss Mary Abrahams is left out, and it's just Mrs Annie Abrahams. I wonder what happened.'

'Perhaps she died.'

Mary's expression changed; her nostrils pinched inwards and her eyes took on a pink, watery appearance. Maggie thought for a moment she was going to cry. 'Well, she had to die sometime,' she said. This ultra-sensitivity was a bit much.

Mary made an effort to hide the distress. 'Yes, but I somehow don't think she did – die,' she said, and then she looked up at Maggie as though testing her out on something. 'Because I looked her up in the parish register, and there's no notice of her death that I can find.'

'You did that?' Maggie was astonished that she had taken the initiative over the matter. 'But how clever of you to think how to find out.'

'There was something else,' Mary said. 'You remember when they had all the floor boards up and we found that old newspaper of 1872? Well I went right through that because I thought it was so interesting and at one point there was a news item underlined. It said two bodies had been found in woods outside Hatfield plus a complete set of women's clothes beside them, though no other body had been found. They didn't know what they died of and couldn't understand about the extra set of clothes.'

'The missing body mystery – nice title for a thriller, but I can't see the connection.'

'The fact that it was underlined means something. It obviously meant something to someone in this house.'

57

'Are you going to write about it? It would make a wonderful short story.'

Mary relaxed, and her tension eased. 'I might,' she said. 'But I've got to find out a lot more first, I feel I'm only just beginning.'

'Well let me in on the next instalment,' Maggie said, picking up her books and going towards the door. 'I can't wait.'

Mary looked back at the passion flower she had drawn at the beginning of her diary. Starting a new page, she drew it again, this time making the three central stigmas into three faces, and the crowded purple stamens became little people, packed closely together and encircling them. The petals spread out behind them and held everything together. The result pleased her, and she contemplated it seriously, chewing at the end of her pencil.

After a little while, she started to write again: 'Once upon a time, many, many years ago,' she wrote, 'there lived a girl called Mary. She lived with her father and her extremely beautiful mother in a mansion in London. Her father was a rich and famous artist who spent nearly all his time painting pictures of his wife and daughter. They were a very loving and happy family until one appalling, dreadful day, when Mary's calm and happy world was destroyed by one single earth-shattering blow.'

She paused, her pencil poised. What, in heaven's name, was that earth-shattering blow going to be? Her mind was quite blank, devoid of inspiration. Whatever made Maggie think she could write a story?

She kissed the passion flower, put it in a thin-stemmed glass and balanced it on the window sill. It was significant, she knew; it had some message or other which she would one day discover. Just at that minute, though, the link-ups and odd half memories eluded her. All would be revealed one day. Of that she was certain.

6

'I have employed a carpenter, Mama,' said Mary Abrahams. 'And I think it's time that you came to see for yourself what I hope to do to our dear little house.'

Annie looked at her daughter with fury. 'A hovel is what it is,' she said. 'That you should attempt to see it otherwise shows that the devil is weaning you away from the truth. You attempt to make excuses for your father by succumbing to his disgraceful suggestions. Can you not support your mother against such wickedness? Do you think so little of your mother that you work actively against her?'

She reminded Mary of a great stone statue that had somehow achieved the power of speech. Her mother seemed paralysed within her life, with only a venomous talking machine left spouting its malevolent utterances unceasingly. She sat in her chair day in, day out, possibly talking on when she was alone, Mary believed.

'Come now, Mama, I am only trying to make the best of the situation. This we must do if we are to survive.'

'Better to die, I say. Much better.'

'If God had meant us to die, He would have arranged for it to happen. We are being tested, that's all.' And how I am enjoying the test, she thought. She heard, with a small spasm of shock, a voice that said, 'It's just so great that Ma and Pa have finally made the split.' Who could have expressed such an evil sentiment? She felt, momentarily, uncomfortable, but then remembered that all this was meant to happen. It was her great testing time; her life's work had been set in motion. The excitement of the challenge was like living on the crest of a wave.

'The house already looks very much prettier than it did, Mama. I want so much for you to see what I have done. It is wonderful what a little cleaning and scrubbing will do for a place. And I have made some pretty curtains for the front room. You will be pleased, Mama, I am sure you will be pleased when you see it. And now I have employed this carpenter, Joey O'Malley is his name. Most highly recommended by Mr and Mrs Smith of the grocery stores in the High Street, because, you see, I wish him to make a door to connect the two cottages and a stair from the little back room up to the bedroom above so that we shall be able to . . .'

'Stop your prattling, child, it makes my head ache. I am not strong enough to stand such chattering.'

Mary smiled to herself, because nothing at all could dampen her spirits. 'I am sorry, dear Mama,' she said. 'I know that I go on alarmingly. But I am so happy that at last I may be really useful to you. I feel I am fulfilled.'

Joey O'Malley was a humble Irishman who undertook many odd jobs for the local people. He was Irish only by parentage, and had lived all his life in the village and its outskirts. He had known of the Abrahams family and had watched Mary grow up with an interest akin to worship. Being cursed with an impediment in his speech, he was unable to string words together, and this meant that he had never managed to get as far as asking a girl to marry him. Girls thought him daft in any case, but he had his dreams, and Mary was now the sweetheart he would never be able to achieve. In his own mind, he had never grown older than twenty-five, which was when he had stopped trying to remember his birthdays because nobody else did, and eighteen could well be the wife of twenty-five. He kept her safe and secure within his imaginings because, of course, she was quite untouchable in reality.

'You see, Joey,' Mary said, 'I need to make a lovely home for dear Mama who has recently had a bad, bad shock from which she suffers every hour of every day.' And she was silent for a moment with the thinking of it.

As if, Joey thought, everyone in the town hadn't heard the rumour. That heathen devil had thrown them out at last. Not that you blamed him all that much, seeing what a vixen was that Annie Abrahams. Mother of God, how those two hell-hounds had managed to produce such an angel of grace – it was like a miracle.

'If we could have a doorway between the cottages and our own way upstairs, then we should have all that we need. Quite separate from the other house and yet a part of it.' The slight flush of her cheeks made Joey's scalp tingle. He nodded enthusiastically and pointed to the ceiling of the back room.

'Up go . . .' was all that came out, while his hands made a staircase in the air.

'Exactly,' Mary said. 'How clever you are, Joey. A little staircase of wood to my bedroom above, and dear Mama shall have the bedroom in the front. How beautiful it will all be; and I will have dimity for my curtains, and perhaps a paper on the wall if our funds will run to it. And you, Joey, will lodge with us, yes? For the work you put in for us will be well worth bed and board, will it not?'

All was falling into place of its own accord, Mary thought, almost as though she, herself, were superfluous, something like Queen Mab waving her wand. And it did not even take very long.

Came the removal day; Joey had hired the horse and cart, for there was not much to remove, just what she had been able to induce her father to part with. A bed for each of them, a table for the kitchen, and a comfortable chair for her mother. There was already some furniture in the cottages; a small dresser, cupboards of sorts, and Joey would make the rest.

Annie moved with resentment and a very bad grace. 'You have cleaned it well enough,' she conceded, running her finger along the mantelshelf and peering at the black leaded grate. 'But those curtains won't wear. Far too flimsy.'

'But so pretty, Mama, and we need not draw them back, for they are just to discourage the neighbours peeping. We have the heavy rep for winter. Is it not cosy? Please say you are not too unhappy with my efforts. Come and see your bedroom . . .'

She took her mother's hand, and led her towards the clean, new timber steps that led up from the back room. 'There,' as they emerged through the small room that was Mary's into the larger front room she had prepared for Annie. 'Is it to your liking?'

Annie, dressed all in sad black, looked out of place in the new brightness with which Mary had imbued the cottage.

'Do you like it Mama? Do you like it?' Her mother's room had to be one in which all that resentment and anger might begin to dissolve and be absorbed.

Annie stood with her back to Mary, staring out of the window into the greenery of the lime trees outside. The blackness of her long, trailing dress still seemed discordant in the room and Mary's disappointment began to creep up her spine like cold water. It was not going to work, there was no way – but as she looked again, through smarting, watering eyes, the blackness appeared to mist and become grey, the weight and depression of the sombre figure seemed to lift and lighten, and when Annie turned back to Mary, her face was not her own at all, but Clare Stein's. Smiling, open, heavily made up and outstandingly handsome.

'You girls are fantastic,' she said. 'I always knew you were, but this just proves my point. You've made it perfect. To think I was actually feeling guilty about leaving you all on your own! God, I was mad. You are much more adequate than I ever was. How did two such reprobates as Sam and me ever manage to produce you? Come here and let me hug the three of you,' and Mary was swept into the quartet of laughing, shouting family, to smell familiar Chanel Number Five and Max Factor foundation, and to feel warm, smooth arms and cheeks, and soft, loving squeezes and hand pressures.

It did not last very long, stiffening up almost immediately, and the wafting scent becoming static moth balls and carbolic. But Annie had her arms round her daughter; her eyes were moist and her mouth was unbelievably smiling.

'It is very nice,' she said. 'You have done your best for me. You are a dear, good girl.'

With a little encouragement, and some practical help, the Johnson family, a mother, father and three children, in the downstairs back, seemed to have taken on a new lease of life and was definitely to be included in her new family, Mary decided.

'He's really quite a gentleman, Mama. A clerk in good employment, and very good to his wife, Tilly.'

'A clerk is not a gentleman,' her mother said. 'Nor ever will be, however he may treat his wife. And three children in the same room – it's not decent.'

'But see what I have suggested, Mama. Now that we have turned away some of those who were not suitable, and since some others have moved on, we have the next door room vacant. This would do excellently for the children, and could be let to them for a few shillings more which I believe Mr and Mrs Johnson could well afford.'

'Your heart is too soft, Mary Abrahams, I don't doubt you have let them have the room for a pittance? You will not make the house pay by being soft-hearted and then we shall both end in the workhouse.'

'We will run a good house, Mama, and if we do that, then I am sure that the good Lord will see that none of us starve.'

'And that Joe O'Malley, getting everything for nothing. What about him, pray? Simpleton that he is.

Are we to run a Bedlam as well as a poor house? These lunatics can be dangerous you know. We could all be murdered in our beds.'

'Mama he is a poor, gentle creature, who has difficulty with his talking, that's all. He is a treasure, not a trouble, and he has merely converted a part of the loft for himself. We truly could never have got this place to be a home if he had not helped us. We owe him much.'

Joey had indeed become an integral part of the household. He brought wood for the fires, he cleaned, he fetched and he carried and Mary gave him broth and bread every day for his pains. The arrangement was ideal.

Before she started to fill the other rooms with suitable paying guests, Mary allowed a period of respite while she and her mother adjusted to their new life. She felt the need to become completely acquainted with the cottage before she allowed strangers to take over. She dusted and cleaned and shopped and cooked and allowed the approval and affection in the atmosphere take her over. She was deeply happy.

She had kept the large front room in the letting cottage as a parlour for her mother and herself. Annie complained. 'We cannot afford to allow one room go unlet in our present unhappy financial state,' she said. 'You are being reckless with our meagre funds.' She blew her nose and wiped her eyes to prove what anxiety her daughter caused her. She felt in a constant state of irritation that all should actually be going so smoothly, when by rights she should be suffering greatly through her misfortune. She resented Mary's sudden character transformation, it was not right that a child should so dominate her mother. 'And where, pray, are all these paying guests you are so sure of attracting to your precious lodging house?'

Mary bridled with anger but pushed it behind her with a sigh. 'Oh Mama, how can you say such things? It is not my house, now is it? It belongs to us both and should be loved by us both.'

'One cannot love a dwelling place or any inanimate object.'

'And as for the lodgers, I am interviewing today and tomorrow several people who have applied. Apart from the Johnsons, there is a Miss Amelia Tripp who takes in sewing and seems most respectable and pleasant, and a Mr Godfrey Grebe who is a clerk and sometimes writes articles for the papers, and a Mr Barber, who is a teacher, with his wife and their baby daughter, Constance; and then there is a young man called Richard Cane who is studying to take holy orders.'

'And what guarantee do we have that they are not all thieves and criminals?'

'None, Mama, none at all, apart from faith in my judgement, which judgement the good God has given me.'

'You are impertinent, Miss.' Annie's voice shook, and her face suffused with colour, but Mary's thoughts had already danced away from the moment as she thought of the great excitement of being able to choose one's family, rather as one might choose dolls to set up in a doll's house.

She stared out of the window of the parlour and saw the light green shimmer of the summer lime trees and heard the chirp of sparrows and the occasional scream of swifts. The gardens of the cottages opposite were full and colourful, mostly tended by their owners, but some left to bloom with marguerites and tall grasses and buttercups. Children played on the railings that guarded the high footpath from the road, and a horse and cart lumbered down the hill. She dropped the lace curtain back in place and turned inwards to the room again to find it full of people, nearly all of them quite young it seemed. There were perhaps sixteen in all, mostly sitting on the floor, but some in the big armchairs, and five sprawled across each other on the sofa. They stared into the corner of the room, in rapt attention, occasionally jigging a little and snapping their fingers. The room was full of smoke. It was Top of the Pops time.

Maggie Stein entered the room from the hall and made a sharp expression of anger. She might have known. It was, of course, Thursday, but she never did remember that on that day the house would be preposterously cluttered. She quite enjoyed the programme herself, but it was this devout quality with which it was regarded that annoyed her. Why did they take everything so seriously?

'I'd like to sit,' she said. 'Some of us have to work for our living, I would remind everyone.'

There were groans, and slight shifts in positions.

'Hi toast.'

'Hi Mum.'

'Oh God, here's the boss.'

'Go make the tea, darling.'

'Sh-sh everyone, I want to *listen*.'

Mary slid off her part of the chair and sat on the floor. 'You sit there,' she said.

Maggie tensed with annoyance. Why did their house always have to be used as the viewing venue? Where on earth did all this crowd appear from each week? Layabouts, drones and bums, the lot of them. She put the plastic bags she was carrying noisily on the floor, so that several items fell out. 'It's all right for some,' she said, sitting down heavily. Mary laid her head in Maggie's lap, which irritated her still further. 'Don't drool, Em.'

No one else spoke again. The concentration had only been rippled by her entry, but now had settled back into its normal, routine preoccupation. She put her hand on Mary's head, feeling she had been a bit unkind. It was good to sit down, and if no one else was going to do anything, she was blowed if she was. There was no actual reason why she should do the shopping for all of them. If only everyone weren't so inefficient, she could let them do it, but it really was painful for her to see a job inefficiently done. She could invariably buy more for less money just by sensible planning. She wondered whether her sisters would ever learn to be practical, and rather thought not. Mary was too conscientious for words, which made her slow and painstaking, and often rather a pain in the neck, while Mim never thought before she acted, and therefore could be depended upon to take the most expensive and least sensible action in any situation. Odd how different they all were, when all had had the same upbringing.

Responsibility certainly lay heavy, she thought, and yet there was a great sense of challenge about it all. In spite of her misgivings, there was a part of her that liked the situation she found herself in. Being in charge of a family and a household gave her a sharp picture of herself at the apex of a triangle; as mathematician, her concepts were always diagrammatical in their precision. She saw her two sisters at the other points, on her right and left, and the hypothetically increasing household stretching away to embrace whoever was to be included within the extending arms of the expanding figure. All very precise, neat and satisfactory. It was easier when Matt stayed over, which he did whenever he could, because he shared the workload with her. She and Matthew Sharpe, who now had a job in social services, had remained together after leaving Essex, where Maggie had gained a BSc Maths, and they found themselves still attached now that real life had begun. He had his own flat in Brixton, but came to Hampstead most weekends.

They had continuous conversations about moving in somewhere together, but Maggie was adamant. 'I've taken on responsibility for my family for the next few years,' she said, 'and that's quite enough for the moment. Anyway, I think we should keep our lives individual for as long as we can.'

'That's a stupid idea,' Matt said. 'It just means that we'll tend to grow apart as different individuals, and that will make it even more difficult to live together later. The younger we are when we shack up together, the easier it will be to blend our lives together.'

67

'I don't particularly want to blend my life with any-one's at the moment,' Maggie said, thinking, as she said it, how untrue that statement was. Was her life not inextricably blended with her sisters' lives? Wasn't the real reason for her reluctance bound up with attach-ment to the triangle theorem? She felt very strongly, though she was not one for unexplained intuitions, that only by being a part of the satisfactory fulfilment of the lives of her sisters, would her own life achieve its par-ticular zenith. Not a sentiment she could possibly put to Matt. Difficult enough to admit it even to herself.

If Mary was the most obviously in need of support in finding direction and purpose in her life, Mim's acting career was only spasmodic. She had been a success in drama school, but jobs in London were hard to get.

'And can you imagine me in the provinces?' she asked. 'If I've got to get my card through rep, then I'll give up the whole idea. I'm just not the type for rep or the clubs, now am I?'

'So how do you think you are going to get your card?' Maggie was irate at the idea of her getting away with things. 'Union cards don't just drop into your lap, you know, however lucky you may have been in the past.'

'Don't worry darling. It'll be all right on the night, I promise you. There's this sweet ad man I met the other day. He's going to give me a contract and then I can get my Equity card just like that.'

'I'll believe it when I see it.'

'But are you allowed to do that?' Mary's eyes widened. 'Don't you have to work for years before they give you one? I thought you had to . . .'

'Oh Em my pet, stop being so gullible. I can't bear it. It's all right I tell you. I'm not going to get clapped in gaol or anything. This James person is so fab anyway, and he'll probably actually let me do the commercial as well as just giving me the contract, so that it might be the beginning of bigger and better things.'

'And then again . . .' Maggie said.

'Then again nothing – you're so negative, Mag, aren't you?'

'Just practical.'

James, the ad man, joined the household ten days later.

'Just needs somewhere for a few weeks because he's split up with his girl friend. He's quite rich, so he can pay his way easily.'

He moved into the small downstairs room next to Mim's. It was damp, and painted yellow to make it look sunny.

'He could share my room,' Mim said. 'That little room is horribly grotty. I'm sure he's used to better things.'

'Better that he doesn't get too comfortable,' Maggie said. 'He probably won't fit in with us at all if he's so superior.'

'He's not superior,' Mim said. 'He comes from Manchester.'

'He couldn't share your room,' Mary said. 'You've only got one bed.'

Mim turned her eyes heavenwards and clenched her fists. 'This is true,' she said between gritted teeth.

'I should charge him more if he shared your room,' Maggie said. 'And you needn't think I'd give you the extra either.'

'But it wouldn't be fair to charge him more,' Mary said. 'Because it would only be half a room, and he wouldn't be getting anything extra or anything.'

Maggie and Mim rocked with laughter and Mary blushed.

'Oh – oh, I see what you mean,' she said, and giggled.

Maggie allowed the suspicion to flash through her mind that while one of her sisters was oversexed, the other might be mentally retarded.

7

Mary Stein continued to survey the changing scenes of her life from a slightly bemused and puzzled distance.

'I sometimes feel this is all happening somewhere else,' she said one morning while helping Maggie to sort out and stack away clean linen.

'What darling?' Maggie had arranged the shelves of the linen cupboard into labelled compartments. 'Can you hold these pillow cases while I get the sheets,' she said. 'We shall have to buy some more if any more people descend on us. But I can put it down to expenses.'

The warm smell of aired linen assailed Mary as Maggie piled the pillow cases into her arms. 'My linen smells sweeter,' she thought, 'because I picked that lavender from the bush before the front door.'

But there was no lavender bush by the front door.

She took sheets as well as pillow cases from the linen cupboard and set off purposefully along the passage and up the ladder to one of the rooms in the attic. It was scarcely more than a box room, with a tiny skylight that Joey had pushed through the roof, but it would be far better than the poor little waif had been used to. The dormitory at the orphanage had certainly been large, but the twenty or so coffin-like partitions which passed for beds, almost entirely filled it, and there were no windows at all, not even a skylight to let in the daylight.

It had not been at all easy to choose; there had been so many queueing silently and desperately, in their supplication to be allowed to escape. But it had been Peg who had finally taken her heart.

'I shall expect you to be good, hard-working, obedient, and to help me in all things.' She said it falteringly, because all she wanted to do was to hug the girl, who was only a little younger than she was herself but whose life had been so much more unfortunate than her own.

'Oh yes Ma'am, I will Ma'am,' with eyes wide with terror in case there should be a change of mind, because of course for her the situation was one of life or death.

Mary laid the cotton sheets and worn blankets on the little wooden bed that Joey had made, and went down into the kitchen again, where Annie was staring with anger and distaste at the new arrival.

'Going into the highways and byways now are we? Is there anyone that you will not invite into my house? It is monstrous, Mary, and if I had an ounce of my old strength left in me, then I would forbid such dregs. You are being wilfully rebellious. You need a whip taken to your back.'

She reverted to tears of frustrated rage.

'Mama, dearest, you must not say such things. Peg has suffered much misfortune in her life even as we, too, have suffered misfortune.'

'You would liken us to this brat? You would dare do that?'

'Peg is going to help me with my work, Mama. It is quite hard for me to keep a good, clean house without some help.'

'I never had any help in my home. Kept it spotless for my dear mother, so that she would have nothing to complain of. It was not too hard for me to work for my mother.'

Mary sighed. It was really better to remain silent. Her mother's mind had become rancid with the shock of the break. But this was all part of the testing. She felt proud to be the one to be tested, and then immediately guilty that she should actually be enjoying what was surely meant to be a penance. It was confusing, as was this fogged suspicion that she did not always feel strong like this. There seemed to be times when she did not feel strong at all, when she felt incomplete and ineffectual. Just now, as she watched Peg eat up her broth, and when she looked forward into a well-ordered, satisfactory future arrangement, she could not even imagine feeling ineffectual and incapable. But there were times when she seemed to be standing outside herself and watching other parts of her slide away and carry on what she herself once did. An element of fear crept into her thinking, because she wondered if she was losing her mind. Those moments of blank confusion were out of her control, and shrouded in shadow.

She showed Peg where the scrubbing brushes, brooms, household soap and other cleaning materials were kept, and left her to scrub the kitchen table while she drew the curtains in her mother's room, to make it ready for her late afternoon rest. On her landing, she ran into Mr Richard Cane from the small upstairs back, and was struck, yet again, by his quite overpowering good looks, really much too good for this world. Hair that was startlingly golden, and eyes that were the sharpest blue she had ever seen. She thought he looked frail. Hands so white and thin that veins showed blue and bones seemed about to pierce the skin. His was not the robust beauty of an imagined Greek god, or mediaeval knight in shining armour. He was like an angel, she decided, and for a flashed second she saw him draped in white, with wings like drifted snow and eyes aflame.

'Good afternoon Mr Cane,' she said. 'May I offer you a cup of tea? I am about to make an after luncheon cup for my mother and myself, which we will be taking in the parlour. We would be pleased for you to join us.' Her mother might like to take tea with this holy young man. He was the only one of the small company of lodgers for whom she could feel any vestige of approval.

His smile lit his face. 'I would welcome such a kind

gesture,' he said, 'so that I might say again how happy I am to have the good fortune to be staying in this delightful house where I feel so much at home.'

He said all the right things as though he meant them. Mary felt warmed by him, as though she was really doing him a favour, allowing him to live there with them. This was how it should be; she should be able to do good for each of her guests. That was why they were there. Their stay should result in some actual benefit. She felt suddenly a clear, direct certainty that she was on earth for a purpose. In order to help others attain their goals perhaps? She wasn't sure, but it was something like that. The afternoon sun shone through the trees into the parlour window, making dappled shadows on the wallpaper.

'How beautiful the sun looks when it shines through the leaves like that,' said Mr Cane.

Annie sniffed. 'Fades the carpet,' she said. 'I've told you time and time again, Mary, to draw the curtains to the afternoon sun.'

'But Mama, the sun is so warming and so pleasant. I do not care to shut it out.'

Annie set her cup down sharply. 'Forever argumentative and contradictory. I am at a loss to understand you these days, Mary Abrahams. Such a rebellious spirit she has shown these last few months, Mr Cane. It would seem she does not heed the fifth commandment to honour her mother.'

Mary blushed. She did not appreciate being reprimanded before Mr Cane. It was true that she found that particular commandment sometimes difficult to keep.

'It is not easy to guide our paths along the straight and narrow,' said Mr Cane. 'I find myself falling beside the wayside so often. One can only pray for strength to overcome one's weaknesses.'

They exchanged smiles, and it was probably at that moment that Mary Abrahams fell in love with Richard Cane, so that when the whole room misted over before sharpening into the brown and gold dragon wallpaper of Mim's bedroom, she was left with a bizarre sense of loss.

James, the ad man, was propped against one of the large cushions on the floor, with Mim entwined and enclosed in his arms. Mary sat primly on the bed, her eyes and her mind anchored on to Mim's television. She made a movement to put down the cup of tea she was holding in her hand, but found there was nothing to put down.

'Spiller's Shapes and your dog,' said the television. 'It's a way of life.'

'I made that one,' James said. 'Like it?'

'It's great,' Mim said. 'But you're not going to put me in one with children or dogs are you? You know what they say, and anyway, I'm afraid of dogs.'

'I never said I'd actually put you in one. I don't have all the say you know. Might possibly get you into a dandruff one. An audition, anyway.'

'That would be fantastic. But I'm only joking, really. I don't expect anything, honestly. If you could wangle the Equity card, that's all I'm asking.'

'Do my best.'

James had long, curly, fair hair that hung down to his shoulders, and a slightly darker, curly beard. He had a black tee shirt with 'The Property of HM Prisons' printed on the front. Mary thought him handsome in a rather frightening sort of way. He made her feel inadequate and young, as though she were not actually there at all.

'What are you staring at, chick?' He was laughing at her, and she switched her gaze immediately back to the television.

'I wasn't staring. At least I didn't mean to.'

'Em's a dreamer,' Mim said, 'never quite with us. If she stares at you, you can be quite certain she's thinking of something else.'

And it was true. Sometimes her thoughts were so vivid,

74

she could see nothing other than her own imaginings. So difficult to know what was real. But she remembered times that were not confused. Well, nearly remembered them.

Mim and James began to talk together, and Mary switched them out of hearing and concentrated on the television. It was a children's serial about life on another planet. There was a heroic figure in white, brandishing a sword.

Maggie put her head round the door. 'I'll make your supper, Em, because I've got something we can both eat. But it'll have to be early – about half past six, as Matt and I are going to that CND meeting after. If you want chips, you'll have to do them yourself.'

'I'll do them.' Mary got up, feeling she was making her escape and they left the room together, Mary back to her normal, unambiguous personality. When she was with Maggie, there was a sense of security and knowing just what was going to happen next.

'I do like this house,' she said as she started to peel the potatoes. 'I sometimes think we are the happiest family alive to have such a wonderful place to live.' She stopped abruptly, remembering the reasons for their being there. 'But I do wish we were all together with Ma and Pa and everything. It seems wrong that good should come out of something bad like a splitting up.'

Maggie was preoccupied with her own thoughts, while her hands and her speech got on with her superficial, outside surroundings. 'Don't dramatise so,' she said, thinking about what she would wear this evening, and wondering whether there would be time for a bath. 'Why on earth do you keep harping on as though Ma and Pa were a tragedy? They had a great life together for a considerable time, and then they just went their separate ways, that's all.' The new jeans would be best, though they were uncomfortably tight, but this top she was wearing now had had it. She gave a quick sniff under one arm. And that only left the white shirt which was too smart for CND. 'You can't expect everything to last for ever. That's fairy tale stuff, isn't it?'

Mary stopped peeling and stared out of the window at the pink summer jasmine flowers that were forever trying to force an entrance. Fairy tales? Or beliefs? She was not yet ready to disbelieve. 'If you really love someone, I can't see that you could ever just stop.'

'You don't have to stop, do you? It can just change a bit; increase if you like, or decrease, or shoot off to one side to include someone else. You can love more than one person, after all.'

Mary returned to the peeling, unconvinced. She was waiting to experience love, retaining an implicit faith that it was really there, waiting to be grasped. 'But it does feel like a family here,' she said, 'all living together like this.'

Maggie laughed sourly. 'Wishful thinking,' she said. 'Could be great of course, but it could be hell if it gets out of hand. It's all very well everyone doing their own thing just as long as that thing doesn't upset anyone else's thing.' In spite of what she said, she had to admit to herself that she found the arrangement very satisfactory. But that was because of the personal pleasure she found in being in control of a large operation. Em just liked being included in a big, loving family. Sweet really, but infuriatingly sentimental. No depth. Odd what different things made people happy.

Mim, still in front of the unwatched television in her own room with James, felt sex beginning to get excitingly out of control. How great it was – this start of a new affair. Nothing quite like it.

'You're so amazing,' James said. 'Let's go to bed.'

Mim wriggled free. 'Let's lock the door. Don't know what it is about this house, it's so – well – enticing somehow, or you might say encouraging. It has a great atmosphere doesn't it?'

She took off her tee shirt and turned the television up.

*　　　*　　　*

The group had assembled more by accident than design. Once the three girls had decided on, and decorated, their respective rooms, there was scarcely any time before the other rooms in the house began to fill up. Julian Smile, who had taken photographs of Mim for Spotlight, moved into the large, upstairs back room with his friend, Louis Tripp, who was a dancer.

'You'll really love them,' Mim told the other two. 'They're so funny. And Julian's a fabulous photographer and really starting to take off. I mean, just look at the ones he took of me, they're fantastic, aren't they?'

'If you mean they don't look anything like you, yes, they're incredible,' Maggie said.

'You're so rotten, Mag, and anyway you have absolutely no clue as to what good photography is. You're heinously ignorant. Julian's a real pro, and usually charges the earth, but he didn't charge me much at all.'

'I hope you told him what we charge. With all the money he makes for his fantastic photographs, I trust he doesn't think he's going to get free board and lodging because of doing you some bargain snaps.'

'Give it a rest, Mag, for God's sake, you do so dwell on the money side, don't you?'

'Only because you attempt to ignore the whole unpleasant subject. You're so intent on wanting everyone to think of you as a dear, sweet, generous creature, who would part with her soul for the sake of others.'

'But she is like that,' Mary joined in, unable to tolerate such harshness.

Maggie snorted.

'Better than a suspicious paranoid who haggles over her pound of flesh,' shouted Mim.

Mary sat cross-legged on the floor between them. 'Maggie isn't paranoid,' she said. 'She's just trying to stop you being too generous, Mim, and you know she's right. Can't we meet them both and see if we think they'll fit in?'

'As it happens, they're coming round this evening to

77

see if they could stand all the ferment of the turbulent trinity of the Stein sisters, and incidentally to look at the room.'

Mim later brought them, self-consciously, into the sitting room.

'Julian and Lou,' she said, suddenly overcome with embarrassment and misgiving.

Julian was over-tall, with an air of massive masculinity. He grasped their hands with a thorough grip, which could be thought to be straightforward and honest, Maggie surmised. Probably put on for that very reason, she thought.

'Known as Jude,' Julian said. 'Like the song.'

'Hey Jude,' Mim giggled, and Maggie winced.

Lou was small and neat, with sharp features and fair curls. 'Hi,' he said.

Shyness affected, Maggie decided, and Mim said, 'He's a fantastic dancer, he was in Hair.'

'Oh I saw that with Pa,' Mary said, and blushed because that meant she had seen Lou with no clothes on.

'I was third from the left in the second row,' Lou said. 'Did you notice me? Probably not, I'm *far* too small and not nearly pretty enough. But how advanced of Papa to take you.'

'Our Pa's an ageing hippy,' Mim said, 'but he's really rather sweet.'

'So am I,' Louis said.

'Darlings *please*,' Jude interrupted, and turned to Maggie. 'We'd like to rent your room, if we can afford it,' he said.

'But you haven't even seen it,' Maggie said, warming to him a little. 'We don't actually want to make money, but we have to make everything pay, if you know what I mean. We add up all the outgoings and divide it by however many people are here and telephone is separate and has a meter so that we can't cheat. Come and see the room.'

Everyone trooped upstairs together, the girls all eager to show off the house and have it praised and appreciated.

'Don't you just love it?' Mim said.

'It looks small, but it isn't really,' Maggie said.

'We love it,' Mary said.

When Maggie opened the door to the large upstairs room, it looked extremely clean, bright and inviting. Lou walked straight in and sat down on one of the chairs quite slowly and deliberately. 'The little lady who had this room before – I *know* her,' he said.

'No kidding,' Mim said. 'What a coincidence. Who was it? We didn't ever meet the people who were here before us.'

'All these frocks,' Lou said, waving his hand at the blank wall, 'She made them all.' He turned to Jude. 'This is for us, darling, she's made me so welcome.'

Jude sighed theatrically. 'He goes like this sometimes,' he said. 'He's psychic you know. Forever in communication with the spirits. But we should love to live here if you'll have us.'

Maggie again felt an unexplained warmth towards him. There was something sympathetic and rather sad which she could not pinpoint. Something beneath the aggressive camp exterior.

'It's full of friendly spirits,' Mary said as they went downstairs again.

'Can't you just *feel* it though,' Lou enthused. 'It's absolutely riddled with them, all welcoming you with their presences.'

'Didn't I tell you?' Mim beamed. 'Didn't I just tell you that it was the nicest place that ever was?'

After they had gone, the three girls discussed the idea of taking them in.

'They're absolutely dying to come of course,' Mim said. 'I knew they would be, and I think they would be a tremendous asset to the place.'

Maggie felt her hackles rise at the foregone conclusion.

79

'I don't particularly relish the idea of the place becoming a freaks' circus,' she said. 'They are a bit far out aren't they? I don't think I could stand all the camp humour.'

'You're so prejudiced,' shouted Mim. 'I can't believe it, you'll be calling them bloody queers next.'

'They can't help it,' Mary said, hoping to forestall a disagreement. 'They're just made that way.'

Mim hit her forehead with her fist. 'Oh God,' she moaned. 'How is it that I am burdened with such idiot sisters? Gays are not freaks, they are consenting adults.'

'Gays?' Maggie screamed. 'What's this gays? We're not living in California you know. They may be gay over there, but this is England, remember.'

'You'd rather keep to queers or pansies I suppose? I can't see anything wrong with calling them gays.'

'Just a waste of a good English word,' Maggie said. 'We shan't be able to use it for anything else in future. And about them coming here, I merely said I wasn't sure if I could stand it, that's all.'

'I think they're funny,' Mary said. 'And they like the house as much as we do, so I think they must be allowed to live here.'

They moved in three days later, and painted their room a deep plum, picked out in gold. The blinds were painted by Jude with the New York skyline at night. The stars on the blinds spread out over the ceiling. In spite of herself, Maggie quite liked it.

Mark Rolling turned up on the doorstep some weeks later.

'Heard you had this place,' he said when Maggie answered the door.

'How did you hear?' Maggie felt a sinking resentment on seeing him there. He had been the worst of the hangers-on at Essex. A hanger-on, she reminded herself, not a student, and one of a trio of campus clowns who attached themselves to any part of the place that would afford them a foot or handhold. They did occasional kitchen or domestic work, and stayed with whoever would take them in. They attended occasional lectures, avoided staff who might question their presence, confusing the more absentminded by insisting that they were bona fide students. The jobs they did seldom lasted, and usually ended with such incidents as the serving up of a goldfish in a lecturer's lunch, or a suspicion as to the origins of the graffiti that appeared regularly in various parts of the campus: 'Peter Pooter is a wanker', 'Black Power is Beautiful', 'George loves Stephen but Stephen is straight'.

Mark Rolling, known as Rollocks, was the most constant of the three, and lived fairly regularly with one or other of three girl students, only absenting himself for a time when the official hunt for him became too threatening and imminent. He was a popular figure, usually possessing a good supply of drugs. The other two, known as Pooter and Bummer, were more occasional visitors, who did not often have the drugs to pay their way, so depended entirely on the support of any who might be willing. Their goonish humour brought a welcome touch of insanity into the anxious undergraduate existence, and their idiocy and amorality gave a sense of balance to the rationalised extremes of university behaviour.

Facing Rollocks again after a gap of a year or so, Maggie remembered that Matt had been irritated by what he termed her lack of humour, and she tried to douse her suspicion and resentment. The others were right, she was pretty bitchy and cynical herself.

Rollocks smiled at her. 'Everyone knows everything about the Stein sisters,' he said. 'Heard it on the grape vine. You still with Matt?'

Again the resentment; this time, furious at his intrusion into her affairs. Just because she and Matt were friendly at Essex was no reason to assume anything. 'Your vine communications don't seem to be very reliable,' she said. 'And the answer is, might be, might not. You'd better come in. He happens to be staying this weekend, so we can all sit around discussing our student days, and bore everyone else to extinction.'

'Maggie's caustic wit still in evidence I see.'

Maggie stretched her mouth into a smile. 'You seem to have forgotten,' she said, 'I'm the one that had no sense of humour.'

Later, as they were sitting on the floor cushions of Maggie's room sharing a joint, Rollocks said, 'I have this friend, and we've been chucked out because of living together, can you believe? The old slag who owns the place keeps a sort of female house and didn't like my maleness. I wondered if there was a chance of putting up here for a bit?'

Maggie retreated behind the shield of the others. 'We run this on a sort of communal basis; everyone would have to agree, and everyone has to pay.' He never had any money at Essex. One of the biggest scroungers on the campus, and that was saying a great deal.

'Oh yes, natch, goes without saying.'

Real con man he was, she didn't want him at all.

'You've still got one of the front rooms empty, haven't you?'

Matt was delighted to see Rollocks again. They had laughed a great deal remembering some of the more momentous escapades of the Essex years.

Maggie contained her annoyance that Matt should interfere. 'Some friend of Mim's is after that,' she lied. 'And it's quite expensive to live here you know.' It was important that cards were laid on the table. 'Expenses come to about £4 per person per week without food but that includes rates, repairs, tv hire and you have to clean one part of the house. And we don't encourage drugs, certainly not the hard stuff because of possible police raids which would upset poor Pa.'

Rollocks smirked. 'Never touch the stuff myself, and you won't have to worry about not getting your sums right because money is not much object at the moment, as I shack up with a rich chick. Big and beautiful, from one of the better parts of Kensington.' He leaned back against the wall and looked at Maggie from under his lashes. She could see the sneer in his smile and felt humiliated. 'Want her to take a means test? I'm sure it could be arranged.'

Matt laughed to cover his embarrassment at Maggie's parsimony. 'She worries too much,' he said. 'She has a heart of gold really.'

'Of course, she has,' Rollocks said, 'You can see the gold shining out of her eyes.'

Rollocks and Penny Smythe, a rather plump, very serious socialist, educated at Roedean, moved in two days later, because there seemed no adequate reason why they should not.

And then there were nine.

8

Naturally enough, there was no sort of admission or even recognition of any feeling, other than a deep admiration on either side, between Mary Abrahams and Mr Cane. For her, there was just the warm, contented glow enclosing the realisation that something very pleasant hung at the back of her mind, and for him, the encouraging thought that all women were not devilish and full of temptation and wiles. He found that Mary reminded him of the Madonna in a painting of the annunciation by Crivelli that he had once seen in the National Gallery of London. It was when, as a boy, he had been serving in the choir of the church of St Martin in the Fields. Distant, paradisal days, when his voice had raised him from squalor into the elevated realms of music, ritual and the Church.

The choir had once been taken, as a group, to the gallery by the young and enthusiastic choir master of the time. All the paintings they saw that day were like a divine revelation to the youthful Richard Cane. In fact, when he finally came upon the Crivelli Annunciation, he equated the experience at once with what he imagined a religious manifestation might be. His mind seemed to be suffused with the brilliance; first of all the gold and the splendour, second the overpowering detail, and third what he considered the sublime beauty of the Madonna herself. He had to be firmly led away to join the others. He was speechless; he felt himself to have been specially picked out from the crowd and sanctified by the vision.

And he kept the moment with him all his life, locked away with other memorable moments, like the death of his mother, and the day he was picked out of the gutter by the same enthusiastic organist at St Martin's to be tested for the choir. Like the strange, unreal day when he was told that an unknown benefactor had decided he would pay for Richard's schooling and eventual training for the ministry. He still did not know, nor had he ever seen, this mysterious person who sent him pocket money every month, paid his school and college fees and occasionally sent instructions to him through the bank.

The last instruction had come a few months earlier when he had become ill while studying. 'Take a short holiday from your studies,' he was told. 'Remove your lodgings to the more healthy atmosphere of Hampstead Heath in order that you may recover your good health. Inform the bank of your address and your progress. Continue your studies privately and at your leisure if you feel yourself to be sufficiently strong.'

Richard did not question these orders because he felt convinced that his benefactor must have been sent directly from God. Who else would sponsor an unknown waif and require no recompense?

He had never been back to see the painting. Why? Was it because the dream might have dispersed in the mature appraisal of what was, after all, merely a graven image? Or because he had perhaps been mistaken in his original belief that he had had some sort of religious experience, and that it had only been the realisation of a delight in (and even a desire for) the sensual beauty of a particular woman? He could not be absolutely sure that his interest in Mary Abrahams was not connected with this baser thought. And she was so very like his memory of that Madonna.

But he did assure himself every so often that there was really nothing, absolutely nothing, unseemly or immodest about his admiration for Miss Abrahams. It was her openness of mind and her obvious godliness

85

that drew him to her. Nothing more. He admired her tolerance of other ways of worship, for instance, in spite of the strictness of her Methodist upbringing. She positively enjoyed attending services at Christchurch on the hill and St John's, in spite of her mother's disapproval. She had even been able to soften some of Mrs Abrahams' suspicions towards Richard himself and his high church ways, so that he was received by her with grudging politeness. He did, however, pray daily that there should be no change in his feelings towards Miss Abrahams herself, and he felt fairly certain that God would give him the support he needed if he were to avoid this pitfall. He had been on his guard for so long concerning the temptations of the female sex. Reserve and caution had been schooled into him since childhood, and he was conscious of the idea of resisting all carnal appetites and remaining celibate, the better to serve God with his whole being. He had been fortunate enough, up to this time, to have been able to keep himself to this ideal without too much stress. Pray God that he could continue thus.

Mary, on the other hand, generated involved and phantasmagorical fancies about Mr Cane. He was the defender and saviour whom she was always managing to save or defend. She knew it was childish, but it gave her great satisfaction and a sense of escape from the realities of her mother, and the tensions of responsibility. He was always there, the knight in shining armour and billowing white cloak. His sword, the cross, held aloft, and the red cross of crusade emblazoned on the back of his cloak. With her fantasies kept for such times as she had a little leisure, Mary took up the task she had set herself – she corrected her thoughts – the task that God had set her – with a renewed vigour and enthusiasm.

She took down her account book after coming in with the shopping. The excuse that she might forget to enter some small item was not really relevant, she knew that, because she never did forget. She had to admit that she enjoyed the sight of the neatly laid out pages: clean, tidy, beautiful. Outgoings, income, rentals; everything ordered and satisfactory. Pride it might be, to admire her own work like this, but the realisation that everything was going according to plan was pleasant, and the sight of it all gave her great strength.

She heard the Johnson baby, Madge, laughing behind the closed door across the passage, and felt the glow of fulfilment yet again, this time with slightly more unease. Was this self-satisfied complacency? If it had not been idolatrous, she would feel disposed towards touching wood. Phrases like 'Don't tempt providence', 'Pride goes before a fall' came back to her with memories of her grandmother, who was forever quoting them at her. But all the same, it was true that the Johnson family had changed beyond all recognition since she had taken over the management of the house. Was it not because she had helped Tilly Johnson to clean the room and put it into some sort of order? And because she had occasionally taken the children off her hands to give her some time to herself? Or because she had looked out some of her own clothes, which were prettier and newer than Tilly's own, to give to her?

It is not that I am smug, she assured herself, but I now have a new friend in Tilly, and I also have an opportunity to be with children, so we have both benefited from each other. She wondered if that made her self-congratulations a little less shameful. She remembered, with a shudder, the smell that had come from their room the first time she had called on them.

Noting the pages in her rent book, where each lodger appeared to be up to date with the rentals, was almost like looking through a list of friends: Miss Amelia Tripp, with her sewing machine. The quiet, serious young teacher, Mr Percy Barber, with his pale, ethereal wife, Grace, and their pale, angelic baby, Constance. Even hot and harassed Mr Godfrey Grebe, who was forever rushing out to report on some disaster or other, and then of course, the saintly Richard Cane, all seemed to have become her special charges, relying on her for their comfort and peace of mind. It was a very responsible position she now held, with the comfort and well-being of all these people, including her mother, little orphan Peg and dear, smiling, mumbling Joey, resting on her shoulders. What a joy to have that responsibility! Small wonder that she felt fulfilled and happy with her lot.

It was this look of content which Richard Cane found so divinely fair in Mary. This, with her youth, and thus her innocence, combined to make her, like the memory of the Crivelli Madonna, a sublime and sublimated love-object. His life moved on an easier plane than it might otherwise have done, just because of her presence. He contrived to cross her path whenever possible; not, he told himself, in any underhand or deceitful way, nor because of any unsavoury or unmentionable desires some might imagine that he had. No, no, not at all. It was just that the sight of her, and the nearness of her raised his spirits and increased his energies towards better and better deeds.

They met thus one afternoon, when Mary had taken two of the Johnson children for an outing; Madge in the perambulator that Mary had salvaged from her own childhood and lent to Tilly, while Georgie trotted beside, holding the handle. Mary hoped that the world might think that she was the mother. How very sweet it was, even to imagine such a thing. So deep in these thoughts was she that Mr Cane had quite caught her up, and was dodging in front of her, raising his hat and smiling at her before she apprehended his presence.

'Miss Abrahams! How very opportune that we should be on the same path. Would it be too unseemly if I should beg to accompany you a part of the way?'

Mary's blush was as sharp as her discomposure. Merely, she supposed, because she had been caught off-guard, when her mind had been running along fantasy channels which were, perhaps, a little too suggestive, even in the confines of her own head, to be countenanced in the presence of one who occupied an important part of that fantasy world. So she blushed, and smiled to cover her embarrassment.

'It would be delightful,' she said, because of course it would, as long as she was sure about keeping her flights of fancy strictly under control.

As he accompanied her down the track between the fields towards the Heath, she was now beset by the anxiety that someone *might* actually believe that the children were hers, *theirs*! The situation became one of deep embarrassment to her, and she quickened her pace a little, so that Georgie started to whimper with the effort to keep up. How silly it all was, she must really keep her imagination in check.

'How splendid these dear children begin to look these days,' Mr Cane said rather breathlessly, because of the pace. 'I cannot help feeling that this must be due to your own sympathetic and understanding support of the family.'

'Mrs Johnson has become my friend,' Mary said, relaxing a little. 'She needs a small amount of guidance and company, and we both profit from that.'

'Of course, of course. I find it splendid, Miss Abrahams, that you are able and willing to make the lives of others less burdensome by your administrations. It is a true gift you know. One I so much admire.' He found himself irritated with the conventional words that emanated from his conventionally controlled mind, and he heard strange, unrecognised sentences forming in his head. 'You are fabulous, Mary Abrahams,' he heard himself thinking. 'The girl of my dreams.' This girl had all the qualities he felt he lacked. Why did he have to be so ineffectual and so dull? Her very presence filled him with a spirit of exhilaration.

'You are very kind, Mr Cane.' How delightful it was to be praised! Did he really admire her? Did he really think that she lightened the burdens of others?

There was a silence between them, that for Mary was full of excited anticipation, try as she might to suppress it. She felt warm, with a new sort of confidence, and in her mind there was a sudden clear picture of the two of them, side by side, in a positive aura of – what? She could not explain the rather shocking revelation, but she did, at that moment, feel as though they actually belonged together, and that each could only achieve his or her life potential in a combined effort. It was exciting, and quite took her breath away.

'I have heard from Miss Tripp,' she said by way of damping down her uncomfortably intimate feelings towards him, 'that you run a mission for poor, unfortunate girls.'

He blushed as easily as she did. He had not dared broach such an indelicate subject as that of unfortunate girls. Did she know of such things? Surely not. How could she?

'Well I – I – well I . . .' He became extremely agitated, and clasped and unclasped his hands behind him as he walked, cursing himself for his inadequacies.

'I do so admire you for that work,' she said, in an attempt to put him more at ease. 'Georgie dear, here are some crumbs for the ducks.'

He relaxed a fraction. 'The mission is actually run in conjunction with St Mary's Church in Somers Town, where the condition of the poor is quite deplorable,' he said. 'I go there to help them in their work. It is no more than my bounden duty towards the fallen women of our society. To help them towards God.' Why be so pious about it? he thought angrily. All these pedantic phrases he had adopted over the years seemed suddenly pompous and meaningless.

Mary frowned a little. He sounded like a tract, the sort her mother encouraged her to read. He was repeating what he thought he should. 'Why fallen women?' she asked rather tartly.

Again he blushed. Of course she did not understand

these things. He had used a term he thought she might accept because of its general use in society. The sort of word one used without having to consider its actual interpretation. But why dress things up? Why not be honest?

'I have often wondered about that expression,' Mary continued into the rather awkward pause. 'I think we should not call them fallen, because that means "Fallen from grace", and I do believe this cannot be the case for many of those poor unfortunate creatures.'

Where were the words coming from? She was astounded at herself. What did she know of poor unfortunate women? Where did this sense of indignation originate? How did she dare to speak thus indelicately to Mr Cane? 'I think, Mr Cane,' she found her voice saying, 'it is perhaps the men who have fallen from grace for being the cause of these girls' misfortune. I would say that the women are merely victims of man's greed and selfish appetites. Take care, Georgie, not too near the water.'

Both Mary and Mr Cane were astonished by her remarks, and Mary hid her embarrassment by plumping Madge up in the perambulator, and giving her a crust of bread to chew on. 'Let us pray that this little pet will grow up with enough sense to stand up to the threat of male domination, and fight for the rights of women.' She clapped her hands over her mouth, and looked round at Mr Cane in horror. 'What am I saying?' she said. 'I do beg your pardon, Mr Cane.'

After the initial shock and the quick readjustment of his thinking, Mr Cane felt a degree of normality creep back into his being. 'You are a truly remarkable lady,' he said at length. She was saying all the things over which he had kept silence. She was what his suppressed conscience had occasionally dared him to be.

'Am I? Am I really?' It was the first time she had been called a lady rather than a girl. How very odd it sounded. She still stared at him rather wildly. 'I didn't

91

know I had these thoughts in me. It was just as though someone else was speaking.'

'Perhaps it was God.' But of course it was God! And He was speaking to both of them!

Mary shot a glance at him beneath her eyelashes. He seemed perfectly serious as he said it. Could he be joking though? But he would never joke about that sort of thing. What a strange remark to make. 'But God does not have those sort of views, surely? The Bible is very clear on the role of women, is it not?'

'Christ interprets God's word rather differently. He did not always agree with the Mosaic interpretation of the law.'

Richard Cane thought to himself: Why have I never thought of this before? What a hypocrite I am. She is opening doors I never even realised were shut.

'I shall never again consider,' he said, 'one who may come to me for help as anything but someone who has been sinned against. God forgive me for my lack of humility, and God be praised for giving you the words to make me aware of my own failings.'

Mary felt just about as radiant as she looked. She picked Madge out of the perambulator and swung her around. 'What a perfectly lovely day this is,' she said. 'I have never experienced such a beautiful day. And please, Mr Cane, I wish to join you in the work you are doing for these sinned-against girls. May I do that? It is exactly the sort of thing I have always wanted to do. To serve and be of some real use in the world, however slight the help I may be able to give. You will surely be able to guide me to someone whose life I may be able to make a trace more happy, yes?'

Mr Cane hesitated. Was it right to take one so young into such degradation and depravity? 'I am not sure . . .'

'Oh but yes, you are sure, and so am I sure. We shall override any problems, confound our enemies and triumph in our crusade.'

The laughter that caught up with them drowned the

doubts in Richard Cane's mind. Of course it was right. 'I shall straightway polish up my armour,' he said, 'and together we shall overcome.'

How immodest the whole thing was. What had come over him? This new personality that was being aroused within him was alarming in its directness. What could it be that Mary's presence had set in motion? Whatever it was, it was quite uncontrollable, and even the children seemed swept up in the joy of the moment. Madge crowed with delight, and Georgie skipped along beside them, as they half ran, half danced their way back over the Heath. They had both decided that it was a blessed beginning – of what, they were not certain, but that scarcely mattered – something was born on that afternoon.

Thus Mary began to pursue another of her life's aims in the role of servant of the people. And with the pursuit, of necessity, came an increase in her own self-assuredness. But her happiness brought with it sudden anxiety and guilt about her father's well-being. It had been immoral to walk away from him without so much as a backward glance, or even a backward thought. Was he happy? What was he doing without them? How could she have wiped him from her mind like this? Could it possibly be resentment?

Beset with guilt, she set out one day with two jars of the plum jam she had made the previous day, and a pair of mittens which she had knitted. He had liked to wear mittens while painting during the winter months. The Downshire Hill garden was overgrown and untended. She was shocked to see the cat, thin and wild, peering out nervously from the bushes.

Aaron opened the door to her, and her heart lurched at the sight of him, not just because of the emotion in their meeting but also because he did not in the least look like the father she held in her memory. Was it that she had formed a wrong image of him for all these years? That he was not really as she imagined? Or had

93

he changed during those months into this small, ineffectual little person with no spirit and no personality?

'Papa,' she said, 'you don't look well. Oh, I should have come before. Forgive me Papa, but I was not sure . . . I thought perhaps . . . oh forgive me Papa.'

As he held her to him, she saw the tears running down his face. What madness was this? He surely should be relieved and released to be without the burden and responsibility of a nagging wife and a self-satisfied daughter? What was wrong?

They walked together into the clutter of the studio, Aaron still silent; with emotion? Or grief? She could not yet tell.

'I have brought some scones for our tea Papa, and a pot of your favourite jam.'

She went into the kitchen and was aghast at what she found. Had nothing been done since they left all those months ago? The chaos was complete, with dirt, decaying food and stacked plates everywhere. Mary felt immediately responsible. How could she have thought . . .? How could she not have thought . . .?

'Papa, dear Papa.' She stirred the embers of the studio stove and set the kettle to boil. 'What has happened to you? Where is the servant girl? Where is Jessie? And where are your paintings?'

All the canvases were stacked face to the wall.

'My life stopped when you left,' Aaron said. 'Just like the blowing out of a candle. Don't ask me why. I could not have believed it. It seemed you were my inspiration and my reason for living.'

Mary spread jam carefully on a scone with her heart pounding. 'What nonsense is this?' she said as gently as her own anxiety allowed. How had she been so blind as to overlook her own immediate responsibilities before taking on those outside?

'I thought, you see,' Aaron said later, as they drank tea together, 'I thought that you were taking over my painting Mary. I thought your influence was somehow too dominant and that you were undermining or overpowering my individual self. But I found instead that without you I was nothing and could do nothing.' Tears again started rolling down his face.

Mary made a wan attempt to control the guilt and panic she felt rising into her throat. 'Papa this is not true. You know that it is not true. I have always had such a respect and such an admiration for you and your paintings. All I have ever wanted to do was to support you in your work. I am just your daughter, and though now it seems that I have not been a dutiful daughter, in future I will do my best to amend that fault. We are still part of a family and I will never let myself forget that from now on.'

So another responsibility. She must see to it that her father was fed and cared for and that his confidence in himself and his painting was restored. Was it possible? There were occasions when her faith in herself faltered slightly, but on these few occasions, God actually joined in the conversations she continued to have with Him, He was quite definite. 'Stop piddling around,' He roared, 'Of course you're capable, or if you're not, then you'll be no good for the real job I've got lined up for you. No more dilly-dallying now, or I'll be forced to make someone else my chosen person.' So there really *was* no choice.

Mary did not tell Annie that she had been to see Aaron. She thought it wiser not to until she believed there might be some chance of a reconciliation between the two of them. Annie, in any case, was still hostile and angry at Mary's obvious control of the situation and the confidence and assurance that showed itself so clearly. She had recently taken to entertaining Millicent Grimsby to tea on occasions. At first she was dubious of the advisability of allowing herself to be on visiting terms with anyone who was so obviously on a slightly lower social stratum than she, but she had to admit that she appreciated the comfort of a listening ear. Mrs Grimsby was both kind and discreet, and Annie was quite at her wit's end with worry about the way Mary seemed to be taking the bit between her teeth in such a shocking way.

'I really don't know what to do about her Mrs Grimsby. Such a dear sweet girl she was until her father took this turn. I do, of course blame the whole thing on him. What can you expect if a father refuses to take proper responsibility for his daughter? Though I am naturally delighted to have a respectable house to myself, away from that dreadful artistic atmosphere which can have such a shocking influence over the young. I was afraid, Mrs Grimsby, positively afraid for the morals of my Mary.' She felt it necessary to convince herself that she had chosen to leave and live a separate life for Mary's sake.

'I had to make sacrifices, of course, but I did it all for Mary, so that she could not be exposed any longer to unsavoury talk or vulgar ideas. It may be necessary for artists to feel themselves free and not bound by convention – though for the life of me I cannot see why they should consider themselves so licensed – but for a young girl to grow up in those surroundings is dangerous, and to be avoided at all costs.'

Millicent Grimsby, though understanding through local gossip the true situation, kept up the pretence. 'You were so wise to realise this, Mrs Abrahams,' she said. 'Painters and poets are wonderfully clever people and to be greatly respected for their works of art, but perhaps their way of life is not as ours might be.'

'But Mary has become so wilful of late, Mrs Grimsby. I am really most upset and pained at her headstrong attitude. Not that I am not grateful for all that she does for me. I cannot fault her for her diligent attitude towards keeping our little house most clean and neat, and our guests contented – for all that she is a mite extravagant at times – but I really cannot fault her on the whole. And yet . . .'

'She has certainly become a quite remarkable young lady in a very short time, Mrs Abrahams. When I think of the young child she was, less than one short year ago, it seems hardly possible, I do confess. Less than one short year . . .'

'I cannot complain about her manners, Mrs Grimsby,

never answers me sharply nor shows me anything but the greatest respect, you understand.'

'Oh I don't doubt that Mrs Abrahams. One can see that her nature is sweet and full of humility. One can see that clearly. Such a beautiful girl.'

'But she is none the less headstrong and wilful. Taking on unsuitable work for which she is far too young and far too inexperienced. Mixing with dreadful people in the name of charity. I said to Mr Cane that he should not allow her to be in the vicinity of the sinful dregs of humanity. It may be all right for a man, I said, and particularly one like yourself destined for holy orders, to be in their midst in order to uplift and save their souls, but to allow a child to see such degradation, and unchaperoned too – well Mr Cane, I said, I think that it is not right, not right at all.' She picked up the corner of her skirt, found a handkerchief in the pocket of her petticoat and blew her nose. 'But she will take no heed of my warnings, Mrs Grimsby. I am being made ill with the worry of it all, and especially with that particular knowledge I possess, in reference to . . .!' she raised her hand to her mouth to shield the information from eavesdroppers, 'the Second Coming, Mrs Grimsby. If the Lord Jesus should appear *now*, what might He not think of such goings on?'

Ignoring Mrs Abrahams' aberrations about the appearance of a new Messiah, Millicent Grimsby did continue to wonder to herself how such a transformation in a young girl could have taken place in so short a time. True, she had always considered Mary to be quite outstanding as a child, and outstanding in its true sense of one who stood out from the normal run of the community. Mary had always been absolutely out of the ordinary. Her looks, for one thing, had always been startling. Beautiful rather than pretty; serene was the word that came to mind, and this description was unusual when applied to a child. Something about the eyes, she thought; the way she looked at you, almost as though she knew your thoughts. Uncanny it was, now she thought back on it.

She remembered seeing Mary quite early on, when

she was in her perambulator and Annie had wheeled her through the village soon after she was born. Everyone was curious to see the offspring of this ill-assorted couple. Millicent Grimsby remembered distinctly the shock she had received when she had first set eyes on her. She had discussed it with others at the time.

'Such eyes!' some had said, and, 'What a beautiful child!' and, 'How can a couple like that have produced such outstanding beauty?'

All through her childhood, it had been apparent that Mary was an angel of a child, wise beyond her years and unchildishly perfect. But this transformation from the model child into the confident and positive young woman in the space of a few months was nothing short of a miracle.

One could not help feeling sorry for her poor mother, to have her position as undoubted head of the family so overturned by both father and daughter. One had to sympathise – and yet, to have such a paragon of virtue and practicality to tend one in one's declining years, well, this could not be all bad, Millicent Grimsby reminded herself. Another point in the favour of the transformation was a noticeable softening of Annie Abrahams' public image. It was not only Millicent herself who noticed it, but other ladies of the village, when she discussed it with them, agreed that Annie's attitude had quite noticeably taken a turn for the better.

'Not nearly so high and mighty,' Mrs Bootle, whose daughter ran the Sunday School at Christchurch, declared at one of the weekly meetings of the group of ladies who made garments for the poor. 'I do declare that recently she has stated that she might be interested in attending our group here on Wednesdays.'

'In charity, one must feel sympathy for her,' Mrs Tombs, the doctor's wife pointed out. 'One feels that perhaps the Almighty has sent these trials for her to bear so that she may see the error of her previous attitude of superiority.'

'I cannot help feeling,' Mrs Grimsby said, 'that if it is, as you suggest Mrs Tombs, a heavenly intervention, then I believe that the Almighty may be working through Mary Abrahams to achieve His own ends.'

'A very remarkable child, certainly.'

'So I would have said,' Mrs Grimsby interrupted, 'as little as six months ago. But have you not noticed the transformation of little Mary Abrahams from child into authoritative young woman this past year?'

The ladies' heads turned towards her. 'She has certainly grown tall and womanly.'

'Such an air of grace and charm about her.'

'Of course she was always beautiful.'

'And she does carry with her an element of *radiance* . . .'

They mused over the idea as their needles tacked and hemmed seams. There was suddenly a small shiver of apprehension to which none would have admitted. There was something about the girl that made them slightly uneasy.

'Mrs Abrahams says she has become very wilful of late,' Mrs Grimsby suggested, and the tension eased. It was the seeming faultlessness that was upsetting.

'Breaking out, no doubt.'

'I am sure Annie Abrahams must have kept a very strict household in Downshire Hill.'

'I believe the father had a violent temper.'

'Very violent I have been led to believe.'

'I dare say some hereditary influences may show themselves.'

'You cannot keep these things controlled for ever.'

'Such a dear child she was. How sad that there might be a blemish.'

The short silence that followed was quite different in character from the last, and the ladies smiled warmly one to the other, reassured that Mary Abrahams, most probably, had as large a quota of original sin as anybody else.

9

The impetus and ebullience which both Mary and Richard Cane experienced in their joint activities served to bring them together in more ways than one. Mary was conscious of the happiness of love flowing through her, and yet was not truly aware what this strange exuberance really was. She did not, as yet, connect it with the phenomenon of which she had sometimes read – the state of being in love. You did not fall in love with one so far removed in virtue and piety from one's own qualifications. She could admire, respect and hold in high esteem, but she did not presume to love.

Richard Cane knew well what the sensation might be, and spent many hours praying that he might keep the baser aspects of the overpowering experience under control. But the more he prayed, the greater was the feeling that his suppression of his instincts was ill-advised. It was almost as though two distinct sides of his nature were becoming apparent. Something which before he had understood to be the Devil and All His Works, was emerging as his own legitimate individuality. And this particular individual seemed to be someone he was beginning to approve òf. No longer an evil presence from which he averted his eyes, but more an emergent strength. Mary was the woman he had sought all his life; the woman without whom this same life was as nothing.

'I was considering travelling into London to attend evensong at St Martin in the Fields one day,' he finally brought himself to say. 'I have a dear friend who is serving there, and he writes to me often of the beauty of the singing of the choir in those very splendid, architectural surroundings. I wonder if you might care to share this experience? Whether you might also consider it propitious to initiate young Peg into the benefits of attending worship in such an elegant house of God?'

It was just another way of saying: I want to share my life with you. I want you to share with me an experience I have always longed to enjoy again. We could take Peg as our chaperone, and on the way, I can bring you together with my beautiful Madonna in the National Gallery. The whole idea was sinful, of course, because it was a deceit. This was really an entry into some experience he felt was lying in wait for him somewhere in the future.

The astounding suggestion made Mary's heart race with excitement. An expedition in the company of Mr Cane? Something she had never even dreamed of – well yes, perhaps she had dreamed of it, but it was the sort of dream best forgotten quickly because of the very immodesty of such a thing. Apart from that, it was really a request to step out of the accepted enclosure of her present life and upbringing into other surroundings; even other beginnings. She had, it must be said, already attended services in the churches of other denominations, and she remembered, with pain, the fierce and agitated reaction of her mother, who considered the treachery of allowing oneself to dabble in High Church ritual to be nothing short of heresy.

Was it the aura of the holiness of Mr Cane that filled Mary with the certainty that she was committing no sin by delighting in the services which they had once or twice attended together? Was she being carried away by all the pomp and circumstance? The incense, the candles, the vestments, were they really the temptations of Hell? She could not believe it to be so. The overall sensations she experienced were full of hope and joy, rather than the grim retribution she had been brought up to expect. It was a blessed release which she found strength-giving and uplifting.

'I am afraid that I do enjoy the spectacle,' she said to Mr Cane, 'It makes me feel happy and excited and full of hope. I would think it most fitting and beneficial to introduce poor, dear Peg to some of the glories of God, rather than let her grow up in the fear of His eternal wrath.'

She had been giving time to educate Peg away from the belief that her life was necessarily one of drudgery and servitude, and to introduce her instead, to the possibilities of happiness and hope. 'She is opening like a flower,' she told Miss Amelia Tripp, the seamstress in the first floor back, on one of the many visits she paid in order to talk with this calm and wise lady. When her work seemed a little too demanding, or when her mother had depressed her spirit by her harsh criticisms. Mary would then knock and slip, rather furtively, into the bright, sunny room where Miss Tripp bent endlessly over folds of chintz or muslin or fine linen. The atmosphere of the room, always seeming to be filled with sun and light, Miss Tripp's smiling presence never failed to have a soothing, calming effect, and renewed her own strength and belief in herself.

'She has indeed become your little shadow,' Miss Tripp said without lifting her head, but smiling, smiling away to herself. 'Quite a useful little chaperone one might term her.'

Mary blushed. Here was another reason she visited Miss Tripp's room every so often. There was usually a bringing to the surface of any unacknowledged doubts Mary might suspect were hiding within her. Was she indeed using Peg for her own benefit? Was this the reason for her interest and affection?

Miss Tripp raised her head and smiled straight at her. 'There is no need for you to doubt your good intentions, my dear. It is good that you both should be able to give something to the other. It is important to take as well as to give, and as long as you know that you are doing so, then the balance is kept and there is no danger of pride and self-admiration. But look, I have made some cambric petticoats for your poor ladies of Somers Town, with some bodices for their babies.'

'You are so kind.' Mary questioned in her mind at that moment why dear Miss Tripp had remained a spinster, while her own mother – she snapped back the thought in an agony of shame. 'So very kind.'

Mr Cane, Mary and Peg set out early upon the appointed day, 'Because I wish to show you some of the beautiful things that are in our city,' Mr Cane told Mary. She was scarcely less excited than Peg, and dressed in the best of her small wardrobe which nonetheless could stand up to the journey ahead of them. It was the day on which Mr Reuben, the fruiterer, drove his wagon into Covent Garden to collect goods, and he had promised them a lift. Mary felt emancipated, daring, and secure in the belief that there was a great fulfilment just around the corner, waiting to explode upon her.

But sadly, on the way there, she lost Mr Cane. Totally mislaid this man who was about to lead her forth into the paths of righteousness – or at least somewhere in that direction.

She found herself, inexplicably, on the steps of the National Gallery, without really knowing where the day had gone. The sky full of the screaming starlings, as cloud after cloud hurled themselves from high buildings and swirled at frenzied speed in huge arcs into the trees in the square. Mary had never seen nor ever heard of the roosting of the starlings before, and was transfixed by both the sight and the sound. There was something unearthly and ritualistic about the drama they performed, aloof from the world of man in their involuntary choreography. It swept thought from her mind, and with it the wispy fragments of a half-remembered dream sequence in the depths of her unconscious.

She stood still on the steps, staring at nothing except

the blur of starlings, hearing nothing but the scream and whistle of their song, and with her mind a great blank screen of nothing. But had she not come to attend evensong at St Martins? What a strange idea. Something about the beauty of the singing of the choir? Who had said that? There was something very strange about her memory these days; so much forgetting. But it would surely pass. She had never had much of a memory; nothing to worry about.

It was too early for evensong. She walked through the doors of the National Gallery. In all the time that she had lived in London, she had never been inside before. What an admission! There was time to kill, just an odd half an hour or so. But it was so big, so much to look at; where on earth to start? It was not until she found herself in the Italian section that her anxiety as to what she should be looking at drifted out of her mind. She was much more certain here, almost as though she were looking for something specific. It was quite suddenly that she found it.

She had wandered at random up steps and through rooms, with a kind of questing anxiety. What was she here for? Why did she not look at the pictures as she passed? Other people were moving slowly, reverently she supposed, pinioned before paintings; rapt, sober, respectful. The further she went, the more urgent she felt her mission. She found herself walking so fast that those who dawdled became a nuisance because they got in her way. Impatiently she brushed past them until she came up against what appeared to be a wall of gold. The whole vista was overpoweringly rich, bright, and at first sight rather vulgar. The walls seemed to be encrusted with bright gold and jewels and white light. The dazzle blistered her sight and took her breath away.

She stood directly opposite the Crivelli Annunciation. She had never seen any reproduction so it was her first encounter with the painting. First encounter, in fact, with any mediaeval painting. The nuns at school had favoured the Raphaels and Leonardos for their illustrations. Mary was startled by the detailed, unsentimental approach, but the first riveting glance had been drawn, with powerful force, to the figure of the angel. The virgin might have the delicate, fine-spun thread of light needling across the sky and through the massive stone building to mark her out as the chosen handmaiden, but to Mary, the star of the painting was undoubtedly the angel Gabriel. With the fragile wings, the stylish, pedantic fingers, and above all, the startling beauty of his features, there really could be nothing else of any consequence to match this exquisite creature. He immediately won her disengaged affections.

She feasted on the picture for some fifteen rapt minutes before allowing everyday surroundings to claim her back into reality. Then she reeled away in a daze, and stumbled towards the stairs and the main hall. There was still time to go to evensong, and it seemed a natural progression to do so. To finish off a spiritual experience with another.

As she came out of the gallery into the shadowed late afternoon, the starlings were still wheeling intermittently, but their shrieks and screams had become less frenzied. It was still clear though, that every single one of those beating, fluttering, black entities outlining every tree and building was uttering its own evening hymn. The sky behind the shaded buildings was azure, striped with surprising pink. It was all unreal and unlikely – a hallucination even. What was she doing at the top of these steps looking out over Trafalgar Square?

Equally, once inside the church, the suspicion of fallacy followed her, though everyone and everything was oddly familiar. The billowing surplices of the choir and clergy; the candles, the light through the windows; the euphoria and the tranquillity; the certainty and the confidence that every now and then wrapped itself around her like an aura as she stood just within the door,

105

watching and listening. The very infallibility she felt was untrue. Utterly confusing.

She talked about it later when she returned to the house.

'It was really so odd. I don't know why I went or anything, it was all very dreamlike and wonderful.'

Maggie was correcting books in the sitting room and eating Indian take-away which was balanced on the chair arm. 'You're going to have to watch yourself, you goon,' she said absently, marking a furious red cross against an untidy mess of figures on a page. 'What this idiot thinks he's doing I'll never know. I've told him over and over again that I have to be able to read it before I can correct it. I loathe teaching.'

Lou and Jude from the upstairs back were milling round the cooker. 'Jude darling, do you *mind*? How do you expect me to cook with you positively seething round me like this? Can you believe the clumsiness of this photographer? Calls himself a balanced personality and spills soup all over the floor.'

Jude smiled benignly. 'Oh go and practise your pliés,' he said.

'I keep forgetting things,' Mary went on as though there had been no interruption. 'I'm sure I'm going mental or something. I am always thinking there's something I ought to remember only I can't think what.'

Maggie looked up at her, 'You're psychopathic and cram full of hypochondria. But don't let it worry you, I expect you'll live.'

'It won't be the cough that'll carry you off,' Jude said. 'But the coffin they'll carry you offin.'

Lou groaned, 'Your jokes are heinous. So absolutely *lacking* somehow.' He poured the soup into a bowl. 'Here you are, now just take, eat and be thankful, and don't forget to do this in remembrance of me or I might be ever so, ever so cross. Or even worse.'

They made their way up the few steps out of the kitchen and into the dining end of the room.

'Am I going mad do you think?'

'Don't be so stupid,' said Maggie. 'Stop worrying about yourself. Think about someone else for a change.'

Mary blushed for probably the tenth time that day. Maggie was right; she must curb this terrible self-absorption.

'You're absolutely right. I'm horribly bound up with myself. I do realise it when I stop to think. I must make myself remember other people's sufferings and ailments rather than my own.'

Maggie tore her mind from corrections and calculations and stared at her sister. What a little prude she was. How to get her out of it? How to shake her free of this sanctimonious godliness she seemed to wrap herself in? How was it that she had become so unworldly? It could be excused in the very young, but Mary should be growing out of it by now. She sighed. 'Why do you have to be so incredibly – well – good? It's not natural.'

Mary's eyes filled with tears at once. 'But I'm not good,' she said. 'Not at all good. I think of myself all the time, and I'm self-satisfied and stupid. I'm just awful.' She covered her face with her hands and cried loudly, like a small child.

Maggie felt exasperated to the point of screaming. Mim burst suddenly and noisily out of her room across the hall.

'What's the matter? What's the matter?' she rushed to Mary and put her arms round her, and then looked at Maggie. 'What have you done to her you ogre?'

'What have I done?' Maggie's scream was released in the reiteration. 'Can I help it if she becomes hysterical at the drop of a hat.'

Lou and Jude, drawn by the sounds of hysteria, left their meal to join the mêlée, and at the same moment, Rollocks and Penny, bundled enormously in woollen sweaters, scarves, hats and gloves, and carrying numbers of packages that included indoor plants and a lamp, jostled themselves past the ever-increasing crowdedness of the kitchen, from the cold of the outside.

Rollocks let the three paper carriers he was holding fall on to the floor, where they split and distributed the contents, consisting of tins, bottles and oranges among the feet of the participants of the affray.

'Who's been dropping hats?' he shouted breezily. 'And who's been upsetting Mary baby?'

'Don't tell him.' Lou clattered the plates into the sink, turned the taps on and started to sing.

Jude held his head. 'What a hidjus din. *Please* – can we discuss – oh God, I'm being got at by a tense nervous headache.'

Penny surveyed the scene with distaste. 'Can't really do with all this emotion. Just too much, yah.'

'Sorry,' sobbed Mary. 'I'm really so sorry. It's nobody fault, it's just me being stupid.'

'Darling, you're not stupid. You mustn't think that. You're so *sweet*, really you are.' Mim looked round defensively. 'You're all so mean,' she said, rather inconsequentially.

Maggie flung herself back into her chair and picked up the pile of exercise books. Her plate fell on the floor, and Lou stepped delicately forward over rolling oranges to retrieve it. 'Seelly eesn't it,' he said, placing knife and fork primly back on the plate. 'Naughty *naughty* tempers when love is really all you need.' He walked briskly back into the kitchen and put the plate in the sink, and the commotion gradually dissipated into a self-conscious pause.

Mim led Mary back into her room with a 'never-mind-I'll-look-after-you' look on her face. 'You must learn to stand up to people you know, and not let them walk all over you. Maggie doesn't mean to be unkind, it's just that she's so efficient and clever herself that it makes her a bit impatient with others.'

'I know, I know,' Mary wiped the tears from her face with the backs of her hands, and the dribble off the end of her nose with the palms. She looked round for something to wipe her hands on, then rubbed them on her jeans. 'I was crying about me, not about anyone being nasty to me. I'm just so much the sort of person I don't want to be. I have such great ideas and hopes and – sort of visions about what I want to do. But things never work out. I mean things aren't how you imagine them – oh I can't explain.'

'I know exactly what you mean.' Mim took a cigarette and searched round the room for her lighter. 'You don't have to explain darling. We all feel like that at some time or other – specially when we're young.' She could have sworn she put it on the table just five minutes ago. She pulled open a drawer and scuffled about inside it through scarves, a hairbrush, make-up and crumpled tissues. Where the hell was it?

'I had such a wonderful thing happen today.'

'Did you love? What was that?' Jamie must have taken it, the moron. And there were no matches either, not even in the kitchen. Maggie wouldn't leave any near the cooker because everyone pinched them.

'I saw this incredible picture. It was by Crivelli.'

'Zeffirelli? Romeo and Juliet you mean? But I thought you saw that ages ago.'

'No, not a movie, a picture in the National Gallery.'

Mim gave a shout of laughter, 'Oh God – sorry! How *sweet*, what sort of a picture?'

'It was the Annunciation.'

'The Annunciation? How *great*. God, back to childhood – do you remember all those bleeding hearts we kept under our pillows at school? I mean when you just think of it, wasn't it frightful? And I really believed they'd bring me luck you know.'

Mary giggled. 'So did I, and they did too.'

'Oh give up, do.' Mim doubled up with laughter. 'You're so hopelessly naive.'

Coming from Mim, the criticism was far less wounding. Mary didn't even feel guilty about it. 'Yes, I know I shouldn't believe such stuff, but I've still got that rosary, you know. Couldn't ever get rid of it.'

'There are things you cling to; I've kept a shirt button from the first youth I ever kissed.'

'I haven't kissed anyone yet, I mean not really kissed. I get frightened.'

Mim sighed. 'You've got to be a bit more – well – aggressive, sort of.'

'I can't be. I don't feel aggressive.'

'I suppose aggressive's the wrong word. But you're a kind of mixture between a baby and a saint, and that's too much for most men.'

'But I don't seem to need men.'

'Everyone needs someone, lovey. You're so inhibited you just keep it down all the time so that you *think* you don't need it. You're probably scared to death and so don't allow yourself to think about it. Don't you ever feel sexy? I mean sort of itchy down there and thinking sexy thoughts and things?'

'No.'

'Not excited by seeing naughty pictures and things?'

'Well this picture today did make me feel most extraordinary, rather like I was floating.'

Mim looked at her quizzically. 'I can't see how an Annunciation could make you feel sexy.'

'There was this great angel, he was just wonderful. So beautiful and everything.'

Mim crowed with laughter. 'That's typical,' she said, 'trust you to get all randy about an angel.'

Mary joined in the laughter because she suddenly felt light-hearted and secure. Perhaps today's experience was a sexy one. It was certainly nothing like anything she had felt before, though she could not imagine making any actual physical contact with the angel in the painting. It was the beauty of those fine, delicate wings that could never have supported a real being, and the absurd frailty of his hands that had moved her most. The unreality sparked off most of the excitement.

'When I looked at it,' she said, 'I felt as though I was witnessing a sort of manifestation, like Bernadette.'

Mim groaned. 'Oh God, so now we're going to have to set up a grotto in the National Gallery are we? Well bags I be Mary in the film of the book – or even the book of the film.'

10

'I don't reckon Miss,' Peg said, as she applied black lead liberally and vigorously to the grate in Annie's and Mary's small back kitchen, 'as any child from that workhouse from what I come from, don't have no better time nor what I do Miss.'

Mary laughed at the mixture of grammatical blunders, and gave Peg a hug. 'I'm so glad you're happy here,' she said. 'I somehow knew we'd get on as soon as I saw you. And one day, when I get a bit more time, I really intend to help you to read and write properly so that you can enjoy life more.'

'Don't reckon I could Miss,' Peg said. 'Enjoy life more I mean Miss. I don't ask for no more than to eat and drink proper, and to please you, Miss. That's real pleasure.'

'You and I are lucky people, Peg,' Mary said, 'because we do enjoy life so much, though many people might consider us to have been quite unfortunate in various ways. Your misfortunes, of course, were far greater than mine, I suppose they can scarcely be compared.'

Peg glanced up at Mary and thought about the misfortune of having Annie for a mother, and having, presumably, as unsatisfactory a father as she had herself. 'Oh no Miss, if you'll pardon me,' she said, 'even though I didn't have no mother and father what I knew of Miss, that's no worsen having them what don't treat you right.'

It all depended on how you looked at it, Mary thought, and was yet another instance of the way both Peg and she were able to admit to the possibilities rather than the insuperability of events.

'You should thank God for giving you a cheerful nature,' she said.

'Oh I do Miss, I do.' Peg's smile positively radiated over her face. 'And I really means it when I say me prayers now. For you, and for this lovely home, and for all them nice people we look after Miss, you and me, and more than all that Miss, for my little room there under the roof, so warm and happy and snug and that Miss.' She paused in her polishing to find a clean place on the duster, and she looked up sideways at Mary again. 'I got a friend up there Miss,' she said shyly, pushing back a strand of hair that had escaped her cap.

'A friend? What do you mean? A mouse is it? Or a sparrow that comes in?'

'Oh no Miss, nothing like that Miss. It's a boy Miss, quite a bit younger than me he is. He don't say nothing, just sits and looks. Quite eerie it is sometimes Miss, because he ain't reelly there I don't think. But he's ever so reel, just sits there or stands by the wall and sort of smiles at me so I ain't reelly afeared Miss, though well I might be when I think about it because he's a little savage Miss, and I ain't never seen a savage before except in pictures. He's as black as your hat Miss. I never seen nothing like it. But he don't mean no harm like.'

Mary's heart seized painfully. 'A little black boy?' she said. 'Where does he come from?' What a silly question, because she knew Peg could not answer it, but it gave her a moment to recover her composure. She felt all the little hairs on her body standing starkly upright, and the flesh at the back of her neck tingling.

'There's certainly something about this house,' she said at length, 'something I don't quite understand, I have to admit. But I can't feel that it is evil. You are not afraid you say?'

Peg's smile radiated out again like the sun. 'Oh no Miss. Don't you be troubling yourself on that score. I wouldn't never have told you if I thought you was going to worry Miss. He's a friend, even though he don't say nothing. He's part of a good luck thing Miss, I know it. Like he wants to tell me something special about something Miss. He makes me feel reel happy when he's there.'

'Then it must be all right.' Mary's smile joined Peg's. Something about two laughing girls floated into her mind from a great distance, and she felt like laughing herself. There was certainly nothing evil; quite the opposite. She wondered if she could tell Mr Cane about it, and knew, simultaneously, that she had to do so, whatever his reaction might be.

They talked as they walked back from the Somers Town mission one early evening, with Peg trundling behind them. That walk was one of the highlights of Mary's week – of both their weeks. It was perhaps a self-indulgence, disguised as an economy. They took the horse bus down, as they usually had food and clothing bundles to carry, but then put the pennies they would have spent on the return fare into the poor box, feeling a little guilty that the self-denial should be so enjoyable. It was a long pull up the hill, which was occasionally made lighter by a lift part of the way from passing carts or hay wains, or even the infrequent doctor in his gig. Carriages passed them, unheeding, which was only to be expected, times being what they were. Richard seemed to find the walk far more exhausting than she did, and she regarded him anxiously as he paused for breath and a bout of coughing while crossing a stile.

'Does all this walking tire you too much?'

He laughed. 'What? You consider me a weakling? No no, the fresh air does me nothing but good.'

She felt illogically reassured. 'Have you ever thought, Mr Cane, that our little house has something special about it?' Mary did not wish to make her meaning too clear so that his answer might be unbiased.

Richard Cane was silent as he considered his reply.

114

He felt anxiety which he did not wish to communicate to Mary. It was something more than special, something that made him uneasy and yet filled him with an overpowering anticipation; something awesome yet benevolent. 'It is indeed a gentle, embracing house, as I have so often said. But whether that is the result of its sticks and stones, or the character of its owner is easy to answer I believe.'

Mary smiled at the compliment, and decided to be more explicit. 'I was questioning more the character of the house itself,' she said. 'Do you not find something – something one might call a trifle *strange* on occasions?' Most probably it was all in her imagination, and Peg could easily have made up the story.

Again there was a fractional silence which permitted grasshopper whirrings and hedge sparrow twitterings to surface and mix with the crunch of feet on the road's gravel. How clear and clean the air seemed as they climbed out of the sad squalor of Camden Town, Mary thought.

'I have noticed,' Richard Cane said hesitantly, 'that at times there seems to be a – what might be described as – a presence.'

So it was not her imagination. Was it relief or apprehension that assailed her? 'A beneficent presence do you think?'

Again he hesitated. 'In that any presence may be considered to come from a soul not at rest, then we have to assume that there may be distress attached to it. But I have to say that the presence I have felt has both warmth and beneficence as its aura. I would dare to say that it comes from God rather than from the Devil, if this is a possibility.'

'I think it must be a possibility Mr Cane.'

'It must be so, Miss Abrahams, I truly believe.'

Yet another glad area of agreement and understanding. They both felt absurdly elated.

'Could we not make some enquiry into the history of

the house?' she said. 'Might we not find something relevant? If there was something unhappy and unable to rest, then it might be possible to help and exorcise such a thing.'

It was the beginning of another combined operation. The reading up of local history, wherever it might be found, and the study of Church and other local records. Richard glowed with the sparkle of Mary's enthusiasm. He suddenly wanted to know. Instead of backing away from the mystery, he wished to forge forward with discovery. No longer content with the suspicion of something mysterious, but eager to go out and find out.

Mary even managed to combine the study with the continuation of Peg's education, getting her to copy out dates and information which might conceivably be relevant. She found the increased overfilling of her time, so that no part of her life was left empty, to be very satisfactory. There was no waste. It was so important to live life to the full. But in spite of the search and the animated discussions on anything they might discover, the only thing of any real significance which turned up was that a witch had once lived in the immediate vicinity; a young girl of nineteen it seemed – also, by strange coincidence named Mary – who was accused, set upon and ducked in the nearby pond by local people. After this, it was said, she mysteriously disappeared from the district.

'What a gruesome story,' Mary said with a shudder. 'How venomous people were in those days, and I expect the poor girl was merely feeble-minded. I don't believe that she could be our presence, do you Mr Cane?'

'I can hardly imagine so,' he said. 'There seems to be no evidence of fear, and certainly no venom in Lavender Cottage. Rather a sense of tranquillity and a certain –' He paused to consider his words. 'A certain quiet infallibility and security about the place.' Like my darling, blessed angel Mary, he heard himself thinking and blushed a little at the idea.

'The tranquil, infallible cottage,' Mary laughed.

116

'What an unusual description. Strange, and a little eerie that the girl should have been called Mary, but I suppose it is a common enough name for all time.'

'A beautiful and holy name,' said Mr Cane.

'I am glad that at least we have found nothing actually connected with the house that could possibly be described as evil or unpleasant; the witch incident could have been anywhere in the vicinity.'

A slight chill persisted in her mind, however, at the coincidence of the name. But what was momentous about a girl called Mary? The question raised a half memory – Em? Em for Mary? Mim for Mary? She snapped her mind back to reality and away from nonsense.

'It seems that this was once the site of stables for the big house,' Mary told Peg. 'But farm stables and cow-sheds, not grand stables for the gentry's carriages. I like to think of cows grazing round here, and perhaps sheep.'

'And pigs,' Peg added.

'And not that long ago either.'

'I expect that boy what visits me looked after the pigs Miss,' Peg went on, 'I don't somehow think he could have done much more than that Miss, he don't seem too bright.'

'You still see him?' Mary had almost lost touch with the reason for their researches. The pleasures of the combined study with Mr Cane had taken over so completely.

'Oo-ar, 'e still comes fairly regular like. But 'e still don't say nothing Miss.'

All just in her mind, it had to be. Perhaps the memory of a long-lost brother. Nothing really here. After all, no one else in the house had mentioned anything. They all seemed so happy now, quite like the family Mary had imagined when they had first taken over.

Her mother appeared to have come to a grudging and disgruntled impasse of disapproving dullness, but she was far less aggressive these days; almost as though she had given up the struggle, Mary decided. The indignity

117

of her position as a wronged wife and an unheeded mother did, however, arouse a sense of condolence among her acquaintances, of which she made full use. The small congregation of diligent ladies bent over their knitting and their sewing, still met weekly. Leaning towards each other in murmured discourse behind unfinished cambric bodices and knitted Spencers. There was an air of secretive self-sufficiency about the assembly which tended to stifle Mary when she passed by the open door of the parlour on the days they met there, and it was as much as she could do to pour the tea when she and Peg served them refreshments at four o'clock.

'Quite a smell they has Miss, don't they?' Peg said as they withdrew to the kitchen later. Mary tried to suppress her laughter.

'Hush Peg, it is most impolite to make personal remarks of that nature.'

Peg eyed her to see how deep her disapproval went. 'Begging their pardons of course,' she said, 'but that Miss Tripp now, she always smells that nice now don't she Miss?'

It was true of course. Peg always appreciated the things that Mary herself noticed, and the mention of Miss Tripp immediately brought the clean smell of Pears soap, and the warm smell of freshly ironed seams to her senses.

'And that Mr Grebe, Miss,' Peg went on, 'now 'e reelly do smell lovely because of what 'e do put on 'is 'air don't 'e Miss?'

'Aitches, Peg, do try to remember them.' Mary smiled as she thought of earnest, anxious Mr Grebe, with his pomaded hair and moustaches, in the room on the first floor that had the skylight to let in the light, and incidentally the rain as well. She felt a little guilty about Mr Grebe when it rained, but he never complained, merely asked for a bucket to catch the drips. Joey was always working on that skylight, but never seemed quite able to track down the problem.

As she worried about Mr Grebe and his bucket, she felt a sudden draught catch at her, seeming to spin her round, and she found herself inexplicably standing in Mr Grebe's room; but instead of the small bucket there was an immense receptacle to catch the drips. The room was all warm and steamy, and smelt strongly of gardenia and there was Mim lying submerged in bubbles in a grossly overflowing bath.

'It's all coming through to the kitchen,' Mary said breathlessly from having charged up the stairs as the stream of bathwater poured through the kitchen ceiling. 'For goodness sake let some out before the ceiling comes down.'

'What?' Mim surfaced through the bubbles with her hair clinging flat to her head. 'What's the matter? Oh sorry – why didn't it go down the overflow?'

'You've got the taps full on, that's why.' Mary turned off the taps and piled bath towels on the floor to soak up the flood.

'I just love the feeling of being under water with the taps on,' Mim said, looking over the edge of the bath at the mess. She started to laugh. 'Oh God. I do seem to have gone a bit over the top in all senses of the word.'

Mary joined in the laughter, rather unwillingly at first, but gradually becoming helplessly convulsed. 'Maggie will go up the wall,' she gasped, and they both let out renewed shouts of, by this time, quite uncontrollable mirth.

Maggie came out of her room and stood, staring and aghast, at the sight. 'Are you out of your minds?' she yelled. 'I can see absobloody-lutely nothing to laugh at.'

The bottle of bubble bath liquid had been knocked over in the commotion, and the bubbles refused to be suppressed; they flowed out on to the landing and started down the stairs. The door to Jude and Lou's room, next to the bath room, opened, bringing a blast of music from the hi-fi. Lou was wearing a long purple evening dress while Jude had shaving soap on his face and wore a jock strap.

'Perleez – what's all the racket? Can we join in or is it private? Oh Judie look, it's snowing.' Lou sat down in the bubbles and started to pile them on his head.

'You'll spoil your frock,' Jude said.

'No I won't, it's hundred per cent pure polyester.'

Mim and Mary were still emitting wails of laughter, which increased Maggie's wrath. 'If one of you raving lunatics could go and fetch some sort of mop at least,' she shouted. 'I don't see why I should wade through all this and get myself soaked.' She leaned to call over the bannisters, 'For God's sake, down there, someone bring up a mop and bucket.'

'A mop and bucket? Why? Has someone been sick?' Rollocks and Penny were drinking coffee in the dining room.

'Doesn't matter why – bring it.'

'Penny, you lazy sod. Don't you hear the girl? Fetch a bucket. Christ, there's a whole lot of water pouring out of the lampshade. Maggie, did you know, there's a whole lot of water pouring out of the lampshade.'

At that minute, Matt came in at the front door, a small, serious-looking little black boy behind him.

'Where is everybody? Go on up the stairs,' he said to the boy, then, 'I've brought someone to meet you all.'

'Splendid,' said Maggie, 'that's just what we need.'

Matt hung up his coat in the hall, while the boy obediently started up the stairs, to be met by the bubbles coming down. He continued slowly, ankle deep, until he reached the landing. Mim, naked and still helpless with laughter, was rummaging in the linen cupboard for a dry towel. The small boy came to a stop beside her as she looked down.

'Oh – hallo,' she said. 'Are you actually old enough to be looking at me like that? Shouldn't someone be putting their hands over your eyes and leading you away or something? The bath overflowed you see.' And she hung

120

over the bannister in another paroxysm of laughter.

Mary began to control her laughter in deference to Maggie's rage. 'Soap dissolves detergent bubbles,' she said helpfully.

'So what do you suggest?' Maggie asked. 'We mix up some soap bubbles and pour them on top of these?'

Matt arrived at the top of the stairs. 'Oh God,' he said, and took the small boy's hand. 'This is John Wild,' he said, 'if anyone wants to know, and he's come to stay with us for a bit.'

Some forty minutes later, everyone was lying, in various stages of collapse, all round the sitting room, drinking tea, coffee and cocoa. Maggie's anger had increased a hundredfold because of the restriction placed on it by the presence of John Wild. It was not possible to continue a family row in front of an unknown, and probably highly disturbed, homeless child. Matt had no consideration. Why did he have to spring things on them like this? How could he dare to bring home one of his cases and expect them all to take him on?

'We've got a very nice room you can stay in,' Mary said to John Wild, more to break the silence than to inform. She felt that the child must be suffering acute embarrassment and shyness at being thrust so suddenly into the demented commotion of a Lavender Cottage community crisis.

John spoke for the first time, turning his head to look at Mary as he did so. 'Is it in the attic?' he asked.

'Why did you think of that?' Matt said. 'Did you sleep in an attic at home?'

'No,' said John.

'As it's about the only habitable place left,' Maggie said crossly, 'there's really no choice.'

'Isn't he *sweet*,' Mim said in an audible whisper. 'How old are you darling?'

'Fourteen,' John said, but Matt intervened, in a quiet, conciliatory, social worker voice. 'No John, not fourteen, you are eight, remember?'

121

'Yes,' John said. 'Will Peg be up there?'

Matt's voice became even quieter. 'No, no, you don't have to worry about a thing, John. You'll be able to have a room all to yourself here, without anyone to bother you.' He turned to the others. 'He had rather a bad time at the children's home,' he said, 'bit of bullying went on.'

'Peg don't bother me,' John said.

'Come and see the room,' Mary said, 'then you can see if you like it.'

They went out of the room together, and Maggie's exasperation exploded. 'You're mad Matt, if you think you can bring your case work back home for us to deal with.'

'Shut up, you boring old bat,' Matt said. 'I'm not asking you to deal with anything. He's just had an extra hard time of it and it would make all the difference if he could stay where there were no other children until we can get him fostered or adopted. He goes to the school at the end of the road and just needs a little love and care, that's all.'

'Poor little angel,' Mim said, 'I think he's absolutely sweet. I'd love to look after him.'

'You'd smother him with love until something else turned up, then you'd forget all about him,' Maggie reminded her.

'I really can't see that it's such a big deal,' Matt insisted. 'Do you mean that all of us here can't together help to look after one small boy for a week or so? What do the rest of you think?'

'Of course he must stay.'

'Can't see the problem myself.'

'After all, we are a sort of commune,' Lou said, 'why can't we be magnanimous and generous?'

'We are not a tired old sixties type commune,' Maggie shouted, 'and don't any of you forget it.'

'Suffer little children . . .' said Jude.

'Oh shut up do,' said everyone else.

'Poor little pet, can't we adopt him?'

122

'We'd never pass the vetting,' Matt said. 'We're all pretty unsuitable in our separate ways.'

'Speak for yourself dear, Jude and I are an eminently suitable couple from any point of view. Nobody could surely object to us.'

'I could,' Rollocks said. 'I think you're shit.'

'Oh go on, we're all right, if you like that sort of thing.'

'So? We are agreed? He stays?'

'Don't say I didn't warn you,' Maggie said gloomily. 'None of you thinks ahead. You don't know what difficulties you're setting up for yourselves and for him. You're so bloody irresponsible, all of you.'

The three sisters looked at each other with feelings of confusion. How was it that they were so divided on this issue? Each understood the reasoning of the other, yet their attitudes wrapped themselves up in separate parcels and remained isolated in their individual personalities. It was a moment of intense sadness for all three.

11

Except that they came through the front door and used the hallway to reach the door into the yard, Percy and Grace Barber, with their baby Constance, from the ground floor back, were more or less cut off from the rest of the community in the house. Mary felt uncomfortable that they did not seem a part of the group. Percy Barber was a shy man who taught in the nearby school, and his wife was a mouse-like shadow who appeared to flit, noiselessly, through the hallway from time to time, almost as though she waited for the moment when no one was looking. The baby was pale and angelic and never seemed to cry. They used the two rooms under the Johnsons' room, one as a scullery kitchen which they entered from the yard. As there was a door at the back of the yard that led into a passageway connecting the stables at the back of the house to the High Street, they often chose to make their entrance that way. They were scarcely a part of the family, Mary decided; the situation had to be remedied.

She knocked one day at the entrance to their apartment, and when Grace Barber's timid face appeared around the door, she found herself bristling with a sense of rejection. This would not do.

'May I come in for a moment?' she asked. 'Is your husband home? I would so like to speak to you both.'

Percy Barber appeared behind his wife, and opened the door wider. 'Of course, Miss Abrahams. Please come in.'

'I see so little of you,' Mary said, 'I hardly know you at all. It is a little disagreeable to feel that we are strangers when we all live in the same house.'

She regretted having to embarrass them, but it was important for them to know how she wished the house to be run. If they did not fit in, then it was better that they should leave. She found her dissatisfaction increasing with her thoughts. Grace Barber looked so terrified, even the baby stared at her as though she might attack it. She was mortified that there was irritation rather than compassion in her approach. Was she really the ogre they seemed to think?

'I am sorry that you should feel that, Miss Abrahams,' said Mr Barber looking rather as though he might cry. 'We did not presume to imagine that you might wish us to be on any sort of familiar terms. We did not wish to disturb you or put you out in any way.'

Their humility was really sickening. Mary steeled herself to overcome her distaste.

'Well let me put that right straight away Mr Barber. I like to feel that we are a family here in a family house. And in fact it was to ask a favour of you that I wished to talk to you.'

'Anything, anything, Miss Abrahams,' said Mr Barber most earnestly.

Mary quelled her irascibility. 'I was wondering whether you might be able to give me some help in my efforts to teach our little Peg some decent English, so that her life might be made less limited.'

'What splendid charity,' Mr Barber beamed. 'How wise a decision, dear Miss Abrahams, if I may say so. What foresight! That the dear child should one day be able to read the Bible herself is just the beginning of a fuller, richer existence that the good Lord meant us all to enjoy.'

Sanctimonious humbug, Mary thought. 'I should also like her to be able to read some of the novels of Mr Dickens,' she said. 'I have read her parts of Oliver Twist

125

already, and she is greatly moved and excited by his words.'

Mr Barber looked shocked. 'I will be glad to instruct her in the rudiments of basic English,' he said doubtfully. 'But I do believe that there is no better way to learn than by the study of the Holy Bible.'

'I think she is not quite ready for the difficulties of the Biblical text as yet. Perhaps you could help her with some of the simpler points in grammar and speech first?'

'But of course, Miss Abrahams, I will gladly take on the task.'

'And in return, we might perhaps make some adjustment to the rent if this is satisfactory to you?'

'You are too kind, Miss Abrahams.'

Grace Barber, with the silent Constance on her hip, seemed to want to melt into the background as Mary got up from her chair and approached her. These two insipid people had produced a truly angelic baby, Mary decided, even if she seemed already on her way to becoming as insipid as they were.

'May I take her?' she asked, holding out her arms, with the sudden desire to enfold something that looked so appealing. She kissed the pink and cream cheek and smiled into the solemn eyes, and she had the momentary sensation that she was holding a stuffed doll in her arms. A doll which had set, glass eyes in a delicate wax face. But as she looked, there was suddenly a remote glow in the glassiness of the gaze; a slow, slow smile emerged from deep down in some unexplored depth, and the characterless little della Robbia putti came gradually to life.

'What an angelic smile she has,' Mary said, and Mr Barber looked round smartly.

'Smile?' he said. 'But she never smiles. Grace, my dear, look how she smiles.' His voice rose and his face became animated for the first time. 'Miss Abrahams, you are miracle worker!'

Grace Barber was also smiling, her hands over her mouth in case anyone should see. They were not really so obnoxious, these people, Mary thought as she buried her face into the softness of baby Constance's neck, they just needed wheedling back into life, that was all.

Peg's lessons with Mr Barber were a success, and she began to master not only reading, but language, and later some fairly adequate writing. She was quick to learn, and her enthusiastic appreciation was a matter of great satisfaction to Mary.

'She's so bright, Mr Cane, and so quick to grasp the meaning of the books she can now read. And the strange, strange thing is what she is doing for Mr and Mrs Barber and little Constance, have you noticed? Such a wonderful change there now is; they are at last truly a part of our family, do you not think? It is all due to Peg's influence; I am so proud of her.'

Richard Cane looked down at Mary as she sat, shelling peas, on the steps at the back of the house.

'Peg is certainly the instrument of the remedy,' he said, 'but I believe you to be the true physician.'

'You flatter me too much, Mr Cane. To think, though, that I had such uncharitable thoughts of Mr and Mrs Barber when I was properly acquainted with them; that was very unchristian and unchivalrous of me, and not to be admired in any way.'

'Indeed, Miss Abrahams, I believe you to denigrate yourself and your great qualities overmuch.' You are just it for me, Mary Abrahams.

His heart brimmed, even as he made strenuous efforts to contain his feelings. This unbounding emotion he felt for Mary was surely not evil? Was it really meant to be controlled? Banished even? Was it really just a satanic temptation to be overcome?

For Mary, as she sat on the steps in the warm spring sun, the tingling sensation in her spine right down into the backs of her legs was unquestionably physical. The same reaction, she thought confusedly, that she had first experienced when her father had taken her to a rendering of Mr Handel's Messiah at the Crystal Palace on one memorable occasion. And indeed, the same that she had felt whenever the church choir soared into particularly exciting heights of harmonious sound.

It was difficult to distinguish one feeling from another. The first time she had seen the Crivelli Annunciation, for instance . . . her thoughts blanked out instantly, and a clear, laughing voice came shrilly into her hearing: 'Trust you to get randy about an angel.' Mary's mouth fell open in shock, and she looked round to see who had made this strange remark. Randy? What did that mean? And what sort of a woman could speak in such a raucous tone?

'Who was it who spoke then?' she asked Mr Cane.

'I heard no one,' he said.

'You did not hear laughing?'

'No.' He listened intently. There was the sound of horses' hooves and a man's gruff command. 'Back up there Beauty, back up now.'

'Yes, now I hear it,' he smiled. 'Old George over the wall in the yard beyond. He is harnessing up his dray I think.'

The intensity of the past few minutes receded, starkly, from both of them, and they found themselves confused and embarrassed.

'I must be getting about my business,' Mary said, rising and brushing the debris from her apron. 'Peg shall finish these.'

She felt strangely put out, and a little afraid. She turned back towards the yard with the basket of unshelled peas on her hip, and looked at Richard Cane, standing there in his sober black suit. Their eyes met and joined in a long drawn-out gaze.

'There is something of vast importance . . .' Mary said slowly.

They were silent for a few moments, and heard only

128

the clattering of hooves and the commands of old George and the screams of the swifts over their heads. Time seemed to be ticking both of them towards an inevitable but unrecognised reality. Mary made positive her escape first. She switched from the locked-in gaze to a disassociated smile that included the surroundings as well as the nucleus.

'This won't do at all,' she said. 'Just standing here in the sun while there are a hundred jobs to be done.' Her smile was far too bright, and Richard Cane was still momentarily transfixed in the previous absorption as he watched her disappear into the kitchen.

'Something of vast importance,' he repeated as he followed slowly up the steps, down the hall and out through the front door. He felt the need to be quite alone to ponder, and directed his steps towards the Heath.

The atmosphere of that morning did not return in the weeks that followed. It could, perhaps, have been that they both made a conscious effort to banish the disturbance that had invaded their persons for an unguarded period. Life was busy, satisfactory and fulfilling for each of them.

In the poverty, dirt and hopelessness of the girls they dealt with at the mission Mary felt sometimes a satisfaction that at least she was widening her sphere of knowledge as to what went on around her, but at the same time, the enormity of the task filled her with dread. Was there any point in making such a tiny contribution?

'We are such infinitesimal grains of sand in this vast desert,' she said once, pausing her task of ladling soup into a bowl. What real use was a bowl of soup once a week?

'Each little drop of water, each little grain of sand,' Richard quoted at her as he added the piece of bread to the bowl. 'They all count. We must not presume that we have been chosen to solve all the evils of the world.' His smile faded rather abruptly from his face, and they looked fully at each other and did not say what was in both their minds because it was absurd and presumptuous. So that the small flicker of certainty that kept attempting to surface was suppressed firmly. Of course it can't be so, Mary told herself, but I can't help feeling that we *have* been chosen. What a disgracefully arrogant idea!

'So it is not entirely vain to suppose,' she said on the way home, 'that we are at least achieving some small success in our work for the poor, Mr Cane? When I see the difference in the expression of some of these poor women who come to us, I do begin to feel that, to a tiny extent . . .'

'Ah yes, Miss Abrahams, as Hamlet might have said – there's the rub, is it not? It is frustrating that the grain of sand is so tiny.'

'It could, perhaps, be considered as the widow's mite.'

'Indeed it could, and perhaps it will suffice until we are able to do more.'

'To do what we both believe is expected of us.'

They smiled together in the combined certainty of the moment. And because of a sudden impulse, they held out their hands to each other, and became, for a very short moment, one complete, unified being, to their intense embarrassment and mortification.

They felt constrained to avoid each other for the next few days, and it was not until a crisis exploded upon the house that they came together again in the mutual co-operation of the whole small community.

Constance Barber was taken ill. At first it seemed only a chill, so that she was kept in her cot, and extra coal was begged from neighbours so that a fire might be lit in the room, and a steam kettle kept boiling; but she did not improve, in fact grew daily worse with heightened and constant fever. The physician was finally sent for and diagnosed pneumonia.

'She is a delicate child, Mrs Barber,' he said. 'and has very few reserves upon which to call. I would expect the

130

crisis within the next forty-eight hours. We can but trust in the good Lord's mercy.'

He packed up his instruments neatly and with a seemly sense of sympathy. Yet another certificate to be written within the next day or two. It was difficult to feign feelings that had long ago dried up among such universal distress and tragedy.

Mary stood at the door. 'But there is surely *something* we can do?' He snapped shut his bag and looked at her. 'Yes Miss Abrahams,' he said rather sharply, 'you can trust in God's goodness, pray, and support the parents.'

Mary was enraged. Something within her refused to accept the inevitability of the prognosis.

'There is a cure, I know there's a cure,' she said to Mr Cane later. 'Anti-biotics can arrest the microbe that causes pneumonia, it's well-known.'

'I beg your pardon?'

'I – what did I say then?'

'Something about a cure for pneumonia, some anti . . . er . . .'

Mary's mind closed as finally as the doctor's bag, and her certainty dissolved. 'I will prepare some beef tea,' she said in some confusion. 'It will fortify poor Mrs Barber, and perhaps little Connie could be induced to swallow a mouthful or two.'

The whole household was imbued with a sense of tragedy. Even the Johnson children hushed their ordinary, everyday chatter. Miss Tripp crept to and from her room with clean linen for compresses, fresh-picked sprigs of lavender for burning in the sick-room, home made lavender water and camomile tea. Mr Grebe made his usual soundless way through the house, emanating sympathy, and there was silence from Joey in the loft; no hammering, no sawing. Peg's daily routine was drowned in continuous weeping and a speechless desire to help, and the grief that even Annie found herself experiencing was alien to anything she had felt before. Unforgivably, she felt resentment against God Himself, and because of the iniquity of this feeling, her emotion overflowed into unaccustomed tears. It was humiliating. Her ladies gathered round to console and commiserate, and the whole house turned into a rendezvous for concern, grieving and condolence.

'Such a consensus of love and sympathy gathered in one place,' said Mr Cane, 'must surely have a meritorious effect upon the situation.'

'You mean it might cure baby Constance?' Mary put it as a challenge.

'I – I am not able even to guess at the outcome. But concentrated prayer is known to have a miraculous effect on occasions.'

'It is also known to fail,' Mary countered. Why had the life or death of this one child taken on such gigantic proportions? Something that was happening every day and everywhere. Why was this particular event so fundamental and disturbing?

It was a quarter-past-three in the afternoon, when the sudden and fearful scream of Grace Barber pierced every room in the house. Mary dropped her mending on the floor, and flew to the Barbers' rooms, with Richard Cane close behind her. Heads appeared at every window overlooking the yard; Annie stood at the back door and Peg set up a wail in the kitchen.

'She's gone! She's gone!' Grace Barber moaned. 'Her little heart's stopped beating, she's stopped breathing ...' and again came the screaming moan of despair. Percy Barber sat at the table, his head upon his arms.

Mary approached the inert and shrouded shape on the bed, and listened to the silence in the chest, where before, rasping breaths had been dragged in and out.

'All may not be lost,' she said, and grasping the body between her hands, she pressed sharply and regularly, with the palms of her hands, on the baby's chest. Why? She had no notion, nor how long she continued to do so, before she felt the flicker of life, and before she breathed gently into the small open mouth to bring

132

breath back into the lungs. There was a minute wail at first, painful and pathetic, a movement in the limbs, and Constance Barber returned to her body to continue her life.

Mary wrapped her in a blanket and handed her to the shocked and silent Grace Barber.

'She had a little spasm, that was all,' she said. 'But I really think she will get better now, God be praised.'

'Oh Miss – Oh Miss – you brought her back to life. It's a miracle.'

'It's a miracle,' echoed Percy Barber, looking down at his breathing, whimpering daughter. 'Just like Lazarus. You are truly blessed among women, Miss Abrahams.'

'You exaggerate Mr Barber.' Mary felt embarrassed and uncomfortable. 'It was God's doing, not mine; but I am very, *very* glad he heard our cry.'

She turned to Richard Cane and smiled. 'You were quite right,' she said, 'concentrated prayer certainly does have a miraculous effect. Your faith was much stronger than mine. To think that I doubted.'

But Richard was looking at her with what could only be described as a radiant adoration.

12

John Wild settled silently and impassively into the community. He seldom spoke and had not smiled to date, but he ate everything put before him, did what he was told, and watched television unendingly.

'Can't see we're doing him a blind bit of good,' Maggie said.

'Do you think he hates us all?' Mim asked. 'If only he'd laugh just a little.' She felt rebuffed and defeated. She had the feeling that he despised her and her efforts to make him talk, or smile, or show some sort of reaction. Almost as though he knew himself to be infinitely superior to all those he found himself among. 'I sometimes feel like pulling his hair to see if he cries,' she said.

'He's just shut up inside himself,' Mary said. 'He doesn't need to talk at the moment, and he's so busy with his own thoughts, I don't think he really hears us much.'

'How do you know?' Mim said rather irritably. 'How can you possibly know what's going on inside his head? You're just guessing.'

'I can't see,' Maggie said, 'that it's at all wise for amateurs like us to be trying to cope with an extremely disturbed child. We're probably doing him untold damage.'

'So you want me to take him back to the children's home?'

Matt had moved in with Maggie on a semi-permanent basis since John had joined the household. 'Personally, I think it would be criminally irresponsible to throw him

134

back into that atmosphere just when he's getting accustomed to peace and quiet.'

'Since when has this house been quiet and peaceful? You must be mad. And incidentally, the only criminal irresponsibility that I've noticed is that of bringing him here in the first place without giving the matter a moment's thought and without consulting all of us.'

Maggie and Matt had been arguing, off and on, for most of the period that John had been with them. Their arguments had been interspersed with passionate and exuberant love-making which always seemed to be made more complete when sandwiched, as it was, between irascible fights.

'I shall take him back tomorrow,' Matt said. The remark was at once greeted with protest from Mary and Mim, their voices raised in a fury of defence.

'You can't do that.'

'I forbid you to send him back to that monstrous children's home, the poor little pet, he just needs to be loved.'

'He likes it here, he feels he belongs.'

'Nevertheless, he'll have to go. I refuse to be considered criminally irresponsible for upsetting the peaceful atmosphere of Lavender Cottage. Never let it be said . . .'

'Oh shut up you wingeing turd.'

John came into the room at that moment, and stood looking round at each one of them. It was obvious that he had heard the argument and that he was quite aware of their guilt and confusion, though none could have described how this last was obvious. Something about the dignity and self-possession of his regard perhaps?

'That 'ome what you want to send me back to ain't my 'ome. This 'ome is, and you can't turn me out of it because I should just come back. However much you turned me out, I'd just come back.'

No tears showed, though it was plain, by the pinched look on his face, that they were near the surface. No one felt inclined to argue further with his declaration.

135

Mim rushed to him and hugged him. 'Of course you're going to stay, there's no question.'

He recoiled slightly from her kisses, and leaned back against Mary, who had approached and put her hands on his shoulders. 'They thought you weren't happy here,' she said. 'But I told them you were.'

'Slight overstatement,' Maggie said under her breath, then she added, 'I'm glad you like it here with us; we thought you didn't.'

'We'll have to see what the Council have to say,' Matt said. 'They may not allow you to stay for very long.'

'Yes they will,' John said, 'because I'll tell them this is my home.'

'Yes, of course,' Matt agreed, 'but it may not be for ever, that's all I mean. You remember that we're trying to find a family for you to live with, you remember me telling you about that?'

'This is my family,' John said. 'I don't want no other.'

Tears ran down Mim's cheeks. 'Oh John, thank you for liking us and wanting to live with us. It makes us feel so proud.'

He stared at her in surprise. 'You don't have to cry about it,' he said.

Maggie frowned. 'I couldn't agree more,' she said, 'but you'll have to excuse her because she's a sentimental idiot.' And for the first time John started to laugh.

The tension eased immediately, and within seconds, the three girls swept him off his feet, rolled him on the floor and were kissing and tickling any part of him that was left undefended.

Later, as he ate beans and chips in front of the television, he made an important announcement:

'My teacher needs somewhere to live. I told him he could come and live in the room next to mine because it's empty.'

'I'm afraid we have too many people living here as it is,' Maggie said. 'There's absolutely no room for anyone else.'

136

'Yes there is,' John said, 'there's the room next to mine. It's empty.'

'Yes I know it's empty, but we use it as a box room, and as I said, there are too many people living here already.'

'There was more in the home.'

'Yes but we're not a home – I mean we're not a children's home.'

'My teacher isn't a child.'

'I *know* he isn't a child, what I meant was that this home is a private home, not a Council home.'

'He's not Council, he's private.'

'And we have got an empty room,' Mary joined in.

'Don't you start,' Maggie said. 'This place is absolutely crawling with humanity, I couldn't stand any more.'

There was a moment's silence, and then John said, 'He's coming back to tea with me tomorrow. I said you'd asked him and that you'd like him to have the empty room next to mine.'

Peter Stone came for tea the next day. Apologetic and embarrassed, he said, 'John wouldn't leave school unless I agreed to come with him. He said you particularly wanted to see me about a room you wished to rent out.'

'We don't . . .' Maggie started.

'We *do* have a room,' Mim interrupted, and Mary continued, 'We can always find room for anyone who needs it.'

'Welcome to liberty hall dear.' Lou came into the room carrying a teapot. 'Can we presume you need tea?'

Peter Stone was a large, bear-like man of apostolic appearance, with wild, shoulder-length hair and an unrestrained beard. He wore a tweed jacket with leather-patched elbows, a red check shirt, brown corduroy trousers and sandals.

'Salt of the earth,' Rollocks said later, 'he obviously believes in things and does a tremendous amount of good.'

'Don't mock dear. He means very well indeed.'

'Tired old sixties, by the way,' Lou added. '*Sho* tired and *sho* shquare sort of thing.'

137

'But you're all tired old disillusioned sixties types,' Penny made one of her rare and unexpected comments, 'all wondering where things huv gone wrong.'

'Penny *please*, stop stating unpleasant truths,' said Jude. 'We are seventies types, and we are not admitting to nasty things like blighted hopes and disenchantment. We are merely fighting back our tears and making brave jokes with our heads held high.'

'Makes you laugh really,' Rollocks said.

'Doesn't make *me* laugh,' Penny said glumly.

'Well I think Pete's sweet,' Mim said. 'You're all very unkind. He can't help being old and humourless.'

'At *least* thirty I suspect,' Matt said, 'but John seems devoted to him, so it might be good to have him here.'

'Don't mind us, will you? I suppose you envisage him as a kind of psychiatric nurse?'

'We'll have to turn out the room. John says he's a carpenter and has a bench and things.'

'That might be an asset.'

'And he did say he was pretty desperate to get somewhere near the school.'

It was about the same time as Pete joined the community, that James Line, who was now universally known as the Ad Man, began to bring Ginny back to the house for the odd night. Mim hid her resentment thinly. Even if they had always gone their separate ways, this was a bit much.

'It's just not on,' she said, 'you can't have two people living in that tiny room, it's unhealthy. And anyway, I can hear everything.'

There was a general snigger of suppressed amusement round the room.

'I know,' Rollocks said, 'you move into his room and soundproof it, and then he and Ginny could set up home in yours. What a good idea.'

The laughter surfaced, and Mary looked anxiously at Mim. Why did Rollocks have to be so nasty? He seemed

138

to enjoy hurting people. Was it really to hide his disappointment with life, like Jude said?

'There hasn't been any suggestion of the Ginny woman moving in permanently,' Maggie said. 'And if there was, then I would be dead against it. Not that that seems to make much difference.'

'What do you mean? We are so repressed in this house that we have all become Freudishly inhibited. Don't you agree Penny?' Rollocks clasped his arms round Penny's neck and raised both his feet off the ground, so that she held him in her arms like a baby. 'Look at that folks! Isn't she magnificently strong?'

Mary joined in the laughter guiltily, because seeing Rollocks clutched in the arms of the large and serious Penny was ludicrous.

'I think you're a toad,' Penny said unemotionally. 'With a measly luck of munners. It's Muggie's house, and she should huv who she wants to live in it.'

'What?' Mim shot upright in her chair. '*Maggie's* house? Is that what you think?'

Mary felt the same wave of resentment well up, but she said nothing.

'This house happens to belong to all three of us,' Mim said, 'though you might not think it, the way some of us carry on, and I think we shouldn't be dictatorial as to who stays and who doesn't.'

'But it was you who wanted Ginny out dear.'

Penny dropped Rollocks on the floor.

'I didn't say I wanted her out,' Mim said, climbing down in some confusion. 'I just said it was unhealthy.'

At that moment, James the Ad Man burst nosily out of his small back room leading Ginny by the hand. 'Morning all,' he said breezily. 'Any coffee going? I'm starving.'

'It's all the exercise you take,' Rollocks said from his prone position on the floor. 'You should relax more.'

Ginny was well over six foot tall, with very large, bare feet. She stepped cautiously over Rollocks, clutching a black satin kimono round herself.

'Why does he lie on the floor?' she asked.

Rollocks rolled over and clutched her foot. 'I am bowled over,' he said, 'because you are so big, so black and so beautiful that I feel impelled to kiss your foot.' He did so, unbalancing Ginny, who fell on top of him, loosening her hold on the black kimono under which she was wearing nothing.

'This is so sudden,' Rollocks said as they disentangled themselves. 'Do let me introduce myself. My name is Mark Rolling, known affectionately by my closest enemies as Rollocks.'

Ginny took his outstretched hand. 'Hi Rollocks,' she said. 'I'm Virginia Stock from California.'

The hilarity that followed this announcement brought all the members of the community downstairs or upstairs from wherever they happened to be, to hear the joke. As they came in, Rollocks waved his hand towards Ginny. 'May I present my friend, the new member of the Lavender Cottage mob, Miss – wait for it folks – Virginia Stock.'

'Why is everybody laughing?' John Wild asked without looking round from Sesame Street.

'You may well ask.' James the Ad Man was visibly nettled. 'But I suspect it's because they are a crude, ill mannered lot.' He took a mug of coffee across to Ginny, who was sitting among the giant cushions on the floor, surveying the giggling group round her with dignified indulgence. She did not appear at all put out by the effect that her name had had on everyone.

'All English people laugh when they hear my name. I'm not at all certain why this is, but I guess it's a kinda English joke. They say it's a kinda flower over here,' she added, as though trying hard to understand why this should be funny.

And of course it wasn't, Mary thought to herself, and then gave another burst of laughter, because of course it was. But it was really unforgivable, this laughing at other people's disabilities, plain bad manners. Like mak-

140

ing fun of the Irish or spastics. She wished she didn't find the jokes about them funny because there was nothing particularly commendable about being the same as everyone else. And there was the possibility that one might end up like Rollocks, making fun of everything and everybody.

Mary took a good look at Ginny, and decided that she looked like a beautiful camel. The thought brought another bubble of laughter, swiftly controlled, but it was those vast, soulful eyes and the way she held her head. Her hair was straightened back, flat against her head and then released in a great bush in the nape of her neck. The neck itself was longer than any Mary had come across before, and had a chiffon scarf wound round it, the ends flowing down the back. Mary wondered if she actually slept with the five inch gold rings in her ears. She was, of course, a model.

'Ginny needs to shack up for a bit,' James said, when the hysteria had died down, and coffee and toast were being consumed. 'Will that be all right? Of course I'll pay.'

There was a deep silence as all eyes were turned towards Maggie and Mim.

'We're pretty full,' Maggie said.

'That room's so small,' Mim said.

'But we do have a bed in the tiny cubby hole next to the washing machine downstairs,' Mary said.

'And then there's the basement which is crying out for urban development,' Rollocks said.

'We weren't really thinking of an extra room,' James said before anyone could answer.

Ginny rearranged her legs among the cushions. 'As it happens,' she said, 'I do have quite a bit of stuff. It might be handy to have a room to put things in, even if it were quite small.'

'If you took the cubby hole,' Mim said, 'you could store the stuff in one room and sleep . . .' she dried up, acutely embarrassed.

'Or Mim could rent the cubby hole,' Rollocks suggested, 'whenever she wanted a good night's rest.'

Maggie fumed silently. Either she would have to come out openly and boldly with 'We don't want you', in which case she could rightly be accused of irrational bias, or she could allow herself to be overruled yet again. Was it worth a fight? Probably not, in the long run, she decided.

So Virginia Stock, a few days later, brought boxes, bags and baubles, and piled them into the cubby hole, so that the bed was no longer visible.

And then there were twelve.

13

Peg climbed up the ladder into her attic for the hour's rest which Mary insisted she took in the afternoon. 'You need rest to help you to grow,' she had said. It was a welcome time; one whole hour in which to do exactly as she liked. How lucky she was. She had always told herself that one day her guardian angel would come and rescue her from the orphanage. It was difficult in those drab days to keep herself believing that he would one day come to her rescue, but she realised as soon as she saw Mary standing beside the Matron that this beautiful lady was indeed that guardian angel. In spite of having expected a male saviour all this time, she still was able to recognise an angel when she saw one.

She took off her mob cap, and let her hair fall freely about her shoulders, shaking her head about as she did so. She was still unused to the freedom of allowing her hair to go loose after years of scraping it back into the twisted bun that had been obligatory at the orphanage. The bun itself was a privilege after the initial shaving of the head to delouse it, and then the close cropping of the hair until you were twelve. It was only then that you had been allowed to start growing it ready for your being sent out into service.

There was absolutely no doubt in her mind that Miss Mary was an angel. They did come down to earth in disguise to serve and help people, sometimes as nuns and sometimes as quite ordinary people, like Miss Mary. If she had needed proof, which she did not, there was the miracle of the bringing of little Connie back to life the other day. That was a miracle if ever there was one. Plain for all to see, before their very eyes. How lucky she was to have been there and seen it.

Still lost in the contemplation of that amazing happening, the appearance of the small black boy at the other side of the room did not cause her more than a faint flicker of surprise. 'And I don't suppose you've never had the good fortune to look upon a miracle now did you? Poor ignorant little savage that you are,' she said.

'I'm not no ignorant savage,' he said.

Then Peg did jump. 'You can talk?' she said.

'Of course I can talk you dummy. What do you think I am? Spastic or something?'

'Why didn't you never talk before then?'

'You never asked me nothing.'

Peg absorbed the sense of the argument. 'Where do you come from?' she asked.

'I don't come from nowhere, I live here.' He looked round the room. 'But you keep changing it,' he said, 'and why are you in my room anyway?'

And then he turned round and walked through the wall.

Peg was disturbed, but decided to say nothing because Miss Mary and Mr Cane seemed slightly put out when she mentioned it before. After the miracle episode, anything could happen. It wasn't her place to question.

She went to the door and looked out, knowing well that he would not be there, and sure enough, the landing was empty, and all she could hear was old Joey's saw going ssher-shi ssher-shi in the room next door. Feeling rather in need of company, she knocked on his door and went in to sit on the stool near his work bench.

'Did you ever see a ghost Joey?'

'Ar, I di . . . I di . . . I ar,' he said, nodding his head and smiling sheepishly. ' 'twere my Da. He w . . . he w . . . Just the once.'

144

Peg felt comforted. It was not so strange to see a ghost then, even to talk to one for that matter. 'I've just been talking to one,' she said.

Joey laughed of course, but it made no matter. It was not a spiteful, disbelieving laugh, just a kind of chuckle between friends. Peg returned to her room, shut the door and stretched out on the bed, feeling exhausted. She was sound asleep within minutes.

John Wild went into Pete Stone's room without knocking. 'That girl keeps messing up my room,' he said. 'I'll kill her if she goes on.'

'What girl?' Pete was working on a lino cut for a poster for the school concert. 'Someone from school you mean?'

'No, there's a girl called Peg who comes and messes up my room. I'll kill her. Can I do a picture like that?'

'You can try. Make a drawing of something first, and then I'll show you what to do.'

John drew Peg with a hatchet, smashing up a chair, and Pete guided his hand with the cutting tool, showing him what bits to cut out and what to leave. They printed it in red and John pinned six of the prints on his door. 'I'll kill her,' he said.

Pete and Matt discussed it together. 'He seems to have the idea that some girl comes into his room,' Pete said. 'He looks really vicious when he talks about it, but he did a drawing of her, so should have worked some of the anger out of his system. He's not nearly so aggressive at school now, just looks daggers at everyone without actually doing anything.'

'He's had a pretty bad time of it,' Matt said. 'No father, and mother beat him up when she was drunk. And the kids in the home were no help. Seemed to have a down on him because he wouldn't talk to them. Kept taking his things and fighting him. There *was* a girl who was particularly spiteful, but she was called Marlene. He's talked to me of someone called Peg. Can't think who that can be. But he said she didn't bother him.'

'That seems to have changed a bit. Just now he said she'd messed up his room and that he'd kill her.'

Matt smiled. 'We'd better watch out, but I think it's probably someone he's invented to wreak vengeance on. Might help him to get the hate out of his system to invent a victim.'

Shortly after Pete left the room, Maggie banged into the house and went straight upstairs to Matt.

'It's just the last straw,' she said. 'Of all things to happen, this is the worst. I'm sick, sick, *sick*.' And she burst into tears on the bed, beating it with her fist.

'What on earth's the matter?'

'You may well ask. I'm pregnant, that's all – PREGNANT.'

'Oh God. Did you forget the pill or something?'

'No I *didn't*. Do I ever forget things? No, I'm just one of the two per cent or however much it is that's unlucky. It isn't fair, I don't want a bloody baby now, probably not ever, but certainly not now.'

Matt hit his head with his open hands. 'But why didn't you tell me before?'

'Well I couldn't believe it. Thought it *must* be a false alarm. Didn't think it was worth throwing us both into a tizzy for nothing.'

'You can have an abortion.'

'Yes, I suppose I can, if I can prove I'd go mad otherwise. We can't afford a private one.'

'Wouldn't your Pa pay?'

'I refuse to sponge. He's done enough.'

'Well why don't we have it? You know I'd like it.'

'But it doesn't affect you, does it? A whole bloody year at least out of my life and then tied hand and foot for years to come. No travel, no courses, no fun. Oh shit, I could spit.'

There was a scuffling outside, and Rollocks shouted through the door. 'Just happened to be passing and heard this astounding piece of news. Did you know folks – Maggie's preggers, isn't that nice?'

Maggie stormed out of the room. 'Fuck off,' she screamed. 'Can't we have the least bit of privacy in this madhouse?'

'Of course you can't darling.' Jude and Lou came out of their room. 'That's why it's all such tremendous fun. One for all and all for one sort of thing. It's so cosy.'

'How *great*,' Jude said. 'I just love babies. Is it Matt's? Do say it isn't because then it would be *so* exciting trying to guess whose.'

Mary's door opened. 'Someone's having a baby? Did I hear someone's having a baby? Who is?'

Maggie brushed past all of them and crashed downstairs with tears of fury streaming down her face.

Mim was in the kitchen making tea, with an untried friend called Tom. 'What's the matter angel? But you never cry, whatever's the matter?' She clasped Maggie, and untypically, her sister clung to her and wailed out her frustration.

'I'm just pregnant, that's all.'

Mary rushed down the stairs and joined her sisters in a clinging group of three.

'But Maggie, that's wonderful.'

'Stupendous,' Mim agreed, 'I'm so glad for you. Tom aren't you glad for her? This is Tom by the way. It's not a tragedy, it's great, really it is, isn't it Tom?'

'Fantastic,' Tom agreed.

'The best thing I've ever heard,' Mary said. 'Come and sit down and be made a fuss of, we must celebrate it, not cry about it.'

'It's all very well for you,' Maggie sobbed. 'You can all sit round and feel cosy and broody, but I've got to have the bloody thing, and I don't want it.' But her original hysteria was waning.

Everyone was gathering in the sitting room, and James the Ad Man brought in two bottles of champagne.

'A bribe from a client,' he said. 'What better way to use it? We have to celebrate.' And the whole thing began to turn into a party.

'A cheeky little wine,' Rollocks said, 'and such unaccustomed generosity to boot, my dear Ad Man, from one who marks the tide mark on his opened bottle of Liebfraumilch in the fridge.'

'Snide remarks to cease for at least the next hour,' Matt said.

'This is a day of rejoicing. And we all know you pinch it anyway.'

'Ah but I always top it up with good, nourishing tap water to the dreaded mark on the bottle, even above it if I feel generous.'

'Bickering – CEASE,' Jude shouted. 'This is a party. Someone fetch the carpenter on the roof.'

Maggie found herself suddenly and contrarily happy, and supposed it to be the champagne. A joint was handed to her, which she brushed aside crossly. 'You know I don't allow that here. It's one of the rules.'

'Aw come on Mag, don't be a drag.'

'Mag the drag.'

'Jude the rude.'

'Rollocks the bollocks,' John said.

'Pete the effete,' yelled Rollocks, collapsing off his chair on to the floor.

'Tom the bomb,' Tom attempted, and there was an immediate embarrassed silence until sniggers surfaced and Rollocks patted Tom on the head. 'Never mind,' he said, 'at least you tried.'

'Go and get a cake,' someone suggested, and the mood eased again, 'but it will have to be a birth cake because we can't add the day until we know it.'

'When is it due?'

'Roughly seven months from now.'

'That makes it about Christmas time – how great. Will you call him Jesus if he's born on Christmas Day?'

'Might do might not.'

'Oh go on – be your best friend.'

'You can't have Jesus,' John said, 'Mary has to have Jesus,' and there was more laughter.

John looked on at all these grown-up people carrying on as though they were about five years old, and he wondered why they did it. Of course they were a bit drunk, but when his mother had got drunk before he went into the home, she got angry as well, and no one was angry here. Even Pete and Matt were laughing, though there seemed nothing at all to laugh at, and anyway, those two never laughed much, because they were usually busy teaching him something. Looking at and listening to everybody now, he decided that it was almost as good as watching the telly. Anyway, they said they were going to buy a cake. And it *was* Mary what had Jesus, Maggie couldn't have him. Her baby would be ordinary, only Mary's would be special.

Maggie, by now, had decided that the whole thing was an enormous joke. What really could be funnier than her being pregnant? She, of all people, who had taken so much trouble to plan and organise her life. It just went to show, she thought, even the best of us can make mistakes.

'I think you're most frightfully brave,' Penny said seriously, and they all fell about laughing again. Penny neither drank nor smoked, but approved of everyone doing their own thing.

'But darling Maggie,' Jude said, 'you shouldn't be drinking you know.' He snatched the champagne away from her.

It was a rowdy, good-natured gathering, much enjoyed by everyone, which continued on through the evening at the William the Fourth in the High Street, until they were finally ejected to make their noisy, riotous way home to bed.

'It really is surprising how things turn out sometimes,' Maggie said to Matt. 'I could have sworn that I was devastated by all this earlier today, but somehow I now get the feeling that it really isn't the disaster I had thought it might be. It's really not like me to be swayed by the opinions of others.'

They lay in bed and watched the light from the street lamps shine through the lime tree leaves to make moving shadows on the ceiling.

'So perhaps you'll realise now that you should listen to all of us more. Our baby could never be a disaster. I can't tell you how pleased and proud I feel.'

'So do I, oddly enough. Though I don't expect it will last. Reason will no doubt return with the dawn and abolish this absurd attitude of irresponsibility and euphoria.'

'If it does, I shall divorce you.'

'You can't, we're not married.'

'Well, I shall marry you so that I can divorce you.'

'All right, let's do that then. What a day it's been.'

'You've messed up my room again,' John said, surveying Peg across it. 'I'm going to kill you.'

'You can't,' Peg said, 'you're only a poor wandering spirit what isn't really there.'

There was a silence while he tried to sort out what she had said. He looked down at the cricket bat he had snatched up in fury when he found the room had changed. He'd jolly well bash her in this time. But he held nothing in his hand. Where did it go?

'What? You round the bend or something? Who are you talking to if I'm not there?'

'Well, I don't understand these things aright because I ain't got no learning, but some people do see things what aren't there.'

'You're barmy.'

'Maybe I am, but how do you keep coming and going else?'

'I never. It's you what keeps coming and messing up my room.' His certainty began to waver, and he looked round for the cricket bat. Where had the window gone? It had changed into a skylight. 'Ghosts are scary,' he said.

'They don't have to be if'n you aren't afeared of them.

You're just some poor wandering spirit of long ago what can't find rest. I'm not afeared of you.'

'Well you ought to be because I'm going to kill you if I can find my bat. And I don't want no rest neither, and suppose it's you what's the ghost and me what's real?'

Peg laughed at the very idea. 'Oh I'm real right enough,' she said. 'Always have been, always will be. So you must be the ghost, some spirit from long ago you must be. What sort of people did you live with in them olden days? Was they cruel to you? Did they murder you in this very room? Is that why you're 'aunting me?'

'But I'm not dead.'

'Ah,' Peg said comfortingly, 'I don't expect you remember that bit. I expect the good Lord sponged your mind of that, but you're still seeking out the truth I wouldn't wonder. What was they like, though? Them people what lived here in them days?'

'Lots of people live here; there's Pete and Matt and Maggie and Mim and Mary and Rollocks and the ad man and Penny and Jude and . . .'

'A lodging house was it? Like this is? Or was it a home?'

'It's not a home,' John said quickly. 'I was in a home before, but then I got put in with the family.'

'You got a big family then?' Peg's eyes widened as she had visions of a great many black savages dancing round the yard dressed in beads and feathers. She had seen pictures.

But she suddenly caught sight of the lino cuts pinned to the door. 'What's them things?' she asked, going over to look at them.

'It's pictures I did of you messing up my room,' John said rather apologetically.

She turned to him, laughing. 'Well I never,' she said.

But he had gone, taking his pictures with him.

14

'Clare? This is Maggie.' There was a pause. 'Your eldest daughter. Remember me?'

'Oh God – darling. I couldn't think for the moment. You sounded so different.'

'Well we haven't spoken for ages, have we?'

'No, no, that's true. I'm dreadfully sorry. I kept meaning to phone you to see how you were getting on, but I thought you might think I was interfering.'

'My dear mother, that's the last thing you would do.'

Why was it not possible just to come out with: 'Mother, I'm pregnant' there and then? She took a breath, and held it for a second, then, 'We want you to come and see us all,' she said instead. 'Why don't you come to tea?'

'TEA?'

'Well a drink then. We think you should see how well your daughters are managing.'

'But darling I am absolutely confident that you are managing so well that I should immediately develop a large inferiority complex about you.'

'Nonsense. It will merely prove how well you brought us up.'

'Well, if you put it like that, I can hardly refuse, can I?'

'Of course you can't, and anyway, you wouldn't be so rude as to turn down a formal invitation from your three daughters now, would you?'

She had meant to tell her about the pregnancy over the phone, but had somehow lost her nerve. Ridiculous

152

that she should feel the need of back up from her sisters. What did it matter what Clare's reactions were?

'The trouble with Clare,' she said to the others afterwards, 'is that she is really so sensible and intelligent, if only she didn't put on that sophisticated act.'

'I suppose we all hanker after the comfortable old-fashioned Mum image,' Mim said, 'which is crazy, because we should hate her to be like that. It's just so great the way she makes fun of everything and is so marvellously laid back and cool. I mean, she's really so with it, isn't she? Considering how old she is.'

'I wish everybody wouldn't make fun of everything,' Mary said. 'It seems like people are afraid of taking anything seriously these days in case they're considered square.'

'What a pearl of wisdom,' Maggie said. 'Making fun of everything shows a great sense of insecurity. Sort of I'll laugh first then you can't laugh at me for being intense.'

'Oh la –' Mim said, 'I wouldn't have said that any of the mad people in this house had the smallest bit of insecurity showing, except me and Em. They all seem outrageously confident and pleased with themselves. But *I* think that laughing is a tremendously important part of life. Things could be so boring otherwise.' What silly nonsense had Penny once suggested about their covering up inadequacies with jokes? Fun was fun, and a thoroughly good thing.

The following Sunday, Clare came to lunch, which the girls had worked at all the morning to prepare.

'You can all come,' Mim said to the household, 'because we think it would be good for your education to meet our mother, and we're going to have an enormous leg of pork as we're only half Jewish and this is to celebrate our gentile side.'

'And chocolate mousse,' Mary added. 'I'm going to make that.'

'Oh sooper,' said Penny. 'Do we dress up?'

'Naturally,' Rollocks said, 'put on your gorilla costume.'

153

'For goodness sake,' Mary laughed, 'do we ever dress up here?'

John looked round at all of them and tried to understand what Mary had said. Did they really think they didn't always dress in fancy dress? He saw Mim's long, long legs in green tights which she wore under her white mini dress that had a high buttoned collar. And all those gold chains that clanked and let you know when she was near. And her silly, clumpy shoes with buckles and great square heels. And those crazy cissies in dressing gowns and pyjamas most of the time, but who sometimes wore girls' dresses. And that new black lady who was taller than anyone in the house and yet wore great enormous platforms on the bottom of her mauve boots to make her seem even taller. And why did she want to look like a gypsy with that flowery scarf thing round her head and all those huge wooden beads? And to make it worse, they sometimes painted their eyes up like clowns did. Even with tears painted on their cheeks. Pete and the ad man dressed more normal like, though even they had trousers that were so tight that they showed their willies quite plainly, the shape and everything. Everyone else was pretty nearly always in fancy dress. Even Mary had a floaty type dress that came down to her feet, and her hair was fair and frizzy and sort of hung all over her face so that she couldn't see out properly.

'I've got this fantastic new wig,' Mim said, 'which I shall wear to give you all a treat and Mumsie a shock.'

'And I can wear my way out leather suit,' Lou said. 'Can we discuss how superb I look in that?'

There were groans, but the air of tense excitement continued to grow.

'Anybody would think you were about to put on a show,' Rollocks said. 'Sort of first night hysteria. Personally, I shall wear the Oxfam jacket and the jumble sale jeans.'

Clare arrived in a taxi at half past one, wearing a long,

154

flowered dress and a large, black felt hat on top of an Indian silk scarf which was tied over her hair. She had a paisley shawl draped on her shoulders, and she looked magnificent. The three girls ushered her in, feeling proud and pleased that their mother should have dressed up to visit them.

'Mumsie, you look great.' Mim flung her arms round Clare, full of emotion at meeting her mother at last on her own level. Maggie glowed with satisfaction that she would be able to demonstrate how well the house was running, and Mary cried a little at seeing her mother after such a long time and realising how little she had really missed her.

Lou stood at the end of the hall, waving a bunch of scented sticks in the air. 'Incense, incense,' he called out. 'Might even be frankincense for all I know, not to mention myrrh. Hi Mum, I'm Lou and this is my friend Jude who is very obscure and we are both ever so pleased to meet you and happy to know you even if it's not in the biblical sense.'

The sitting room was very full and sounded noisy, though there was a brief lull as Clare was brought in, like the show piece that she was.

'Meet a bit of our past life,' Maggie said, 'Our Mum.'

Lou and Jude stood behind her in rapt admiration. 'Isn't she fabulous?' Lou said, while Jude darted out of the room. 'Must just go and get my Brownie,' he said, 'to take some snaps.'

Maggie found herself enjoying the novelty of introducing a part of her life that none of this lot knew anything about. It was almost as though she had half forgotten it herself. There was this great gap between her parents, and herself and the other two. The generation gap of course. What a cliché, but how true. They were miles apart in an odd sort of way, didn't seem to belong at all, never really had done, she supposed.

Clare raised her hand in a rather embarrassed

greeting. She had not expected a party, and felt out of place and defensive, as she usually did among the young.

'You have three very beautiful and very wonderful daughters,' Ginny said in an intense voice, rising to her full six feet plus platform soles, and towering benignly over the astonished Clare. 'They took me in off the streets and made me so very welcome. I would be most honoured if you would take my chair.'

It was one of the few chairs in the room, and Clare took it gratefully, imagining her three daughters hauling a possibly drug-sodden black giant out of the gutter and making her welcome. The floor cushions looked attractively opulent and eastern, but she knew that she was not at her best on the floor and the sagging bean bags that had no supportive backs did not appeal either. She felt, and looked, very queenly as she sat among the floor-strewn company.

'I'll tell you who everyone is,' Mary said. She was always uneasy with the current attitude of no introductions and the consequent constrained awkwardness of strangers coming face to silent face.

'But I shall never be able to remember,' Clare said faintly.

'Never mind,' Mary was not to be gainsaid, 'you may remember some of them. This is James and that's Ginny, and that's Mark called Rollocks and that's Penny and this is Pete and this is John and you've met Louis and Jude and you know Matt. Oh and this is Mim's friend – er – David.'

'Simon, actually,' Mim corrected.

Penny had been watching Clare with admiration in her eyes. 'I think thut hut is funtustic,' she said.

'Hut?' Clare looked bemused.

'Your hat,' Mim translated. 'She likes your hat.'

'Oh really? Do you like it?' There were murmurs of approval from the others, and Clare's tension began to ease. 'Mim darling,' she added, 'what have you done to your hair?'

Mim's hands went to her head, adjusting here and there, and winding curls round her finger. 'It's my new wig. Don't you think it's over the top?'

'But *white* darling, don't you think you're a bit young?'

'Mumsie you're so *quaint*. White's just an in colour, it doesn't have to mean anything.'

'Oh I see.' Clare looked round the company. 'Do you all live here?' she asked. 'I mean is there actually room for everyone? I thought it was a tiny cottage. And who does he belong to?' She indicated John, and looked at Ginny.

Matt laughed, 'John is mine and Pete's,' he said, enjoying the look of non-comprehension that this remark caused. 'Fostered,' he added, relenting after an appreciable pause.

Clare was given a glass of wine, and again felt as though she was holding court. They seemed to be waiting for her to speak – almost with bated breath. Was she really of such historic interest? she wondered. Or did they think that anything she might say would be hopelessly out of date and therefore funny? It was not a situation she had met before. She had always considered the young of the day to be rebellious, rude and unpleasantly contemptuous of their parents' generation.

Jude was kneeling, lying and leaning about the floor and furniture, taking picture after picture of her, interspersed with exclamations like 'Fab. Great. Hold that darling – fantastic.' It was really rather nice. She relaxed, visibly, and lay back in the chair, abandoning the hat, but keeping the headscarf in place. Then she lit a king size cigarette elegantly and theatrically, and crossed one leg over the other.

'I want to know about you all,' she said. 'Do you get on, living on top of each other like this? What do you all do?'

'I take photographs,' Jude said.

'I dance,' Lou said.

'I make commercials,' said James.

'I am John's teacher,' said Pete.

'I'm just a visitor,' said Simon.

'I work for CND and Ulcoholics Unonymous,' Penny said.

'And she also keeps me,' Rollocks said, 'as a pet and also in a manner to which I have become accustomed. Both she and Social Security are doing a bloody good job of it too. I even got a clothing allowance the other day.'

'Only because you joined the dole queue dressed in a blanket with no shoes on,' Maggie said sourly. 'He really is the long-haired layabout par excellence,' she said to Clare.

'Lazy, good-for-nothing parasite,' Rollocks agreed. 'It's an art form you know, and a full time occupation if you want to excel. As a social security collector I'm the greatest. I mean they sent me for an interview as a butcher's assistant the other day, but they didn't seem to like the nail varnish. Just sent me back as unsuitable. It's the subtle approach that wins every time.'

'Your really are abject,' Matt said with feeling.

'Oh – thank you very much,' said Rollocks. 'Can I have that in writing?'

'I am a fashion model,' Ginny said. 'In California the competition for such work is intense, so I came to England in the hope that I might do better over here. And I would also very much like to marry a rich English man. I do have a great respect for the English aristocracy you know. We do not have that kind of thing in the States.'

'She hasn't landed one yet,' Rollocks added, 'but we have very considerable belief in her chances in the extremely distant future.'

'We're just one big, homogenised happy family,' Matt said.

'And we secretly hate each other's guts,' Rollocks added.

'Your lovely daughters keep us in excellent order,' James the ad man said. 'They throw us out if we don't behave.'

Ginny turned on him angrily. 'Indeed they do not,

Jamie Line. This is a downright lie. They are three very beautiful people who are trying to help us all. Living here is so *fun*,' she said earnestly to Clare, 'and the house is just darling.'

'Funtustically okay,' Penny agreed.

They moved in a body to the dining room, and after settling Clare at the top of the table, fought each other amicably for chairs, or settled for the floor. Lou sat on Jude's lap. John remained clamped in his normal position in front of the television, and took his plate without moving his eyes from the screen. The meal was good, the wine was good and the atmosphere sparkled with a brittle goodwill.

Afterwards, Clare drank black coffee from a mug, and smiled round at the company.

'And what about my three darling daughters?' She considered them all, affectionately. 'I want to know exactly how things go with you. Your home life seems to be a success, what about your careers? I'm quite out of date, you never tell me a thing. What are you all up to?'

Maggie remembered that she had suggested Clare's visit so that she could tell her, in the course of conversation and in a suitably laid-back manner, about the pregnancy. There was a fractional silence while all three girls wondered whether or not this was the moment of truth.

'I've got two auditions tomorrow,' Mim blurted out, rather too loudly, deciding that it wasn't. 'Did you see my commercial? It was pretty heinous I know, but it did get me my card with all the other little things I did when I was young, and all thanks to darling James who's been unbelievably helpful.'

'But it's all so insecure,' Clare said. 'Shouldn't you take a typing course so that you can do something while you're resting?'

Mim sat back in her chair and scowled. There was really no sense in trying to explain if Clare couldn't even congratulate her on the auditions. To take herself out of the running to do a typing course would be disastrous. All the things she might miss in the meantime; it didn't bear thinking about. And in a year, or however long the course took, they would all have forgotten her and she would have to start again from scratch without even the additional boost of having been seen by producers at auditions and parties or in theatre bars or anywhere else.

Mary watched the disappointment and frustration in Mim's expression, and tried to take the sting out of the situation. 'I think I might be going to write a book about this house,' she said. 'I've been doing a whole lot of research about it, and it's so interesting, you wouldn't believe. You see there was this girl called Mary living here a hundred years ago and she just disappeared and I thought I might sort of make up a story about her and what might have happened to her. I've started it actually.'

Clare looked through her in a remote way, because she was still considering what a lot of time Mim was wasting, trying to get into the closed world of acting. 'But I thought you were singing and joining choirs and things.' The idea of Mary writing a book seemed so ludicrous that Clare could not bring her mind to envisage such a thing.

'Yes, I am doing that,' Mary said apologetically. 'This is just in my spare time and because it's so interesting. At least it is to me,' she added, seeing Clare's inability to imagine anything remotely interesting in the subject.

'I'm pregnant,' Maggie said, and they all looked at Clare to judge the reaction. Nothing, however, showed on her face. The smile was as bright, as disinterested and as transparent as before.

'We're so pleased,' Matt said. 'A little surprised perhaps, but very pleased.'

'I hoped you might like the idea of becoming a grandmother,' Maggie added for want of anything else to say, and realising, as she said it, how unlikely a prospect that was.

160

John wrenched himself from the television to fetch himself a banana. 'He will be my brother,' he said, 'and they want to call him Jesus but they can't because Mary has got to have Jesus. So we shall probably call him Chips,' he added as an afterthought.

'Aren't you pleased?' Mary said to the silence as Clare retrieved herself from shock.

'Of course, it's wonderful.'

'I want a girl,' Lou said, 'because I have this far out pink mohair wool, and I'm going to knit her a duffle coat with swansdown trimming.'

Penny turned to him sharply. 'But mohair's not really on for babies,' she said, 'it goes up their noses and forms balls of fur. Like cuts,' she added by way of explanation.

'Don' be s' stupid,' Jude said, 'wool is wool and fur is fur.'

'And cuts are cats,' said Lou.

Ginny grasped Clare's hands in hers. 'This must be a truly great moment of your life, Mrs Stein,' she said. 'I would like to be the first to congratulate you on being an expectant grandmother.'

There was stifled laughter all round, and Ginny turned her great black eyes reproachfully on the company. 'It's perfectly true. Old people do particularly appreciate the birth of their first grandchild. It takes them back you see, and makes them feel needed.'

Clare's smile looked unreal, but Ginny remained imperturbable. 'It does too,' she said. 'Why, my grandmother took on a new lease of life the day I was born, and joined the Seventh Day Adventists.'

'So am I to be asked to the wedding?' Clare asked as the laughter died down.

'Oh we're not getting married. I mean there's really no point in getting married.'

'But now you're having a baby, isn't there some sort of point?'

'Absolutely none. A piece of paper makes no difference at all.'

161

The rest of the company sipped their coffee and began to talk to each other self-consciously. James got up and moved to the door, trying to sign to Ginny to follow, but she was absorbed in the conversation, watching each speaker with rapt attention.

'We rather think, you see,' said Matt in a non-involved voice, 'that the feelings we have for each other and now for the coming child, are strong enough in themselves to keep us together, and don't really need an official stamp of approval.'

'Don't you believe it,' Clare said, 'nobody's feelings are so strong that they can do without the help of all the official or unofficial binding agents they can get if they are to last.'

'But we don't want to "last" as you put it, if we are no longer compatible. We don't want to be stuck together like limpets so that we have to go through all the sweat of a divorce if we want to live separately again.' Matt's smile was persuasive and kind. It irritated Clare, but then she had always been irritated by Matthew. Particularly the logical condescension, the steel-rimmed glasses and the drooping, untidy moustache.

'We don't think for a minute that we will want to split up in the near future or even distant future,' Maggie said, 'but we don't want to go through the sort of fights and bad vibes that you and Sam did for so long. If we don't get on, then we shan't fight it, we shall just agree to part and go our separate ways. No fuss, no hassle.'

'You have a great deal to learn,' Clare said, 'but I'm sure it's better for you to learn it the hard way.' She raised her cup of coffee to Matt.

'Welcome son-in-common-law,' she said, and the mood relaxed again quickly.

'You have a remarkably trendy mother,' James said. 'My parents are still complaining about the length of my hair.'

'Und mine won't hvv Mark in the huyse,' Penny said. 'They call him a long-haired lay-abuyt. Duddy's in the army you see,' she explained to Clare. 'But I do think you are prodigiously tolerant Mrs Stein. Do you smoke hush?'

'Of course she doesn't,' Mary said crossly, 'she just happens to dress very well and understand young people.'

Maggie, Mim and Clare swung their astonished gazes towards Mary. Did she really think that? Or was she trying to butter Clare up for some reason, both Maggie and Mim wondered, while Clare mused on the continuous idiotic misconceptions with which her youngest daughter seemed to be burdened. Understand young people? She must be mad. Clare allowed the thought that she actually disliked the lot of them to hesitate in her mind for a moment, but then decided that it was perhaps only fear that made her so uneasy in their presence. While it was true that this crowd actually did seem a little less alien than most, you never could tell. They were probably all jeering at her privately and thinking her an old fogey. Silly little idiots. Bad vibes with Sam indeed. Sweat of a divorce. It was ludicrous. Thinking they knew it all. Really believing it was all going to be easier because they didn't tie themselves up legally. She felt impatient with them, but at the same time sad for them because eventually their dreams would founder and their certainties would fail to materialise. Just as the hopes and beliefs of her own generation had collapsed in the post-war years. Although she and Sam had not noticeably been involved in the belief of a brave new world, she was nonetheless aware of the let-down of disillusion and the sense of hopelessness for the future.

Maggie considered her mother with a modicum of tolerance. Clare really wasn't a bad example of that previous generation. She couldn't be expected to sympathise with the wave of new confidence that was beginning to be apparent among the young. Maggie thought with satisfaction that the protests of the young were perhaps at last being heard, so that the influences of the decrepit old could finally be ousted. The '68 riots in Paris, the Aldermaston marches and peace demonstrations, the Vietnam war protests; the signs were there for all to see – it would happen in spite of opposition. The more tolerant oldies, like Clare, had to be won over. It was all possible.

Mim rushed to her mother and hugged her, so that the coffee was tossed over the chair and carpet.

'Darling, trendy Mumsie, you're so *sweet*, I just couldn't love you better than I do.'

Mary ran to get a cloth, and started to scrub the coffee stains from the chair. She was quite taken aback when her mother said, 'Get up off your knees you clumsy child. Peg, can you not see that the tea has been spilt? Do you let your young mistress do your job for you? What are you thinking of, pray?'

Peg hurried to take the cloth from Mary. 'Let me do it Miss,' she said.

Mary rose to her feet uncertainly and stared at Annie. 'However did I manage to spill that?' she said.

'Because you were not attending I have no doubt,' Annie said irritably. 'You have been becoming most inattentive of late. I am at a loss to understand what has come over you, mooning about like some lovesick peasant girl. Are you sickening for something?'

'I don't think so, Mama,' Mary said. 'Though sometimes I feel a trifle strange and rather confused.'

'Picked something up in the slum you visit I'll be bound. If I were a little stronger, I would lock you in your room. That's what your father should have done when you were younger, but he was far too weak with you. I always said that it would bring trouble later on, but he would have none of it.'

Peg looked sideways at Mary from the floor and gave a huge wink, so that Mary had to cover her own smile with her handkerchief.

'I am sure you are right Mama,' she said.

15

'Tell me about your people,' Peg said to John on his next visit.

'What was they like in them days? How did they dress? Beads and things I suppose?'

'Yes, they all wear beads and great rings and things in their ears. Even the men.'

'Reelly? Do they reelly? And rings in their noses too?'

'Not in their noses, stupid, they only do that in hot countries.'

'And do they wear feathers and things in their hair?'

'Sometimes they do; feathers and big hats and bits of stuff all tied up round their heads. They all have very long hair, specially the men.'

Peg's imagination took off, and she saw hordes of black people in beads and feathers dancing and chanting round a heathen idol, like they did round the golden calf when they disobeyed Moses's command. 'And do they dance and sing to their gods?'

'Well, sort of. They have festivals in the Isle of Wight and go a bit mad.'

'Like go into a trance and that?'

John was not sure what a trance was. 'They go very silly, and scream and cry. At least the girls do. Boys don't, except if they're in the band, and then they shout and yell and break their guitars over the microphone.'

Peg took it that Microphone was the name of the idol, and that guitars were perhaps weapons of some sort. She felt proud to be learning so much history in such an unusual way, and looked forward to discussing it with Miss Mary afterwards.

'Well I never did,' she said. 'A holy frenzy I dare wager. We don't do that no more in these days.'

They eyed each other doubtfully, suddenly suspicious that each might be having the other on. What did she mean by 'these days'? John wondered. Did a whole lot of black savages really have religious frenzies in the Isle of Wight? Peg knew of someone's auntie who had lived in the Isle of Wight and she'd made no mention.

'Are you having me on?' she said.

'No, I'm just telling you.'

'Who do you live with then?'

'With my sisters and my social worker and my teacher and a whole lot of others. This house belongs to my sisters.'

'Go on with you, there ain't no black girls what could have owned a house like this.'

'They're not black, you silly cretin. I'm fostered, so they don't have to be the same colour.'

'Fostered? I s'pose you're a little black slave boy brung back from foreign parts are you?'

'No, I'm not. I'm English. And I'm not a slave. They was in Roman times and it isn't Roman times. And anyway, what are you? Are you an au pair or something?' He was getting hot and angry and uncomfortable. 'You're stupid,' he said, and turned back into his own time.

Peg was left feeling physically cold and irritated. She found herself shivering from the sudden draught that swept through her room. She sat on her bed and wrapped the blanket round her, wondering if John was sent from the devil to do her a mischief. Or had that old gypsy who roamed the streets trying to sell clothes pegs, put a curse on her when she cheeked her the other day? It weren't natural, and if it weren't natural, then like as not it weren't Christian. She would have to ask Miss Mary.

'Was there ever a tribe of black savages what worshipped idols in the Isle of Wight Miss?'

Mary laughed at the question. 'Not that I know of, Peg. I understand that the ancient Britons painted themselves with woad, but I believe that was blue rather than black. Why do you ask?'

'It's my little black boy, Miss, he keeps telling me these tales. 'E says that in 'is time they 'ave festivals in the Isle of Wight Miss where they dances and sings round an 'eathen idol called Michael Finn and they break things called gritters at 'is feet Miss.'

Mary looked at Peg in astonishment. 'I think you must be eating something most indigestible before going to bed, Peg, and that must be inducing these strange and fanciful dreams, or else your imagination must be getting the better of your good sense. It is important to know what is true and what is fancy.'

'But it's not my fancy Miss, honest it ain't. 'E do come into my room Miss, bold as brass, and since 'e's begun to talk, 'e comes quite regular like Miss. 'E's not a dream that's for sure. But I was that worried Miss in case 'e was sent by the devil for some bad reason, or perhaps 'e was a bit of black magic what's got loose and come to 'aunt me for my sins Miss. 'E don't look it, except that 'e's black, but 'e ain't got up in rags Miss, though you can't tell if 'e's dirty because of 'im being black and that. 'E ain't dressed classy – funny like, but not like a savage ought to be dressed Miss, in beads and feathers. Someone must have given him some clothes because of the cold I suppose Miss.'

'But how does he come, Peg? And where does he go? If he's real, then he can't just disappear, can he?'

'Lord bless you Miss, when I say reel, I don't mean reel reel, because of course he's a poor, wandering spirit isn't 'e? 'E must be, because he can walk right through my wall Miss, without so much as a by your leave.'

'Is that what he does?'

'Sometimes 'e does Miss. And sometimes 'e just

167

vanishes – pouf – like that Miss. Ever so clever 'e is like that. Don't really know 'ow, though they do say that that Mr Maskelyne can make people disappear at the music 'all Miss. Something to do with mirrors they do say, but I only got that little cracked glass in my room, so I don't think 'e does it that way. Do you think 'e's a wicked spirit Miss? Sent to plague me for my sins? I don't reelly know what I done to deserve it Miss, honest I don't.'

'Of course not, Peg. Your sins are very tiny, if indeed you have any at all; I am sure that the good Lord has already forgiven them a hundredfold.'

Peg's smile always illuminated her face. Mary could scarcely refrain from hugging her when she smiled because of the look of trust, innocence and untrammelled happiness it projected.

'Do you reelly think so Miss? I'm ever so relieved, because it do seem so queer that I've been picked out so to speak for 'im to visit.'

'Some people have certain powers,' Mary said, 'of being in touch with things most people's understanding cannot grasp. I, too, have these – these moments when something I do not quite understand seems to happen to me. But I do not remember them well – not like you do – I am even doubtful that anything actually does happen. It's just that my thoughts sometimes get a little out of tune . . .' She groped for words and did not find them. Peg sensed the anxiety.

'Don't you be afeared Miss,' she said. 'Begging your pardon I'm sure, but you're too good for anything bad to visit you. If there is anything haunting you Miss, it can't be nothing but a good spirit.'

'I hope you are right.' Mary returned the smile because it was impossible not to. 'So let us decide that any spirits who do visit us must be good ones and should be treated with respect, do you not agree?'

'Oh yes Miss. I try to be ever so polite to my little blackamoor in spite of 'im being an 'eathen, though 'e did get a bit short with me the last time, so I'll have to watch me tongue.'

'Should I attempt to curb her extravagances, Mr Cane, do you think?' Mary was mending sheets in the parlour at the same time that Richard Cane had used the opportunity of Annie Abrahams' rest period to pass by the open door.

'How opportune!' He had tried to sound genuinely surprised and amazed at his good fortune. 'To find you alone.'

Mary had wondered whether the encounter had really materialised through pure chance, and hoped that it hadn't.

There had been quite a considerable pause while he wrestled with the problem of finding words in which to make the daring suggestion that he might once again accompany her on some small excursion. Perhaps even repeat the magic experience of viewing the Crivelli; an experience that had been so overwhelming the last time that neither of them had been able to discuss it at any length afterwards. She had indeed seemed to fall into some sort of trance, which lasted right through the service they attended at St Martin in the Fields. He had even begun to wonder at the time if perhaps she was unwell.

'Miss Abrahams, might we . . . I mean would you consider . . . that is to say . . . would you consider accompanying me once more on some small . . . excursion . . . perhaps even to view again the beautiful painting of the Annunciation we both so admired previously.' There, it was out now. Would she agree?

'But what an admirable idea Mr Cane.' Her excitement showed itself more clearly than she would have wished, but her thoughts were a little confused. Both so admired previously? She drew her brows together slightly. 'A painting of the Annunciation . . .? Did we . . .? I don't quite recall . . .' But she did recall . . . something.

He glanced at her, surprised, shocked almost. 'When we saw the Crivelli Annunciation.'

169

Memory flooded back and the colour rushed to her cheeks. 'But of course, of course! It was not that I did not remember – but that moment was so supreme that I had thought of it always as a dream rather than a reality. It was such a revelation – like a vision. My mind does strange things sometimes. I seem to forget things that are and remember things that are not.'

Jumbled recollections fought in her mind to gain a place. Gold was dominant, and a shining angel with delicate wings. Trust you. And whirling starlings seething overhead. Get randy about an angel. Trust you.

To hide her confusion, she told Richard Cane about Peg's hallucinations. 'Should I attempt to curb her extravagances, Mr Cane? What do you think?' The turmoil in her head settled down again like a cloud coming to rest. Like the starlings.

'You think she may be deliberately inventing these tales?'

'A tribe of black savages in the Isle of Wight?'

They both burst out laughing.

'It seems almost too fanciful for one of her limited experience to invent,' Mary said. 'Where could she have got these idea? It is a mystery.' She looked up at him. 'But I do think, do you not also, that this place is full of mystery? Something which you and I both feel and yet cannot explain. These strange lapses of memory on my part for instance.'

'And this conviction that I have a mission to fulfil,' he said. 'Can this also be just a figment of my imagination? Sometimes it is so strong that it seems to become –' He demurred to consider his choice of words – 'become – well – almost a – a divine revelation.' He blushed furiously at the enormity of the suggestion. Chosen to fulfil some mission? How presumptuous, how ridiculous.

'My own sense of mission is more humble,' Mary said, 'but none the less strong. I feel fired with a great sense of the injustice of man towards woman and the desire to help to put that wrong right. But I am not sure that I have the strength or the ability to do much more than join my poor efforts to those real heroines of today. I read only yesterday of the exploits of a Mrs Josephine Butler in her uphill struggle for the rights of the poor, distressed and destitute women in most of our big cities. Those who are driven, willy nilly, into – into prostitution, through no fault of their own. Perhaps I may someday feel strong enough to join in this battle with my whole being.'

There was a shocked silence. Mary's heart beat strongly with the sense of daring which had allowed her to broach the subject. What would Mr Cane think of her outburst? But then the hot feeling of injustice took her over again, and she found herself becoming incensed on behalf of that poor Mrs Butler who, it was said in the journal she had read, was pelted with eggs at the meeting she addressed. She waited, taut, for Mr Cane's reply. Much hung on his reaction.

Richard Cane looked straight ahead of him in great confusion, his heart troubled by the idea of her fighting raucously and flagrantly against debauchery of this kind. A chill of apprehension and anxiety overtook him.

'I don't much like to think of you in battles of that sort.' He looked at her almost pleadingly and with an intense concern.

Mary melted inwardly as she saw the expression in his eyes, but there was no denying this inner voice that had taken possession. 'Being a young woman rather than a young man does not – or should not – make me less able to deal with the world as it really is,' she said. 'I could not respect myself if I should be cowardly enough to leave the unpleasant things to others. Men, both good men and bad men, have neglected the depressing and pitiful result of their own greed and depravity for far too long.'

She glanced again at Richard Cane to see his reaction. But it was not as though she could hope to control the flow of her own words. They kept tumbling out of her mouth quite unbidden. She even found herself

171

interested in what she might say next, because it did not seem to be anything of which she had previous knowledge. Had she seen those reports of the bellicose meetings of Mrs Butler? She had no real recollection of reading about them anywhere.

'And then there is the Queen herself,' she continued, frowning. 'I was yesterday shocked and most upset to read that she is reported to have announced – I can scarcely believe that she can truly have said it – but it was reported in the newspaper that she had remarked on "the mad wicked folly of women's rights". Can you believe that? And she, a woman who should, above all, see that her own sex is treated fairly and neither put upon nor misused by men.'

The silence between them hung very heavily, and Mary was trembling when she turned towards him. 'Who is it that speaks through me?' she said unhappily. 'I don't know where it all comes from.'

He took her hand, quite firmly, in his own. 'Wherever it comes from, I think you do believe in the things you are saying, do you not? Because I do, and I feel ashamed that I should not have come out with them myself. That I should not have probed below the surface of my own paltry propping up of a rotten system, because I did not bother to look further. However, I do not believe even this cause to be the one – the true one – for which you and I are intended. You have a far greater, more spiritual destiny ahead, and I feel that I am fortunate enough to be somehow connected with this destiny. I would count myself a coward indeed if I did not stand by your side to support you with my whole heart and soul in any holy and courageous stand which you see fit to take.'

With a startling boldness that emanated suddenly from that same hidden source, Mary took his other hand in hers, and drawing him towards her, she kissed him on his virgin pink cheek, and laughter immediately engulfed her.

'Swalk,' she said, 'or to put it more plainly, sealed with a loving kiss. But I do believe we shall be whisked up to heaven to join the saints if we are not very careful. Is it that I am holier than thou or that thou art holier than I? Are we not two precious prigs, just brimful of our own goodness and loving kindness? And must we not come sharply down to earth if we are to remain two ordinary, humble, no-account little mortals?'

'You never will be that to me,' he said. 'I consider you to be truly a heaven-sent gift from God.'

The boldness of the previous moment collapsed, and her laughter, and the attempts to rescue the situation from intensity faltered, but she persisted, because it was imperative to escape from the frightening, emotional tangle. This was altogether too big a thing for her to accept at the moment. She was not ready. She might never be ready, even though the inevitable finale loomed menacingly. Far too frightening for confrontation.

She got up and swept, with a rustle of skirts and a gilded smile, out of the room, down the passage and into the kitchen and the safety of Peg preparing vegetables among the gleam of saucepans and everyday domesticity.

'Mr Cane suggests we might once again make a trip to London to view the paintings,' she said. 'Would that not be very pleasant?'

But in spite of the flight from danger and the escape from the emotional abyss, Mary knew that the first step towards the inevitable had been taken.

16

Mary Stein bought herself a typewriter. She somehow imagined that this was an important step in her life which prefaced a newish start. It was something she needed to do in order to become someone in her own right. But what a silly idea that was. A typewriter did not make you into someone; it was merely a prop, she supposed. She was never sure why she did things at all, or at least could never find the sensible reason for doing some of the things that she did. She wondered if everyone felt like this, but at once assured herself that other people were far more likely to know what they were doing and why. Her own stupidity must be unique.

Just now, she saw her singing and harp lessons and her position in the Lavender Cottage group of people as coincidental to what she now believed was her story telling role. There was a powerful urge just under the surface to write something down. To tell a story. The story, whatever that might be. This would be the Gospel according to Mary.

She typed that across the top of a clean white page and underlined it. Then she put Page 1 in the right hand corner, and Chapter One underneath the title. After that, she leaned back in her chair and folded her arms, staring out from her bedroom window over their back yard, which was now full of plants that Mim had put there and tended. Above the yard, and the high wall that divided them from the surrounding houses, were roofs and chimneys and television aerials and pigeons. She could see the tops of two trees, and beyond there was London, stretching on and on over more roofs and more chimneys and tall blocks and spires, right down to St Paul's gold cross and dome – dwarfed now by impersonal squares and rectangles crowding in. No longer rising supreme, but struggling to exist among the monstrously encroaching tower blocks. But you could just see it. It was still there.

Mary hankered after the view that Victorian Mary would have seen. Fields like Constable painted them, and many distant, delicate spires round the pivotal dome. She would have looked down on a distant London, instead of craning to glimpse the centre of her own scattered galaxy. But it was good to be able to look out and down at distance, however crowded and encroaching that distance might be. Gave you the feeling of being in a god-like position of control. And whatever blocked the view, it was still beautiful, still impressive, still awe-inspiring.

She brought her mind back to the piece of paper in the typewriter. Had she any real ability? Was there any point in writing something that no one would ever read? A diary might be interesting. She could write Mary Abrahams' diary. Pretend that she *was* the nineteenth century Mary?

'My name is Mary Abrahams,' she typed slowly and deliberately. It probably would take for ever, but it was a good way to learn.

'And we have just come to live in Lavender Cottage in Hampstead. It is the first of January in the year 1871 and everything just now seems very cold and bleak. It is the beginning of a new year so I must look forward and not back, I must hope and not despair. My life will be very different from this time onward. I do not know what to expect.'

The typing was laborious, with constant mistakes, and Mary found that her thoughts also emerged sluggishly and without inspiration. Perhaps the whole thing was a mistake. She slumped back rather hopelessly, then forced herself up again immediately, so that her back was ramrod straight. It was only an exercise to teach herself typing after all. Didn't matter what she turned out; that was of secondary importance. Could just as well write rubbish about brown foxes jumping over lazy dogs. Far more interesting to attempt to imagine what the thoughts of her namesake in 1871 might have been. Probably not very different from her own in 1971.

'Why did Father throw us out?' she wrote. 'How dreadful that moment was. I think I shall never forget it the whole of my life. He had always been so quiet and so gentle before, and yet here he was, a madman almost. Someone I did not know, someone I had never met before. Of course dear Mama is a nag, and had treated him most shamefully for all the time they were together. She cannot help it, she is just made that way and one must not mind her sharp tongue. He did not mind, or did not seem to mind for so many years; just stayed quiet and gentle, almost as though he did not hear her. And then, so suddenly, the explosion, and the blowing away of our lives in that single moment. How can this have happened? My heart is too full of despair to dwell upon it for any length of time. It is too painful.'

Mary got up from her chair and started to pace backwards and forwards in the small area of her room. Her heart was beating noisily, and she felt a very great distress and at the same time an elation, because of the profusion of ideas that suddenly seemed to fill her head. It was really too much, and quite overpowering. How to get it all down? Her present rate of typing was too slow, it would have to be longhand. She took her spiral notebook and her newly sharpened pencil, and for the next two hours lost herself in chronicling the diary of Mary Abrahams of 1871.

It was Maggie's voice that finally broke the concentration. Her face peered round the door. 'What are you doing? Couldn't you hear? I've been yelling at you for an age.'

It took several seconds for Mary to adjust. She had been at the orphanage, searching out Peg. Peg? PEG! Of course – Peg! She jumped up and hugged Maggie in her excitement. 'Oh Mag, you just can't imagine – it's all clear. I know who Peg is.'

Maggie stepped back from the embrace without understanding. 'Peg? Well who is Peg?'

'She was the little girl the other Mary picked out of the orphanage to be their sort of maid.'

Maggie's expression still registered blank incomprehension.

Mary laughed. 'Oh you *know*, the Peg that John's always talking about. I know who she is now. She's the little waif that Mary picked out of the orphanage in the 1870s.'

'So you just said. How do you know?'

Mary's exuberance shrivelled like the air going out of a balloon, 'Well I – er – I . . . Well it's this story I'm trying to write about the house. You know. I sort of started it today again and – and this Peg character is coming into it.'

'Oh I see. What a good idea. I told you you could make up a great story if you put your mind to it. I just came to say I do really need some mince if I'm going to do spaghetti bolognaise for this evening. Could you possibly? I just seem to lack energy these days. It's so irritating because I swore I wasn't going to give way to pregnancy vapours. Would you mind?'

'Of course I wouldn't mind. You really must stop doing so much or you'll have a miss. Why don't I do the supper?'

'Because I'm not an invalid and refuse to be treated as such and you hardly ever get miscarriages at six months anyway. Pregnancy is a normal, natural process and should make absolutely no difference to one's life. It's certainly not going to to mine. I just happen to be a bit hot and tired today, so be an angel.'

Mary bounded through the streets to the butcher, wrapped in total exhilaration and the knowledge of how

177

the story would proceed. It was all so clear, and the sun and the small autumn breeze intoxicated her still further. The Gospel according to Mary. What a good title. There was no doubt that this was her true vocation. She wanted to tell everyone: I am a writer. I'm writing an inspired book. This is what I am going to do from now on. Two pounds of mince and some chrysanthemums from the flower lady on the corner. 'Five shillings a bunch darling. Lovely and fresh.' Life was wonderful.

'I can't see,' she said later to Maggie as the three of them ate their spaghetti together in the dining room, 'why I can't take on all the shopping and the cooking to save you a bit of work now that you're pregnant. You should really take things a bit easier.'

'I've told you before,' Maggie said irritably, 'I don't intend to let this baby make any difference to my life. It has to fit in with everything in a perfectly normal way. The fuss some people make is absolutely unnecessary. I mean you don't see African or Indian mothers giving up work because they're pregnant, and they have far less trouble over the birth because of that. It's a natural process and shouldn't be made into anything different.'

'But anyway it's daft you doing everything and us just poncing about on our fannies,' Mim said.

'You do the housework.'

'Not any more than anyone else does.'

'But you're so hopeless at cooking, both of you, and appallingly extravagant. It's much easier if I do the whole thing. It would be hopeless to divide up the cooking and the shopping.'

'We can't cook because you've never let us try.'

'It's much easier to do it myself than try to teach you.'

'Oh *charming* I must say.' But it was scarcely worth fighting over, and Mim, rather gratefully, did not pursue it.

Maggie turned to Mary. 'I suppose you *could* do the shopping as you're not doing anything else.'

Mary blushed, because she had begun to think that

she actually had started something worthwhile that very afternoon. But of course it could not be considered seriously. Not yet anyway.

'Oh yes do let me, I would so like to,' she said. 'You could make a list of the things you wanted and I'll soon learn to be economical.'

It would be good for her, Maggie thought. Give her a sense of responsibility and help to her to become more practical.

At that moment, Matt came in from work, and Maggie looked at him with discomfort. 'Oh God, I forgot you. We've eaten it all.'

'I haven't finished mine,' Mary said, pushing her plate towards him. 'We could share.'

Matt's expression was thunderous. 'That's the sort of thing one really likes to come home to,' he said. 'I've had a hell of a day and it seems I'm not going to be able to relax here either.'

'*You've* had a hell of a day,' Maggie shouted, 'and what do you think I've had? Trying to din maths into the heads of hundreds of resistant, aggressive, smelly idiot children all day.'

'You really don't like kids do you? Seems a bit pointless having one.'

'If I had the smallest amount of co-operation from its father, the tiniest amount of all this sharing we've heard so much about, then things might be very different. Why should you expect a meal when you get in? Am I already delegated the female role of kitchen and kids?'

'That's hardly fair, your hours are shorter, you come in at four.'

Maggie banged both fists on the table. 'My God that's typical,' she said. 'You know perfectly well my hours are no shorter than yours. If I ever do happen to get in before five, then there's at least two to three hours of corrections. You know that you bastard. And you don't have to come in so late, you just choose to spend more time with your cases than you do with your family – if you can call

179

me that. You can bloody well get your own food in future.'

Mim sighed, and sprawled back in her chair. 'Are you planning to split up now or later?' she asked. 'If I remember rightly, we weren't going to have any of this bad vibes syndrome à la Clare and Sam.'

'But I'm going to do the food in future,' Mary said, 'because I have nothing else to do.'

'That's right,' Maggie said, 'encourage him in his bloody male chauvinist piggish attitude. Always some woman or other ready to pander to him.'

Mary tried to think her way round that one. 'It's just that I have more time,' she said, 'not because I'm female.'

'Male and female role-playing could only be dragged into an argument like this by a biased, unbalanced feminist like your sister,' Matt said. 'It's all so boring.'

'So are you,' Lou appeared suddenly at the dining room door in white satin trousers and a pink silk shirt. 'Having a tincey wincey row are we? Anyone for tennis or tea?'

'Any food attached?' Matt asked gloomily. 'Doesn't look as though I'm going to get any here. Because it's seems I am both male and chauvinist and a pig into the bargain.'

'Be our guest dear,' Lou said, 'share our trough. I was just going to run up a little something for my friend Jude.'

'Did I hear food mentioned?' Rollocks' voice came from the front door, 'because we have company folks. Voices from the distance past and county of Essex.'

'Bummer and Pooter!' Matt shouted, emerging at once from the irascibility of the previous moments. 'Where the hell did you come from? God, but that's great man. We're just about to have coffee and some food. I'm sure we've got something. Bread and cheese at least, or we could order something from the Chinese. So what's new?'

'I found them wandering about Hampstead,' Rollocks said, 'they accosted me and asked for sixpence for a cup of tea. That was before they beat up the old lady and took her handbag.' The four of them laughed uproariously, transported back into the gilt nostalgia of university life,

180

and away from the silent disapproval of the rest of the company.

'I'll phone Moonlight for a take-away,' Matt said dialling. 'How many are we? Six? Eight?'

'We have eaten, remember,' Maggie said stonily, but only Lou noticed the grim line of her mouth and the embarrassed anxiety of the other two girls on her behalf.

'Tea while we're waiting then?' he asked. 'But it won't be green and middle class, just Typhoo tea bags and common.'

'So what are you doing? Where are you living?' Matt clutched gratefully at the chance to revert from present day pressures.

Maggie retreated still further at his ability to switch. She sat, tensed and still, with Mary in the role of guarded supporter, and Mim relaxing hostilities briefly to survey the two visitors. Unattractive, she decided, because she was not into grubby, hairy types. Her nose wrinkled at the thought of the inevitable smell.

'Well well, how nice, how nice,' Bummer said, rubbing his hands. 'What charming, middle class premises, my dear Rollocks. I always said you'd make it in the end.'

'We are living in our car, parked at the bottom of the road,' Pooter said. 'Just temporary, mind you, until they give us a nice Council flat.'

'But how do you manage to run a car?' Rollocks asked.

'It's not easy,' Pooter agreed, 'but not impossible either. There's the little matter of licence and insurance. But run is perhaps the wrong word, we push it mostly. And then of course we do tend to borrow some of the necessities of life.'

'How can you live in a car?' Mary said.

'Again – not easy. I suppose you don't happen to have any floor space you could loan out?'

'No,' said Maggie.

'We have a coal cellar,' Matt said at the same time.

'Splendid,' Bummer said. 'Temporary of course.'

'You'd be far more comfortable in the car,' Lou said

bringing in the tea. 'You have to share the cellar with mice, spiders, black beetles, and the remains of nineteenth-century coal dust, not to mention cobwebs, and Maggie will probably charge you extra because there aren't any windows so you don't get any draughts.'

Matt laughed. 'Floor space in the cellar is non-chargeable. We are kindly landlords, brimming with high ideals and moral fibres and always ready to help friends in need. You can stay as long as you like.'

The atmosphere remained frigid and divided, the girls silent and tense, while the four men reminisced and laughed over-loudly.

Lou took himself and his tea back to his room. 'Bored now, bye,' he said. 'I never could stand the embarrassment of confrontations, specially when they're combined with reminiscences. Haven't the stamina.'

The four men went out to fetch the take-away, in a gregarious, matey bunch, full of noisy laughter and the loud-mouthed, self-conscious blatancy of an aggressive gang of school boys.

As soon as they had gone, the bitterness exploded.

'Well really, that's pretty cool I must say.' Mim strode to the window and stared angrily after them. 'I mean, taking it all for granted. Not even asking us or anything.'

'I shall move out,' Maggie said. 'Just move out and stay out until they've gone. Matt can bloody well look after his own precious friends if he's so keen on them.'

'You can't move out,' Mary said. 'That would be crazy. That's cutting off your nose to spite your face.'

Mim turned round to stare at her in surprise. 'That's a very worldly wise speech for little Em to make.'

'But I'm right, aren't I? It doesn't help to fight over this.'

'But he can't be allowed to get away with it.' Maggie was beside herself. 'What right has he to land these bums on us?'

'They won't actually be much in the way down in the coal cellar.' Mary started to laugh. 'Perhaps we could catch a few more mice to let loose down there. I think Matt might get fed up with them pretty quickly anyhow.'

'But it's the principle of the thing. Matt can't be allowed to ride roughshod like this.'

'I think he's probably only being sort of kind, like he always is. Just likes to help people all the time.'

'The veritable, authentic social worker in extremis.' Mim laughed at the whole idea. 'How priceless. Looked at in that light, I suppose you can't be angry with him. He's just doing his job.'

'I can,' Maggie said. 'He may consider everybody else, but he doesn't consider me, does he?'

'But you don't need considering,' Mary said, innocent of any barb in her words. 'You are so good at looking after everyone – yourself included. I think we shouldn't mind so much them being here for a bit. If they're a nuisance, I'm sure Matt will get rid of them.'

Mim stared at her again in continuing surprise. 'You sound so wise suddenly little Em. Where has all this wisdom come from?'

Mary looked perplexed. 'I don't know, but I hate fights and quarrels. I think we should try just being ordinary and together like we usually are, because I think that will make everything easier for everybody.'

The anger crumpled, because it suddenly seemed to matter very little to any of them.

John had been sitting silently in their midst during the whole incident. He watched the television screen intently, though the sound was turned right down. 'Mary is a peace lady,' he said. 'She should carry an olive branch in her mouth and be a dove.'

'Where did you learn about that?' Mim asked.

'We're doing Noye's Fludde and I'm Mr Raven.'

'How sweet,' said Mim smiling.

John turned round in his chair to face them. 'It will be quite all right to have those two men to stay,' he said, 'because Matt will find out that they are bad men and he will get angry with them and send them away quite

183

soon.' He then swivelled back in his chair, put his chin in his hands, and continued viewing.

'Talk about pearls of wisdom coming from the mouths of babes and sucklings,' Mim said.

'All this talk of wisdom,' Maggie said, 'anyone would think you actually knew what it was. But it seems I've been voted down as usual. I really do think that perhaps I should opt out of the whole thing and go and live by myself somewhere.'

Mim and Mary gravitated immediately towards her, and twined their arms round her neck and waist. 'You know that's just not possible,' Mim said.

Maggie frowned at them. 'You'd probably do much better without me.' She hunched her shoulders, put her hands in her pockets and slammed out of the room. 'Your turn for the washing up,' she said to Mim as she went up the stairs.

But when Matt came home that night, she found her resentment had melted into unexplained affection for the type of personality which would offer house, home and himself to anyone who asked.

'I can't imagine why I put up with you,' she said. 'It must be the influence of my idiot sisters, but I do appreciate the fact that you are really a very good person. Quite the opposite of me.'

'My god, she's human after all.' Matt held her close and kissed her. 'I always suspected that it might be the case. And I'm sorry I'm such a bastard. It's just that I can't say no to people. You know that, don't you?'

'Yes, I know that. Whereas I simply can't say yes.'

'So you're a selfish bitch and I'm a cowardly slob.'

'I suppose we deserve each other in an irritating sort of way.'

'If the infant gets half of each – providing they're the right halves – he should be well balanced.'

John's prediction was borne out in a fairly short time. Pooter and Bummer stayed on relentlessly at first, wisecracking and taking advantage of everything and everyone. Graffiti began to appear on the lavatory door, the bath was not cleaned, food and drink began to disappear out of the fridge, and Mary discovered unexpected items on the shopping list: 450lbs of pink rice, 2 nerds, 1 pr elephant's knees. Telephone messages came, asking Mim to audition for important film parts; down and outs appeared at the door saying that they had been told that ex-con Matt Sharpe would be glad to put them up.

'It may be frightfully funny,' Mim said, returning from an audition, which turned out to be for the part of the witch in an amateur production of Snow White. 'But it's also nasty.'

'Oh come now,' Rollocks said, 'it was only a joke. Where's your sense of humour?'

'So when are you moving on?' Matt said to the other two. 'We may love you, but you tend to disrupt the group.'

'Like so many of your thwarted generation,' Bummer said, 'you have reverted to type. The brief, lucid spell of the Essex experience was merely a veneer.'

'Joined the inevitable rat-race generation,' Pooter agreed. 'Even poor Rollocks here has succumbed to bourgeois-type manners.'

'Given up principles for comfort in fact.'

'OK, yar. So?' Penny's irritation surfaced briefly. 'It's not uctually a sin to have money.'

'Oh come now Penny, money is the root etc etc, you *know* it makes sense.'

'You're so bigoted,' Maggie said, 'and so narrow.'

Her remark was greeted with delighted laughter from the three. 'Am I hearing aright?' Pooter said. 'I believe there is an expression about a pot calling a kettle black isn't there? Very droll, very droll indeed.'

'All these jokes,' Mim said, 'they're so boring, and so unfunny.'

'And so unkind,' Mary said. 'You're just so unkind.' Bummer and Pooter sobbed loudly on each other's shoulders, but Mary persisted. 'That job Bummer is doing, taking all those awful pictures painted on black velvet round from house to house and saying that he's painted them and that he hasn't had anything to eat for three days.'

'Or telling people that if you don't sell three sets of encyclopaedias you'll get the sack,' Maggie added.

'Anybody silly enough to believe that sort of rubbish deserves death by hanging. And if they live in Hampstead they can afford to share their money with the deserving poor.'

'Like you I suppose?'

'Exactly like us. You wouldn't believe what these cretinous millionaires – and more particularly their wives – will fall for.'

'Specially if you lay them first.'

'You're revolting,' Mim said. 'And you don't have to be rich to have faith in people and to believe what they say.'

'No, but it helps.'

'The trouble with practical jokes,' Matt said, 'like everything else in life – a sense of humour, kindness, faith in human nature – all those excellent qualities we strive after, if they are carried to their logical conclusion, become absurd or evil. Humour becomes cruelty, love becomes obsession, kindness becomes maudlin, faith becomes gullibility.'

'So let's stop being obsessive and allow ourselves to drift into eternity on a cloud of tolerant nihilism,' said Rollocks.

The laughter from Bummer and Pooter that greeted this statement was even louder than usual, to cover any embarrassment and to make an end to confrontation in any depth. The rest of the group remained cohesively stony-faced.

The final crunch came suddenly, with an offer to pick up Mary one evening from her singing lesson in Golders Green.

'Let hatchets be bygones and bygones be buried,' Pooter beamed. 'Let us, in fact repay. We happen to be

186

covering the Golders Green area with a group of young friends this evening.' He gave a burst of unexplained laughter, echoed by Bummer. 'Let us be at your service, holy virgin, to transport you where you will. We might even treat you to a coke and soda at some gourmet's paradise.'

So they are trying, Mary thought. I would really much rather go by bus, but if they want to prove they have taken our criticism to heart, I should at least let them do it.

'I can easily get the bus.'

'Nonsense, nonsense – not to be considered. And this will surely prove how public spirited and generous we really are.'

'Well, if you're sure it's no bother. I finish about eight o'clock.'

'We'll be there, never fear.' And to Mary's surprise, the battered car was waiting outside the house of her singing teacher when she emerged.

It seemed rather full, and when she looked in through the windows she saw that it was indeed crowded with several extra young people and a large collection of garden gnomes.

Explosions of laughter and shouts greeted her. 'Ah Mary, can we introduce you to our friends, the gnomes of Golders Green and Temple Fortune.'

Mary squeezed herself into the car and sat on top of some unknown body who handed her a headless gnome holding a fishing rod.

'This one sadly became hysterical and lost his head you see,' Pooter said, 'tried to resist arrest in fact.'

'But where do they all come from?' Mary asked.

There was increased laughter and a variety of explanations were offered: 'From a fairly wide area.' 'But they're all strictly kosher of course.' 'Attend all the best and most orthodox synagogues.' 'We're demanding a ransom from the owners.' 'Some of them have been really ill-treated, we're reporting the owners to the NSPCG.' 'We're taking them into care.'

187

Someone gave a scream, 'Look! There's another.'

The car screeched to a halt, and Mary fell out with gnomes and parts of gnomes crashing into the road beside her. Two occupants of the car piled out after her, ran into a nearby front garden and snatched another gnome.

There were shouts of 'Charge!' 'Got you, you shitty little bastard.' And then, at the far end of the road, flashing lights and a police siren and hysterical panic.

'Quick you goons, the fuzz.'

'Come on, get in.'

The car started to move off but Mary continued to sit, dazed and bruised, in the middle of the road among the abandoned gnomes, watching it gather speed with the doors open and a pair of legs half in, half out waving wildly in the air.

Mary was arrested, questioned, charged with, and subsequently fined for, the theft of certain garden furniture, viz. three plastic gnomes. She insisted that she had merely been a passenger in the car, and did not know the names of any of the other occupants who were not traced.

Bummer and Pooter never returned to Lavender Cottage after the incident, even to collect the few things they had left behind in the basement, and the outrage among the community was solid and shame-faced.

'Allowing people to stay without actually knowing their real names,' Maggie fumed, 'seems the height of idiocy verging on the insane. We're all to blame.'

Rollocks weathered the storm without too much trouble. 'Just a bit of bad luck,' he insisted when paying for his share of the fine, 'but you can't help laughing, can you?'

Mary sat down at her desk with a deep sigh that was full of relief. There had always been something so altogether nasty about having Pooter and Bummer in the house and it had filled her with unease. They had made her feel disillusioned and hopeless. There they were, making sick jokes to hide their disenchantment. Not being able to admit to failure. Using cliché-ridden, hackneyed humour as a cover-up for their anger and frustration.

She felt sudden hate for her peers and their bigoted opponents. All these useless, stupid creatures who peopled the world, and more particularly her own fragile neighbourhood of family and friends. 'Oh God,' she said out loud, 'send us down someone to get us out of this mess. We don't seem to be able to do it on our own.'

It was far too depressing to dwell upon, she thought, as she sat at the window. There was no way humanity was going to extricate itself from its own destruction. There had to be some intervention – magical, divine, call it what you will. She sank deeper into hopelessness. There was nothing, absolutely nothing she could do about it. Just sit back and demand action from God. What a demoralising admission.

She felt the need, as she sat at the window looking over London, to absent herself from present day unpleasantness, where the threat of violence seemed always imminent. She took up her pencil as though it might be the key to escape.

'Today,' she wrote, 'we took in a poor but deserving couple with their dear little daughter, Constance. Such a frail little thing she looks. I hope that I will be able to help the mother to nurture her, so that she may become healthy and strong. Mama does not consider that they will be able to afford the rent, but Mr Barber is a teacher at one of our schools, and therefore receives a regular wage. In any case, I feel it incumbent upon me to give special terms to the deserving poor, who may find it difficult to acquire decent accommodation. For however can a teacher give of his best if his circumstances and surroundings are degrading and decadent?'

189

17

'I have decided,' wrote Mary Abrahams in her private diary, 'that whatever Mama may think (and I have no doubt that she will both think and say a great deal!) I must show my appreciation of God's goodness to me in some material way. With Christmas approaching, I intend to spend some of my savings on entertaining the members of our little household to Christmas dinner. I believe that there are some fine geese at Mr Dearlove's farm, and I will make a plum pudding myself. Miss Tripp said that her mother had an excellent recipe. The thought of a big, family celebration, such as Mr Dickens had described in his writings, fills me with quite absurdly pleasurable anticipation.'

'Madness I call it.' Annie was incensed at the indignity of the idea. 'Putting yourself on a level with the common herd, although I have tried always to make you understand your superior position. Your father has much to answer for, subjecting you to such a degenerate neighbourhood. Surrounded as we are by the dregs of humanity, what hope have we to keep our reputation unsullied?'

Mary laughed. 'Oh my dear Mama,' she said, 'I cannot really claim to be the paragon of virtue and good breeding you would wish for. I do believe that Joey has more goodness and humanity in his little finger than many so-called respectable people one might meet today have in their whole being.'

Annie fished for her handkerchief in the under-

190

petticoat of her black bombazine morning dress. A dress which had seen better days but was still wearable, by dint of careful patching and mending. She dabbed at her nose, which tended to drip in any case during the cold weather, and emotional upset made it worse.

'Such extravagance,' she said. 'Such wicked waste squandered on those who will be quite unable to appreciate it, or to express true gratitude.'

Mary counted on her fingers. 'I think we should be able to seat everyone in the front parlour. Let me see, there's Mr Cane, Mr and Mrs Johnson and their three children, Miss Tripp, Mr Grebe and Mr and Mrs Barber and little Connie; that makes seven adults and four children. Add to that you, me, Peg and Joey –'

'*Joseph*?' Annie's voice became hoarse through what could have been shock. 'You intend to include a feeble-minded working man and the servant girl among your guests? What ill-advised foolhardiness is this? You think I would sit down at table with such as these? But you –' the handkerchief dabbed the nose again. 'You – my only daughter – will no doubt prefer their company to mine. May I hope that you will find the time to serve me my Christmas dinner on a tray in the next room?'

Mary gazed at her mother with an expression of hopeless compassion. 'Mama dearest –' How to chide without berating? Should she not, in fact, berate such arrant inhumanity? But that would be like punishing an innocent child, and have little effect in any case. 'Think what pleasure you could give to these poor people by honouring them with your presence,' she said instead, and asked God's forgiveness for the sly strategy. 'Could you not bend your principles just this once dear Mama? It being Christmas and the season of goodwill. We should all be so happy if you could.'

Annie blew her nose loudly, as though putting an end to both the drip and the conversation. There was something in what the child said. It was a valid penance at Christmastime to launch oneself into some sort of charitable work, however disagreeable. But it would not do to appear to be swayed by immature arguments, so she turned her head away from her daughter and glanced towards the chimney piece.

'That fire will be out long before Peg thinks to tend it. Good-for-nothing slut that she is.'

Mary tensed with fury. It was more difficult to be indifferent to insults aimed at Peg, and she knelt down by the fire to hide her anger and to pile more wood on to the embers. 'Peg is a child, Mother,' she said, 'I wish that you would treat her as such, and help to make her remaining childhood years happier than her early life has been.' She got up quickly from her knees, and left the room before Annie had the chance to retaliate.

Mr Cane was entering the front door as she came into the hall, and she felt her spirits lift like a flight of birds as she saw him.

'Ah Mr Cane,' she said, 'just the one I wanted to see. I have such a jolly idea for Christmas day, and I would like to have your opinion on it. First, would you be good enough to aid me in measuring up the front parlour?'

She was embarrassed by her own boldness. She could perfectly well measure up the parlour by herself, but it seemed very necessary to have the presence and support of Richard Cane to help her out of the despondency and anger concerning her mother she was harbouring in her heart at that moment. A dose of goodness must help to eradicate the unpleasant atmosphere of Annie's inexorability.

Richard Cane looked delicate and ethereal as he listened to the plan for Christmas day. He felt a little guilty that he had been scheming how to arrange to spend it in Mary's company without giving a thought to anyone else. But the idea of a Christmas dinner transported him at once to a childhood memory of an orphan's treat with stew and suet pudding. The remembered pleasure shone out of his face.

'Oh yes, yes, what a splendid plan! And we could easily fit that number in this room somehow or other. A series of tables added to the big one, and children could sit on their mothers' laps. May I help?' He checked himself. 'Though I suppose there is not much a man could do concerning the cooking – or any of the other arrangements either, except perhaps the moving of tables.' His enthusiasm wilted lamely into embarrassment.

'Of course you can help, Mr Cane,' Mary said. 'There is nothing a woman can do that a man could not.' She stopped and burst out laughing. 'Well, perhaps one or two little things. But I am sure you can peel potatoes as well as any woman, after a little practice that is. Peg would be only too glad to have some help with that, and with cleaning the brussel sprouts; and plum pudding is very heavy to mix in large quantities.' She watched his reaction rather warily, saw his initial shock and then the dawning of resolution.

He marvelled at his own bigoted attitude. If Mary could do his work, then he could equally manage hers. The rigidity of his unquestioned childhood training dissolved in the presence of this remarkable girl. 'You are perfectly right,' he said. 'There is no reason why a man cannot help in all ways. If you have had the courage to venture out of the shelter of feminine gentility and to set yourself, against male selfishness and dogmatism for the sake of our Somers Town girls, then I should at least have the humility to take up some of the humbler tasks of life myself.'

Mary had an immediate thought of the world being turned upside down in the past year. From a dependant, submissive daughter, she had changed into a parent to her own mother, the head of the family group and a partner to one Richard Cane Esquire, who was studying for Holy Orders! How was it that Mr Cane and she appeared to be on a level with one another? Had she really dared to call him a *partner*? What a confusing metamorphosis. Quite alarming when you considered it. She felt that she had changed into another personality.

It was cold, that December, though the rain had not turned completely to snow. The sleet that stung her cheeks was far colder and more vicious than snow would have been. Richard Cane battled with her towards the horse tram on one of the Thursdays that they attended the Somers Town mission. It had been altogether too cold for Peg, they decided, so they left her at home on this particular day. Richard Cane's own wasted fragility also seemed less able to withstand the weather than did Mary's tougher physique. A momentary frantic fear clutched at Mary's heart. The frail being beside her suddenly looked as though he did not belong to this world and as though he might, at any moment, be whisked away by the wind to other realms.

'Are you eating well?' she asked him, shocking herself by the intimacy of the question. 'You are so very thin, I feel that you may not be looking after yourself as you should.'

She had a comforting vision of a warm cosy parlour in a country vicarage, with a log fire, lighted lamps on the tables, and her offering soup to a relaxed and smiling Richard Cane. There may have been children playing before the fire, and certainly a kitten or two. She checked herself sharply.

'This cold tends to make my cough a little worse,' Richard said, holding his muffler over his nose and mouth. 'But I must not complain. This year away from studies in the fresh Hampstead air has done me the world of good, so that I should be quite ready to carry on at the college in the New Year with my health quite restored. It is essential that I do so, that I may not let down my saintly and long-suffering benefactor who makes life possible for me.' The realisation of the limitless opportunities that the future held in store for them both came suddenly, piling into his head and his heart like the rush

194

of rapids and the roar of a waterfall, and all but overwhelmed him.

'Tell me about him.' He was brought back to reality by Mary's question.

'Alas, there is nothing that I can tell for I know nothing, save that I call him my godfather because I feel he has been sent from God. But I have no contact and am not allowed to know his name. I live in eternal gratitude for the life he has given me.' And gratitude to the benefactor for making the meeting with Mary possible was mixed in with the torrent.

Richard was undergoing some sort of metamorphosis. The flood gates had opened, and he was changing into someone he had never been. Someone else had slid into his personality, and this someone else wanted to sweep Mary off her feet into his arms, so that he could kiss, crush and love her. And what was more, he was no longer afraid of this scandalous creature he seemed to have become.

He turned to look at her and stretched out his hand to clasp hers very firmly as they hurried down the hill towards the tram station at South End Green.

'I love you Mary,' he said loudly and clearly. 'And I want to spend my life with you if you will have me.'

The affirmation astounded them both as they ran (or did they actually fly?) hand in hand down the hill. The fusion had been inevitable all along, but it had also been unadmitted and quite unreal. In the open, and actual, it took on a different aspect altogether, and the enormity of the situation stunned the two of them into a well of silence. Mary's cosy country parsonage vision faded, abruptly, into a gates of heaven vision. It was a more triumphant scene of two flames blending into one amid a welter of swords and shining light. Was this the reality?

'But,' she said, after the moment of beatitude had passed into a more tranquil stage of dazed euphoria, 'does not your projected calling insist – what I mean to say is, is a woman – a wife – is it not prohibited?'

195

But of course it was prohibited, she told herself. He was an Anglo-Catholic was he not? Catholic priests did not marry. What was he thinking of? He must have lost his head momentarily. Already he must be bitterly regretting and not knowing how to draw back. The deluge of icy shock stopped her heart and her feet, and she felt again the bite of the east wind and the sting of the sleet in her face. Breathless, she leaned back against the tree beside which she had stopped. It was all a mistake. He had not really meant it. It was all a mistake. In a moment he would say: I'm sorry, I didn't mean to say that. He had not thought.

He stopped also, and rounded to face her, taking both her hands in his. 'There are certain things,' he said, 'which one knows to be right, no matter what has gone before. I had thought previously that my life was bound up only with God and the Church. In my ignorance, I had considered myself complete.' He shook his head. 'I now discover that I am most woefully ignorant and most incomplete. Something has taken me over today, Mary. I feel a different man, a whole man, and it's a wonderful feeling.'

The moment was very solemn, and a still focus at the centre of the maelstrom of joyful exultation which was just then swirling Mary round in uncontrollable excitement. It was all too much to hold in check for long.

'Oh dear, darling Mr Cane, I mean Richard, complete or incomplete, I must be quite the most fortunate, the most felicitous, the most blessed woman in the world.'

'You are indeed blessed among women,' he said, and they both were a little shocked at the awareness of what he had said. 'I mean,' he added hurriedly to offset the sacrilege of the statement, 'that you are blessed with such a sweet and heaven-sent nature, that I am the fortunate one, should you see fit to accept my proposal.'

'But of course I shall see fit,' she said. 'How could I not see such a proposal as being fit?'

And the wind surged round the tree where they stood,

and rustled the dead leaves on the nearby bushes. And the horse tram took off from South End Green with two fewer passengers than it might have carried.

Richard Cane and Mary, meanwhile, walked together in the freezing sleet and wind, across the Heath, past the ponds and up the summit of Parliament Hill.

'My denomination does not disallow marriage,' he told her. 'Only Rome insists upon that. The Anglican brethren do not encourage their priests to marry, because of the distraction a wife and family might cause; but in our case, I know myself to be incomplete without you, and therefore less able to do justice to my religious duties. My superiors cannot help but see that, when I speak to them.'

'And when shall you speak to them?'

He hesitated for a moment. 'At the earliest possible moment, dear Mary. Though alas, I think it would be wiser to wait until I am fully recovered and able to take up my final training again. They may demur a little, even try to persuade me against it. When I am back at my college, then I will feel in a stronger position to convince them and induce them to understand my feelings.'

Mary gave a short burst of laughter. 'I'm going to have to do a bit of convincing myself,' she said. 'Mama being a little prejudiced, it might be wise to wait until our financial situation is a touch more conventional. I think we shall keep it a secret for the time being perhaps.'

'You don't imagine that this would be deceitful?'

'I think we are entitled to our own private feelings without necessarily disclosing them to the world until we wish to do so.'

They stood there together on top of the hill, resistant to the unkind gale, Mary's cloak whipping viciously round her, her bonnet secured by means of her shawl tied over it. Richard held his hat in his hands for fear of losing it, and his hair was swept this way and that, like a ravaged cornfield, in the ferocity of the gusts. But the cold seemed only to enfold them. Clouds raced over the sky. Kentish Town, Camden Town and Somers Town were clustered in their separate hollows on the hillside, and St Pancras and King's Cross spread their rails out to link London with its neighbours. Smoke swirled upwards to join the hurrying clouds and to dye the sky a blacker black.

But they neither saw the landscape nor felt the weather because of the phenomenon that had bonded them together. It could be said that they had left time and place behind them, and stood ready to take the next step into an inevitable new beginning.

18

The Christmas Day dinner was a joyful and prodigious success. Annie, who had been cajoled into occupying her high winged chair in a corner of the room, was seen to smile, and even consented to take Connie on her lap for a short time. Mary and Peg had decorated the parlour with holly culled from the Heath, and Mary had wrapped presents for everyone in paper coloured and decorated by herself with painted robins, and tied with ribbons she had bought from the gypsies. She had piled the presents high on the hearth rug before the fire: tobacco for Joey; a frock for Peg, stitched in deep secrecy in the weeks before; a small but special crucifix in Cornish granite for Mr Cane; a cap for her mother, laboriously and beautifully worked; hand-knitted socks for Mr Grebe; a pipe for Mr Johnson that had been carved by Joey; toys for the children; warm gloves for Tilly Johnson and a lace pocket handkerchief for little Miss Tripp. For Mary herself, the household had contributed towards an engraving of Dignity and Impudence by Mr Landseer.

'Such an admirable daughter you have Mrs Abrahams,' Miss Tripp told Annie. 'So good, so *wise* she is.'

Annie sniffed. 'Wise I doubt,' she said. 'Far too headstrong I would say. It will be her downfall if she does not make the effort to mend her wilful ways.'

Miss Tripp smiled her disagreement as though she knew something that Annie Abrahams did not; and there was every chance that she did.

'Go and put on your new frock Peg,' Mary said. 'I want to see if it fits and becomes you.'

'Oh Miss, I dursent Miss. I'm too rough for all that prettiness.'

'Nonsense! Be off with you; this is a party, and everyone has a right to look pretty.'

Her eye caught Mr Cane's for the hundredth time that day, and she turned the small silver guard ring in the shape of a belt on the little finger of her left hand. Their eyes exchanged the message of their vast secret. It was suffocating in its excitement. Mary thought that happiness could not be deeper nor more heart-warming than that which she felt at this moment. What a fortunate being I am, she thought. Can I dare to expect that life could ever be better than it is at this moment? I cannot believe so. But must it then deteriorate from now? And a small shadow of fear passed quickly through her. Was life too good to her?

But when Peg appeared at the door, transformed from the small brown waif into a radiant and appealing young girl, with her brown curls caught up with a bootlace bow, the anxiety slipped back into its proper perspective.

'Peg, you look lovely.'

There were murmurs of approval from everyone and Georgie Johnson stared, amazed. 'Cor,' he said, 'you don't half look all right. Are you a lady now?'

'Indeed she is not,' Annie snapped. 'Fine feathers do not fine birds make. I'll have you remember that Miss.'

But it was a remarkable transformation, and all part of that magical Christmas afternoon.

When she went to bed that night, Peg delayed taking off the new dress, and lay very carefully on her bed, just so that the magic could continue a little longer. She closed her eyes, for the imaginings to take on a more realistic feeling, and she proceeded to have a very extraordinary dream.

She thought that John was leaning over the bottom of her bed. 'What are you dressed up like that for?' he said, and she sat up on the bed, embarrassed to be caught out in her daydream.

'We just 'ad a party,' she said, 'and I was that tired I couldn't get meself changed.'

'You look different,' John said. 'We're having our party tonight. Would you like to come?'

Peg did not relish the idea of dancing a war dance with a troupe of savages. 'I wouldn't fit in,' she said. 'I'd feel silly.' And frightened into the bargain, she thought. They were probably cannibals. That could be why he wanted her to go.

'Oh come on.' John came round the side of the bed and seized her hand firmly.

' 'Ere, you stow it,' she said, but he caught her off balance, and before she knew it, she was stumbling across what appeared to be a perfectly strange room – or was there something familiar about it? It was very full of a crowd of noisy people in fancy dress, but none of them was black except John. She stood absolutely still, pressed back against the wall, waiting for someone to ask her what she thought she was doing there, but no one seemed to see her.

'John darling,' Mim said, 'go and fetch the gravy in would you? You're hopelessly in the way, standing there like that, no one can get past.'

'I've brought Peg to the party,' John said, moving fractionally out of the way.

'Oh sooper,' Penny said, looking round, 'where is she? Is she too shy to come in or something?'

'She is in,' John said, pointing to Peg. 'She's there.'

Everyone in the room stopped talking and turned round to stare at Peg. She stared back at them in an agony of confusion, but their eyes wandered, and they looked at each other with rather bewildered smiles.

Matt took charge. 'Peg is John's pretend friend,' he said. 'She often comes around. Glad you asked her in, John, she can sit next to you.'

John fetched a chair from the next room and squeezed

it in between two others. 'You sit here,' he told Peg, and pushed her down on to the chair. Everyone relaxed and laughed indulgently.

'Isn't he sweet,' Mim said. 'Go and get the gravy, there's a lamb. And bring a plate for Peg,' she added, giggling. 'Isn't it amazing how they can imagine things like that?' she said as he left the room. 'Must seem absolutely real to him.'

Peg watched and listened to the extraordinary scene that was going on all round her. Though she had never actually been to The Play in a proper theatre, she had been told about how a body of persons, known as actors, acted out stories in front of people who paid to see them. She had no doubt that this was what she was now watching. It was all very confusing, but quite enjoyable, though she felt unable to eat the food John kept putting in front of her, mainly because she had eaten such a large dinner, and felt a little sick. There was so much laughter and noise that she found it almost impossible to understand what was being said. She thought it might be some scene in a common ale house that was being enacted, because the actors who were taking the women's parts were so crude and vulgar, and none of them ladies in any sense of the word. Only one of them did remind her very much of her own Miss Mary because she talked gentle like, and looked almost like a proper lady. Very like Miss Mary she was. Quite uncanny she thought.

She stared round the room, trying to remember what it reminded her of. The big window all down one side, where the pale winter sun shone through now and then – but of course! It was just like the big window in the Johnsons' room; just the same sort of shape, and this room had steps leading down out of it too, only it was somehow all open into the next room instead of coming out into a passage, like it did in Lavender Cottage. She was curious to see more, and slipped off her chair when John was taking out some of the dishes, following him down into the next room. It was very untidy, and seemed to be a kitchen, though there wasn't no kitchen range, she noted, so how did they cook? The one that looked like Miss Mary was stacking dishes in what she supposed was some sort of cupboard contraption, funny to put dirty dishes away like that, but they probably didn't need to do things properly in the play, because it was only make believe.

She stood watching, and wondering, until Mary looked up and saw her. 'Hallo Peg,' she said, 'so you've decided to come and give me a hand stacking the dish washer have you? Don't spoil that nice new frock now.'

But Peg for some reason, was assailed suddenly, with a cold terror, and she turned and ran across the room straight back into her own little attic bedroom, where she slumped down, breathless, on to her bed, and fell at once into a deep sleep.

Mary went slowly back into the dining room. 'I just saw Peg,' she said. 'She was in the kitchen.'

But no one heard her because they were all pulling crackers and laughing too loudly.

It was about half an hour later, when they were drinking coffee and opening presents round the tree in the sitting room, that Maggie rolled into a ball on the floor and gasped 'God, that was a big one. I think you'd better send for the nurse.'

There was immediate panic among the whole company, except for Maggie herself, who was quite unmoved. The place became a maelstrom of movement with bodies barging and bumping into each other, and voices raised in barely controlled anxiety.

'What do you mean – big one? Have there been others?'

'Where's the Nurse's phone number? Where is it?'

'She'll never come on Christmas Day.'

'Don't you have to put water on to boil? They always do that in old films.'

'And you tear up petticoats for bandages.'

203

'Don' be s' stupid, that's in war films, she's not going to have her diggie bandaged up is she?'

'We might have to wrap the babe in swaddling bands and lay him in a manger.'

'Anyone got a manger handy?'

'For God's sake, where's the phone number of the NURSE?'

'It's by the telephone,' Maggie said in a loud, clear voice that surged with ill-concealed laughter. 'And you don't have to go mad, all of you. There's plenty of time. I've been having contractions since eight o'clock this morning. I wasn't going to let this baby break up the party.' She sat down suddenly and clutched Matt's hand with both of hers. There was a dead silence and stillness while the contraction ploughed through her, and then Mim rushed to hug her.

'Darling you're so *brave*, but how tremendously exciting it all is.'

Mary was telephoning, and the first surging panic dwindled into a fairly hysterical unease. The party began to break up, with members of the household backing away with diffident excuses.

'Well, you won't want us around at a time like this,' Rollocks sidled towards the door, but Penny hovered with interested curiosity.

'They say buck mussage is good,' she said, 'and some people find it helpful to walk abouyt.'

Rollocks grasped her firmly, 'Come *on*,' he said. 'People having babies like to be left alone.'

'No, no,' Ginny insisted, 'this is actually very seldom the case. I read somewhere that most primitive people have all the village women in to help because it takes the mind off pain.'

'Then you and I can go out and collect up some village women,' James the ad man said, taking her by the shoulders and propelling her out of the room.

'Do be sure they're really primitive,' Jude called after them. 'Otherwise it won't work.'

204

'Isn't this all splendidly basic?' Lou said. 'I mean, Christmas Day and everything. Shall I go out and see if there's a star hovering or anything? Or even three queens coming up the High Street.'

'See you then, then,' Jude said, backing up the stairs. 'Come on Lulu, you know you can't stand anything like this, even on the telly, it always makes you puke.'

John refused to go to bed. 'Not when it's Christmas and there's a baby coming and there's all that good stuff on the telly,' he said. So Pete stayed with him in the hope of persuading him by dint of compromise.

It was then that Maggie began to change from an excited, laughing mother-to-be into a frightened, swearing harpy. She was on her knees, clutching Matt round the waist. 'Get the bloody nurse,' she screamed. 'They never said it was going to hurt this much. Relax, they said, and it won't hurt. It's fucking murder.'

'They're coming every three minutes,' Matt said. 'We must get her upstairs.'

Mary was stricken by the sudden horror and ugliness of the situation. It shouldn't be like this. Maggie should be able to cope with it as Maggie always coped with things. She should not be turned into a shrieking, swearing victim in a matter of minutes. She felt the necessity to take over for her sister on whom she had relied all her life.

'The nurse is on her way,' she said. 'She'll be here very soon. You'll be all right then.'

'She'll know what to do,' Mim said, also visibly shaken. 'Don't worry darling.'

Maggie and Matt walked towards the stairs in the intervals between the contractions, leaving the rest of the Christmas party standing awkwardly among the tinsel and the Christmas wrappings, and feeling useless and unhappy. Except for John. He sat on the floor, less than a foot from the television, and with his new skateboard on his lap.

'My mum made much more noise than that when she

205

had Elvis,' he said. 'And the nurse didn't never come till he was borned.'

But this nurse did come. Smiling, confident and large, she made her way through the hastily and inadequately tidied Christmas chaos, beaming comforting platitudes as she went. 'So it's another little Christmas cherub is it? How jolly. What a pretty little house you have.' She stumped up the stairs to Maggie's room. 'Hallo my love, how are things? Nice regular contractions? Let's have a look at you then.'

Matt, Mary and Mim melted away from the closed door with feelings of unmitigated relief. 'I've never felt so useless in my life,' Mim said.

'Of course she did keep on convincing us that the whole thing was just a straightforward, natural process and nothing to make a fuss about,' said Matt.

'Which it is.'

Mary was white-faced. 'But she *did* make a fuss, didn't she? She became a different person somehow, like some sort of trapped animal. She wasn't Maggie.'

'I suppose it's because we've never seen her when she wasn't in control of her immediate situation.'

Later, when Matt was beginning to recover a little of his self-composure, the nurse bounced out of the bedroom. 'Where's prospective Dad?' she called down the stairs. 'You can come in now if you like. I think we're going to need some help after all, bit of a complication. Can I use the telephone?'

The panic was not far away, and returned promptly.

'What's the matter?'

'Is she all right?'

'What sort of complication?'

But the nurse kept smiling while ordering the ambulance and alerting the hospital, and quite soon afterwards, a writhing, unrecognisable Maggie was being carried awkwardly down the small white staircase, enveloped in a giant white blanket. Matt hovered and dodged behind the ambulance men, strained and unsmiling, and the whole group was packed neatly and efficiently into the ambulance, to take off, screaming and flashing, down the hill.

There was left behind a sense of stunning anti-climax mixed with a strange aftermath of guilt. But why feel guilty? Mary wondered. For what possible reason? Mim slumped in a chair and chewed at her nails as doors began opening cautiously, and other members of the household crept curiously back to see what had happened.

'How awful that all of us were enjoying ourselves when she was actually *suffering*,' Mim said. 'I mean – so fearfully brave, not wanting to spoil the party.' She did not add the appendage: supposing she dies and all just because she didn't want to spoil our fun.

'Oh, come on,' Rollocks came back into the room wearing a striped woolly cap and scarf knitted for him by Penny. 'She didn't care about spoiling the party, she just didn't want to miss it.'

Penny hit him sharply. 'Stop denigrating,' she said. 'What's huppened? Why did they take her to hospitul?'

'We don't know. Matt said something about blood pressure and breeches, but he was too distraught to be coherent.'

'Poor, dear, competent Maggie,' Lou said, with all the camp, comic-strip pertness missing from his voice. 'How unfair that it should all go wrong for her, of all people.'

They sat, drinking and smoking, silently and grimly, for several hours. John lay asleep on the floor, having continued to refuse bed before news came through. Pete smoked his pipe and drank beer. The others grew progressively more smashed on a mix of wine, hash, vodka and beer.

Mary, being starkly sober, snatched the phone when it did eventually ring, and took in the news at the centre of an electric stillness. It was the smile that preceded her

207

words, which signalled the death blow to the concerted anxiety.

'She had a caesarian,' she said. 'It's a girl and they're both doing fine.'

And the clock struck midnight, quite unheard among the shouts, yells and crows of rejoicing.

19

Alas! The inner warmth of the love that had glowed through Richard and Mary on that December day on Parliament Hill, was insufficient to ward off a return of Richard's illness. He became feverish, he coughed and gasped, and early in the new year, he retired to bed.

'You must rest,' Mary said. 'I thought that you had been looking as though you were doing too much. I thought it at Christmas time. You look so thin. But I will build you up with nourishing and wholesome food and I will nurse you back to health.'

She felt strong and confident, and tremendously pleased that she would have the chance to help in his recovery. He would never have looked after himself properly, but this could now be her pleasurable duty: to restore her beloved, who might otherwise have passed away through neglect of himself, to perfect health and the calling of his choice. How providential that they should have reached their understanding when they did, because now it was so clearly her bounden duty to nurse him, when before it might have seemed improper and a little inappropriate.

She took him his meals on a tray, and went out of her way to boil up calves'-foot jelly and beef tea in order to build up his strength. It was a mission, and she was filled with satisfaction. He improved slowly but was weak and exhausted.

Annie grumbled incessantly. It was inexcusable, unpardonable, reprehensible and immodest. 'Not to mention the fact that he is probably infecting the whole house.' She hung a carbolic sheet over his door. 'There's no knowing what we may all pick up. You must send for the physician and have him put away in the hospital.'

'But Mama, he is improving. Can you not see? Just a little careful nursing and a modicum of good nourishing broth. Will you not come in and see that there is colour in his cheeks now, where before there was that haggard look that comes from lack of care?'

Annie glanced at her daughter sharply. 'I have not made such a detailed study of the gentleman's face as you seem to have done,' she said, 'and I am astounded by the brazen way you choose to discuss his appearance in this way. I would certainly not enter a gentleman's bedroom at all, and I consider it highly immoral for any daughter of mine to do so.'

She folded her hands in her lap and sat upright in her chair. Why did the good Lord see fit to punish her through her daughter's wickedness and folly? What had she done to deserve such an unvirtuous offspring?

'Oh Mama.' Mary tried to be gentle, but found her anger rising in her blood. 'I am only attempting to practise a little charity.'

Annie snorted her contempt and Mary adjusted her bonnet and pulled on her gloves in some confusion, because of course it was not actually true, she was not acting out of Christian charity, she was acting out of love for Richard Cane.

'And where do you think you are going now, pray?' Annie was still making feeble and useless attempts at clawing back her daughter into the aura of parental control.

'Why, to the mission, Mama, it is Thursday, and after, I shall be attending Mrs Josephine Butler's meeting in Clerkenwell, so I shall not be home until later. As Peg will be escorting me, I have taken the liberty of putting your supper on to cook on the slow hob. It should be ready by six o'clock, and Miss Tripp will come in to help

210

serve you with it.' She hurried from the room, to forestall any further argument.

'Come Peg,' she called, 'we must be off or we shall
miss the bus.'

They crossed the back yard and stepped out of the
back gate into Bird in Hand Passage, to wait until
the horses were changed and the bus set off down the
hill towards Camden Town.

'I didn't never tell you my dream Miss,' Peg said as
they trundled slowly down the hill with sparks flashing
from the brake shoes.

'I did not ever tell you,' Mary corrected. 'Or you could
say "I never told you". The two negatives *not* and *never*,
if used together will make the sentence positive.'

Peg did not know the meaning of positive or negative,
but listened attentively: don't use "not" and "never"
together.

'Say to yourself, "Not ever, not not never",' Mary
continued. 'That will help you remember.' And she
began to intone 'Not ever not not never' in time to the
bumps and lurchings of the bus until Peg was convulsed
with laughter and giggles.

Later she said, 'That little savage boy what I see . . .'

'Who I see.'

' 'Oo I see sometimes, 'e fetched me back into 'is time
like. In my dream 'e did Miss. But it was ever so real, it
didn't somehow seem like a dream at all Miss. Only
those people there Miss, they never saw me, except one
of them did. And she was ever so like you Miss she was.
Give me quite a turn reelly when she looks at me and
says, 'ullo Peg she says, decided to come and 'elp me 'ave
you? she says. Only I got reel scared some'ow then I did,
something so scary about 'er being like you Miss, like
almost she *was* you Miss, and she was called Mary and
all Miss, and I got that confused that I ran away and
found I was back in bed. Ever such a strange dream it
was.'

Mary heard the story with a feeling of unease,

211

because it seemed that she had somehow shared the dream. Could it be that this poor little witch girl who had lived in the street all those years ago had left her wandering spirit behind her? To protest her innocence perhaps? But that was much too fanciful. Peg had obviously become muddled. Then again, Mary remembered the incident in the kitchen quite clearly; it had been on Christmas Day, and she had warned Peg about not spoiling her nice new frock. But immediately a doubt surfaced, because the surroundings she envisaged were not the kitchen surroundings. They were . . . Her mind clouded. Where had she been when she had said that? She tried, unsuccessfully, to recall, but could only remember that it was soon after that that she had suffered the first of the violent colic pains which had plagued her all through that Christmas evening and which had finally forced her to retire to bed early. Terrible spasms they were, she remembered, but they had mercifully cleared up the next day after a dreadful night of nightmares.

'I had bad dreams that night too,' she told Peg. 'It was all that rich food we had for Christmas dinner. It seems we both have a lot to learn about moderation and restraint.'

The lurching and rocking of the bus began to make her feel slightly unwell, and to wish that they had taken the horse tram instead. So much smoother, but the omnibus was so convenient, starting, as it did, from their own back door. She closed her eyes, overpowered suddenly by the desire to sleep, and found that the journey at once became smoother and more comfortable. They seemed to be flying, at tremendous speed, and there was a roar in her ears and indeed all round her, that made her wonder if she were about to faint. It sounded more like the steam train than the horse bus.

When she opened her eyes, she was carried forward, for a fraction of a second, the hundred years that time had swallowed. She was momentarily in an unknown world.

212

She had been carrying a carpet bag filled with cast off clothing and woollies, and bones wrapped in butcher's muslin, for the making of good, wholesome broth. It was a heavy, bulky load, but when she looked down, she found in her hands a bunch of unopened daffodils and a rolled copy of Private Eye. She leaned forward in her seat to search for her carpet bag; she must have put it down on the floor of the bus. Then she glanced round to see if Peg had, by chance picked it up; but Peg was not there, she saw only some creature who seemed to be half undressed, showing a shocking length of white-stockinged leg, visible practically to the thigh. Only the moment was revealed, and then total obliteration of recollection.

Off at the next stop for University College Hospital; they were letting them home tomorrow, and arrangements had to be finalised because Matt might not have time to buy all the necessary stuff. Mary felt relief and excitement and anticipation all mixed together within her, after the trauma of the week's anxiety. It had been touch and go for both Maggie and the baby, because of their unexpected difficulties in recovering from the operation of birth. It had been a perfectly successful caesarian section, but mother and baby did not recover and thrive as they should. For several days, in fact, both lay torpid and almost lifeless; disinterested in life. There seemed no medical explanation.

Mary had been appalled when she saw the baby for the first time. She had not been allowed in at first, only husbands were admitted; particularly if things had not gone right. But finally they had let her and Mim into the nursery where difficult babies were monitored, and the two of them had stood silent and stunned at the sight of the tiny flickering baby in the glass box, connected by tubes and wires plastered on to her nose and chest.

'It can't be right,' Mim whispered. 'That can't be Maggie's baby.'

'She's not being loved,' Mary said. 'How can she grow if she's not being loved?'

'But what went wrong? Why doesn't Maggie love her? What's happened to Maggie?' Mim turned away in horror. 'I don't ever want babies. I mean Maggie was so sensible and so clever about it all. Maggie always does the right and sensible thing. It was all going to be so easy, and now it's all so horrible.' Tears spilled down her cheeks. 'Do you think it will die? I shall never have a baby. I never liked the idea anyway and seeing all this has proved me right.'

A nurse passed them as they stared bleakly through the glass into the nursery, and they watched her unhook, disconnect and lift the shrimp-like creature deftly, gently and very cheerfully. 'Let's see if we can interest your mummy in you,' she said, smiling into the contorted and wizened face in front of her, and she packed the bundle neatly into a shawled parcel and bore it aloft into Maggie's room. 'Now mother,' she said jovially, 'what about another little try to feed your daughter? She depends on you you know.'

Maggie hurled herself over in the bed to face the wall. 'Take it away,' she shouted. 'I don't want it. It all went wrong. It's obviously a monster. It refused to be born. It refused me as a mother, so I deny that it can be my child.'

Matt attempted to hold her to him, but she pushed him away furiously.

'Please give the baby to me,' Mary said to the nurse in such an authoritative tone that both Matt and Mim looked up in surprise. 'All she needs is a little love.'

The nurse handed Mary the stiffly wrapped, unbending white parcel with marked approval. 'Of course that's all she needs,' she said. 'A nice loving cuddle will work wonders,' and she stepped briskly out of the room.

Mary closeted the bundle in her arms, pressing the solitarily exposed face into her own cheek. There was an immediate and overwhelming reaction inside her. A sudden welding of herself to what had before seemed

214

merely an inanimate object, but at that instant became a portion of her own humanness, part of her own being. It was an awesome experience, and she rocked from one foot to the other and crooned quietly, with the baby's face still clamped, wetly, to her cheek. It could have been for five seconds or five minutes or five hours that she stood there, swaying.

Mim could finally contain herself no longer. 'Come on,' she said, 'you can't stand there all day exuding love, let me have a go.'

Mary came to with a start and handed over the inert packet. 'But where's the baby?' Mim said rather angrily. 'This, this – package isn't a baby. I want to see her.' And she set her down on the end of the bed and started to unwind the layers of blanket, jacket, nightgown and finally towelling nappy that dwarfed the minute, stick-like legs, waving feebly in the unaccustomed freedom.

'There,' said Mim, 'that's better. Now you're a baby and not just an imprisoned thing.' She laughed. 'Isn't she *sweet*,' she said.

But the released baby gave a wail of protest, and Maggie turned her head from the pillow. 'What are you doing?' she said. 'She'll freeze to death.'

Mim scooped up the handful of flaying arms and legs. 'Nonsense,' she said. 'She just feels released and liberated enough to yell. Emancipated woman in fact.' She held the baby against her chest.

'Oh you poor lamb,' she added a minute later, 'you don't like Auntie Mim's woolly jumper, do you?' and she pulled up her large, loose pullover, and sat down on the bed with the baby cosseted between her breasts.

There was an immediate silence, which lasted until Mim looked up to see them all watching her. She smiled at them rapturously. 'God,' she said, 'this is really it isn't it? What bliss, what heaven. Did I say I didn't want to have babies? I must have been insane. I want one tomorrow, I want one *now*.' She gave a little shriek, 'Oh but

215

look, look – she's actually sucking! She's got hold of my tit and she's actually sucking! How absolutely great! But darling, I can't do a thing for you, my poor pet. I'm terribly sorry – here Maggie, quick, you're the only one able to save the situation.'

She transferred the baby into Maggie's arms with a quickness and dexterity that deceived the eyes of all present, and attached the open mouth to the nipple in a matter of seconds. She then sat on the bed with her arms enclosing both of them. 'How perfectly sweet and how perfectly wonderful it all is,' she said, wiping her eyes on a corner of the sheet. 'The poor little thing never knew we all adored her, she just didn't know, did she?'

And after that, of course there had been no more trouble. It was almost as though that harrowing week had never been. The baby fed and thrived, Maggie came back from death and despair into everyday life.

Mary was now on her way to finalise arrangements for tomorrow's homecoming. Silly to take flowers at this late stage, but they were so symbolic, closed up and unborn as they were, to blossom tomorrow into a mass of yellow flowers. New life, new blossoming, new vistas ahead, visions of spring – the lot. It was exhilarating.

There was discussion over a name, but Matt and Maggie were adamant. 'She's Gabrielle,' Maggie said. 'I never thought about girls' names before she was born, even though Matt kept coming up with daft suggestions like Rebecca and Rachel and Hannah and Martha, just in case it was a girl.'

'Nothing daft about a good biblical name,' Matt said, 'I like them.'

'So we've compromised and settled on a New Testament one. I knew at once on that day Mim and Mary woke us both up. I just looked at her and knew she was Gabrielle.'

'The angel Gabriel from Heaven came, His wings as drifted snow, his eyes as flame,' Mary sang, feeling an

216

emotion that was quite out of keeping with the domestic ambience which encompassed them all at that particular moment.

John was standing beside them, and he suddenly, and very unexpectedly, finished the couplet in the sort of treble that brings immediate tears to sentimental eyes:

'All hail said he, thou lowly maiden Mair – air – ree,

Most highly flavoured lady, Glor – or – or – or – or – ria.'

Mary rushed at him and snatched him up in a hug. 'Oh you *angel*,' she said, 'What a fantastic voice. Why didn't we know about it? Oh dear, it makes me cry,' and she put him down and burst into tears.

Lou and Jude appeared from nowhere and joined in the crying.

'Can we please discuss the flavoured lady bit? I *like* it,' said Lou, laughing between his sobs.

Rollocks came in and sighed deeply. 'Don't know if I can lodge here much longer,' he said, 'now that it's become a crèche. I don't really understand why the advent of a baby can at once reduce a fairly intelligent group to a maudlin, gibbering compilation of revolting sentimentality.'

'You're absolutely right,' Maggie said, 'much as I hate to agree with you. It is ridiculous and rather sinister.' She smiled down at her baby. 'But she is rather a duck.'

'She smells of sick,' Rollocks pointed out, 'and the whole house smells of shit.'

He was shouted at by the rest of the company, especially Penny, who hit him with the boots she had just taken off.

'Can't we put John in the church choir?' Mim said. 'He'd look great in one of those white nightdress things with a ruff round his neck.'

John scowled. 'I don't want to sing in no church,' he said. 'We sang that song at school before Christmas, but it isn't meant for Maggie, it's meant for Mary.' He

217

turned to Mary seriously. 'I'll sing it for you and your baby,' he said. 'When you have Jesus, I'll sing it for you.'

Rollocks snorted, as the others attempted to control their laughter. 'You'll have a bass voice and a bald head by the time Mary gives birth,' he said.

'No I won't,' John said. 'She'll have Jesus next Christmas and then Mim'll have one the Christmas after. But Jesus will be the best, he'll be the chief.'

'The three Supremes, the Holy Trinity, how great,' Lou said. 'Bags I be their manager.'

'Talking about singing,' Mary said, 'you do sing well, John. Fancy us not knowing that. Would you learn some songs to do with me? We could do concerts with my harp.'

John made a face. 'I might,' he said.

Pete was full of enthusiasm. 'But you never sing at school,' he said, 'and yet you have this fantastic voice. Just exactly what I want for the school's Easter play. I didn't think we'd be able to do it because no one could sing well enough, but now – would you do it? It's a very important part.'

'I might,' John said, adding, 'It's the baby what made me sing. I couldn't before. I just remembered the songs but I couldn't sing them till just now.' And suddenly embarrassed, he ran out into the street and took off on his skate board with a great flourish.

'Obviously we have a magic baby here,' Matt said. 'One that has a supernatural influence on its surroundings. Gives John a voice, makes Rollocks look for other digs and turns Maggie and me, who were so indisputably intelligent before, into maudlin, gibbering sentimentalists.'

Whether or not the direct supernatural influence of the baby was responsible, it was certainly at this time that all three sisters noticed a marked change in their attitudes to life. Each felt dubious about confiding in the other, and each was convinced that she was alone in sensing a change.

Maggie continued to be amazed by her unexpected depth of feeling for her baby. How could I be so wrong? she wondered to herself, bowled over yet again by Gabrielle's look of glazed adoration while she was feeding. I thought that pregnancy and babies were just a common or garden happening to be taken in one's stride. It was only when Mim and Mary came to see us and started taking over that I came to. She wondered how she would ever be able to bear going back to work after the regulation maternity leave. Impossible to leave this adorable infant to the care of anybody else.

Mim sat back in her chair, enjoying the sensation of being quite alone in her own room, and looked out of the window. How wonderful this place is, she thought, you look out of the window and it's not like being lost in the middle of a great city, because you are, after all, one of a trinity of sisters within the family group of the Lavender Cottage community, which itself is within the closeness of the cottage, which is within the neighbourliness of the small street, which is within the village atmosphere of Hampstead, within the borough, within the city. And she drew a collection of fat Russian dolls split round their middles, and opening up to reveal smaller and smaller dolls within. It took her some time to draw as she took great pains in the decoration with felt tips of each doll.

That strange hospital session, she thought, with the three of us giving life to a little dead baby keeps reminding me of that frightful film, Freaks. As though we were all rotating in a circle and chanting, one of us, one of us. We accept her, we accept her, one of us, one of us. Oh weird, weird. And then that sexy feeling I got when I held her, it just seemed like it was a complete love experience. I'd never thought about sex in that way before.

Mary took the new Biba diary that Ginny had given her for Christmas, and which had a page for each day. She sharpened one of the pink and white striped pencils, with *Mary* inscribed on each one, from the set which was Jude and Lou's present, and the rubber in the shape of a gorilla from John.

'I almost feel it's my baby,' she wrote. 'Something to do with the fact that it was a kind of joint venture. Almost as though Maggie couldn't do it by herself, and this in itself was extraordinary. I have never known Maggie to take something on she couldn't finish. And then to find that I was actually able to help her to finish the job – well, it was quite an eye opener. It seems I'm not the useless nincompoop I once thought I was!

'Ever since I started writing the story of the other Mary of the 1870s, things began to change a bit. I almost felt I *was* her, and because she was strong and competent and good, then so was I, because she was taking me over so that I could tell her story for her.

'And now, with the taking part in Gabrielle's birth, I feel that I may have taken over a bit of Maggie's character too. And I can understand Mim much better as well. So strange.'

She stopped writing, and read it through, wondering whether she should tear it up and throw it away. Her hands were poised for scrunching up the paper, but she finally closed the diary and put it away in a drawer. It would be an interesting thing to look back on, after all.

John opened up his composition book at school.

'Once upon a time,' he wrote, 'a baby was borned called gaybril and her mother was called maggi and she mite of been hily flayverd like wat the lady was in the song but she never becos it wasnt the rite baby becos he was jesus and mary has to have jesus and heel be much better than gaybril and theyl proberly get marrid and live hapily ever after and rool together and evryboddy will be saved and mary will be hily flayverd like it says.'

20

1st April 1871. A day which should be filled with spring flowers, smiles and happiness, and also be a harbinger of summer days to come. Sad to say, it is not so for me. My poor, dear Richard still does not seem to improve, no matter how diligently I nurse him. He is so thin and weak that I sometimes fear a small breeze will blow him away from me. He has resisted so vehemently the idea of my contacting a physician that I have refrained, but I now feel that my small knowledge of nursing and of the popular remedies of care and love and a good handful of herbs are no longer sufficient. I am beside myself with anxiety and worry, and I have decided that I must, today, call upon Dr Lucas, and ask him to visit us. Perhaps Richard will be vexed with me, but I must take that risk in order that I may administer a more satisfactory treatment for his illness. I am much afraid for him.

Dr Hilary Lucas spent a considerable time with Richard, and came out smiling. Mary saw the smile with much relief; so it is not serious, she thought, as she waited for him to speak. 'May I offer you some cowslip wine? Or tea?' she said into the silent pause. Perhaps he thought it was not her business to know what Richard's indisposition was. 'I am afraid that my nursing experience is meagre, I would be glad to know of anything I might be able to do for Mr Cane.'

'Thank you,' Dr Lucas walked towards the parlour, 'I need no refreshment, but would appreciate a short

discussion on what you might be able to do to make
Mr Cane less uncomfortable.'

Mary was relieved that her mother had not yet
emerged from her own room. Dr Lucas sat in the winged
armchair beside the fireplace, while Mary faced him, sitting a little stiffly in the black windsor that had belonged
to Annie's mother. How right that she had sent for the doctor at last. Such relief to know that she would now have
professional support in her task of nursing Richard back
to health. She cast about in her mind rather despairingly,
trying to think of a suitable topic of conversation that
might put off the essential advice she awaited with such
unadmitted trepidation.

Dr Lucas was no longer smiling. 'I think we both know,
do we not,' he said gently, 'that we can only hope to make
the rest of Mr Cane's short life as comfortable and as
happy as possible.'

So then Mary knew, blindingly, what she had really
known for some time.

The shock was none the less severe. The fact that the
knowledge had been confined and buried for some time
past, only served to increase the potency of the final
dénouement.

'Galloping consumption, of course, as I am sure you
must have realised. All you can do is to burn sulphur
candles in the room, change his clothing when it becomes
saturated with perspiration; give him milk and broth
when he is able to take it; allay his distress, and administer the syrup I will prescribe.'

He was business-like, discreetly sympathetic, but
treating her as the philanthropic neighbour that she
appeared to be. 'Has he relatives? They should be called
immediately. We cannot tell how long.'

'I will find out – I am not sure.' Mary found a smile
stretching her lips as she answered. She and the doctor
were discussing medical details of treatment in a
detached way. Medicines; food; care of the sick; relatives
to be called because he was dying – *because he was
dying.*

The wave of despair all but deluged her, but she clung to the everyday, and saw Dr Lucas to the door, thanking him for his advice and for the prescription, and handing him his fee from her purse. She would inform the relatives. Everything under control. But when he had gone, she could not face Richard immediately. He had known all along. Of course he had known. Her mother must not hear her weeping. No one must hear her weeping. No one must know.

It was a full hour later that Mary was able to compose herself sufficiently to go into Richard's room. Though it lay just beside her own, and she could both hear him and feel his presence through the thin wall, she felt that she needed to gain a little control before they came face to face in the tragedy. To dissolve before him in grief and despair would only serve to ensure his own collapse into hopeless desolation. She wanted to wail and mourn and to shriek her anguish out of herself and into the world about her, but this was unacceptable.

She splashed cold water into her face and tried to reduce the ravages of weeping. She blew her nose and brushed her hair and straightened her dress; all actions of a living being, bearing no relation to the dead residue she had suddenly become. It was she who had died that very morning; she who was now engulfed in the limbo that preceded hell, even while Richard began his elevation towards the prospect of paradise. She had no prospect at all.

She entered his room, smiling. 'I have the prescription,' she said, 'and I had thought to set out straight away to fetch the elixir that will soothe you. Is there anything else that you would wish me to collect for you?'

She had avoided looking into his eyes, and he was silent until she did. After that, all the preparation of the previous hour towards control were swept away in the cataclysmic torrent that drowned them both. Though the grief was still silent and secret from the rest of the house, there was mutual devastation between them.

They clasped each other as a safeguard against being torn apart, and she kissed his face and lips, as though to bring the life back.

'I could not bear to consider your suffering,' he said. 'That was why I did not wish you to call the doctor.'

'You knew it all along.'

'I had suspected for some time, but I did think that perhaps I had been cured by the rest and the Hampstead air. And I would not allow myself to admit that the illness had returned. So deceitful, so cowardly. I should never, never have involved you in my life like this while I had even the least suspicion. I am an unworthy wretch.'

'It was not you who involved me. I was already involved from the very first. We could not have avoided it. It was meant to be.'

They lay entwined in each other's arms as though they were one person.

'That feeling that we have something momentous to fulfil – it still remains strongly with me. And yet how can it be? We have so little time left to us.'

'That we do not know,' Mary said sharply. 'What we do know is that every moment from this one is precious, and must be savoured. And there are such things as miraculous recoveries.'

It had happened once with baby Constance after all. Why not again. But she immediately knew that this was not a part of the present design. This was no oversight that could be remedied; this was all predetermined and predestined. There was nothing she could do.

'Your family,' she said, suddenly sitting up and becoming an individual person again. 'They would like to see you. May I inform them?'

He, as quickly, became Richard Cane, the young man, fatally ill with consumption, who had to get his affairs in order. 'I have no family,' he said. 'I never knew my father, and my mother and elder brother died from cholera when I was six. I was in a foundling hospital, and it was there that my blessed benefactor supported me and

224

saw to my education, so that I was able to start my studies to enter the church. I have failed him most miserably, even as I have failed you.'

'You have failed nobody, my most loved angel. Should we not inform your benefactor?'

'But I know nothing of him, as I told you. I receive bank notes from him in a plain envelope each month. Sometimes an unsigned note to show that he is watching my progress and approving what I do. He seems to see everything, and I cannot tell how.' He took her hand. 'He knows about you for instance. In his last note he wrote: "Your Mary is indeed favoured among women. God blesses you both." It was this that made me more bold than I might otherwise have been in speaking to you.'

'Then he will know that you are ill?'

'I think that he will. Strange as it may seem; almost as though he sets guardian angels to watch over me.' His eyes searched hers anxiously. 'They will guard you too, I am certain. They will support you when . . . You will continue with all the good work you have embarked upon will you not my beloved? And our mutual work? You will keep that up after I . . . even when I am not physically here?'

Tears ran down her cheeks. 'I cannot see any future for me just now. I wish most earnestly to die with you, because to me there now seems no sort of life without you. I pray that God will somehow take us both. I really feel that he will. I think that God will arrange it without either of us having to be responsible.'

'But there is so much we had to do. Perhaps he will show you the way to achieve it on your own.'

'We shall make our contribution together or not at all. We were brought together for a purpose and God will see to it that we achieve that purpose.'

He took her small cool hands in his. Those long, fragile fingers, white as death itself, and that frail smile that drifted almost unnoticeably round the corners of his mouth. 'Into God's hands then . . .'

225

She snatched her hand away and placed it over his mouth in case he should consider adding the remaining words. 'We are still on this earth together,' she said, 'and we have something to achieve *together*, before either of us takes leave of it.'

After the first overwhelming shock of the confrontation with tragedy, life took on the immediate day-to-day unreality of no future and no past. They both clung to the desperation of walling themselves up in each consecutive moment. It was possible to do this, Mary found, as long as she kept herself continuously occupied. She kept a meticulous diary, quite different from the self-indulgent ramblings of any of her previous diaries. She ruled a firm line under the first of April entry, in order to emphasise the ending of her life. After that, it was all short, pregnant statements such as: 'Richard very feverish. Took a little chicken broth. Small dose of laudanum before he retired.

5th April. Very bad attack. Coughing much blood. Left him exhausted and desperately weak.

7th April. Spring cleaned the parlour with Peg. Mr Porter the sweep swept three chimneys; such soot there was.

It was all bearable because it was not real. She was a clockwork toy that had been fully wound, and was now performing perfectly, according to plan until the clockwork ran down.

Mary Stein practised her harp in her room, and listened to the blackbird singing in the lime trees. She was greatly disturbed, but found it hard to discover why. She sensed that there was some convulsive explosion looming just beyond her grasp, and it filled her with an anticipation that was between dread and exhilaration. Something that was just out of her reach and out of mind, that was waiting to engulf, and probably destroy her.

Life at Lavender Cottage seemed to be proceeding without much incident, after the bouleversement of Gabrielle's advent. The sense of maturity and change stayed with the three sisters, unexposed, into the aftermath of the birth. They did not discuss it, but each kept mulling over the new beginning idea in her head, trying to decide whether or not she was imagining it. Maggie and Mim convinced themselves finally that the whole idea of such symbolic reawakening was ridiculous and rather crass. Absurdly euphemistic. The incident of Gabrielle's birth might have brought them closer together, that was all. Don't let's go over the top.

Mary, on the other hand, knew that the bonding of the three of them was deep and very real. Because her mind was still, in spite of the new maturity, devoid of cynicism and guileless in the extreme, she was quite able to accept the union as a probable magical event, and to decide that she was indeed part of an enchanted trinity of sisters who might possibly have some spiritual significance in the world. But one didn't say such things. It would be thought to be a joke.

There was actually no question but that each of them had suffered some sort of sea change. Mary and Mim had both taken on some of Maggie's confidence and practicality, Maggie had realised some of her own shortcomings, and found that her love for Gabrielle actually did pass man's or woman's understanding, and Mim came to the conclusion that sex in a vacuum was fairly unsatisfactory on the whole and began to think in terms of what she took pleasure in describing as meaningful relationships.

Mary realised, in spite of her new-found confidence and a greater sense of security that went with it, that in her case, only a small step had been taken, and that she was still woefully ignorant of many aspects of life. The dig from Rollocks about the likelihood of John being middle-aged before she produced a baby rankled unpleasantly. The eccentricity of her still being a virgin,

227

and of her showing no eagerness to change this state of affairs seemed to strike everyone. No one was able to understand or tolerate it. There were continuous hints of lesbian tendencies. Before, she had thought that perhaps she was as unattractive as some of them seemed to infer, but now she considered more than surface values. The very idea of going to bed with anyone, male or female, and of being moved, or roused, or whatever one had to be, in order to perform the necessary physical connection, left her literally cold. Not horrified, not disgusted, not amused, just completely uninterested. Perhaps this was a part of her that had not matured. She could not see how it would ever do so.

As she sat in her room, considering these questions, a sudden wave of depression, anxiety and fear swept through her with a force that destroyed all thought. It was like a net dropping down on top of her, so that her very movements were constricted, and breathing became an effort of will. She shrank, crouched on to the floor in an attempt to escape the desolation of something she could not identify, and still less comprehend. The fear paralysed her, though she felt that there was an escape somewhere if only she could find it.

After perhaps fifteen ominous minutes, the intensity of the attack lifted minimally, leaving her with a fierce, pulsating pain in her head. It was hardly bearable, and she crawled back to her desk, scarcely conscious of what she was doing, knowing only that it was important to record something. Leave a message? What did she have to tell? Who did she have to tell? Imperative to get it down; that was the immediate task. Something about the newspaper they had found under the floorboards. She took it out of the file and laid it on the table, folded at the marked page. No other body had been found. What had happened to nineteenth century Mary? It was important to find her and rescue her – rescue her. She must be rescued.

'Richard is most desperately ill,' she wrote, 'and my

own life draws to a close as surely as his. God must, I pray, in his mercy, take us together. I have absolute faith that this will be so. We must pass from this life as one.'

With a shudder, Mary stopped writing and put down her pen. Was she mad or something? She had had no intention of writing her book at that moment. She had thought to write up some of her own problems as a possible way of taking her mind off the pain in her head. She had not, in any case, meant to write about illness in her book. Who was this Richard? Mary, Annie and Aaron Abrahams and Peg, these were the only characters she had imagined so far, and the story about them had not revealed itself as yet. But Richard . . .?

Distraught, and with an unreasoning fear, she burst out of her room and ran down the stairs. Maggie was feeding Gabrielle and Mim was telephoning. The room seemed full of people, so she could not rush to her sisters for comfort as she had hoped to do. There was a great deal of noise. The television was on loudly, with John on the inevitable stool far too close to the screen. Mary saw Pete lift John and stool bodily, and place them further back. She saw Penny and Rollocks locked in a passionate embrace. Matt was filling the washing machine with nappies. Jude and Lou were giggling and talking very loudly with a crowd of unknown people invited in for tea. Ginny was there. James was there. Rollocks and Penny; John, Pete. There were people, people, people; a great jumble of people everywhere. Just like hell would be, Mary thought. I have to get out, to get away from the noise. Why can't Maggie and Mim and me be alone together like we ought to be? This isn't a family, it's a mob. This isn't a peaceful, loving community. It's anarchy. I don't belong here. Who are these alien people? I don't know them. They're noisy and crude and vulgar and cruel, and they laugh and jeer and sneer and point fingers at me because I'm a virgin . . .

Her voice came out of her mouth unexpectedly, without any seeming command from her mind.

229

'I'm going out for a few minutes,' she said.

Only Rollocks took note. 'What a very Oates remark,' he said. 'Remember to be gallant and a gentleman, and watch out for the blizzard.'

Mary walked up the street towards the shops. There had been a gypsy selling primroses in the High Street yesterday, and she wanted to put a bunch on the table beside Richard's bed. He so loved primroses. They were a sign of spring and new life. Thank God she had escaped from all that noise and laughter. Street noises were far less worrying. Just the sound of horses' hooves and of children and neighbours calling across the street. Very peaceful and comforting, and the headache and that tearing, ghastly grief that had held her in its grip was kept in check by the simple, everyday fact of walking up a village street to buy a bunch of primroses for her sick lover. All that unreality that appeared to be hanging in a great cloud over her head was no more than a slight indisposition and forgetfulness, brought on by the migraine attack she had obviously suffered. Or was this a dream? Hard to tell, because there was a dream-like quality about this bright spring day in a street that was in some small way so well known to her, and yet vaguely unfamiliar at the same time.

She bought three bunches of primroses and some early, sweet-smelling violets and made her way back to Lavender Cottage. The haven of her life. The heaven of her life. But only a few moments ago it had been hell – hadn't it? Was there not disaster, devastation – obliteration even – behind this elegant black door, with its old-fashioned (or was it chic and trendy, being genuine Georgian?) god's head knocker and its big, clumsy keyhole with the giant key still in it? But there had surely never been a key for that old keyhole; there were all the Banham security locks instead. Such confusion. Unfathomable chaos and distress surged into her mind again, and she rushed into the house, stumbling in panic, up the stairs, for fear she might be

230

too late. There might, after all, be nothing there but the room she had left earlier.

But it was all right. As she opened the bedroom door, and the sun streamed out into the passage, she saw that he was still there, lying whitely in his bed, with the blinding glow of sunlight all round him. Her angel was there, halo and all, waiting for her in all his Crivelli glory. At once, all the apprehension disappeared, leaving only the exhilaration and joy.

'Look,' she said, 'primroses and violets, because they smell of spring and new beginnings.' She knew this idea should fill her full of tears and despair, because this was an ending rather than a beginning. She held the flowers out for him to smell, and as she did so, an instant release of a long-buried desire exploded into her consciousness with frightening force.

They stared profoundly at each other, as though probing towards this unexplored new territory. His eyes were fever-brilliant.

'Mary, beloved Mary, lie beside me and cool me. I am burning. I cannot bear to be alone now. We belong together. I cannot die alone, Mary. I am incomplete, I cannot die when I am incomplete.'

The flowers scattered out of her hands, on to the pillow and all around him. There was no longer confusion in her mind, only strong, bright certainty that all this was ordained, predestined, and meant to be. It was the obvious thing to do.

The stifling restriction of prohibitive clothing rustled and slipped away smoothly. So this, then, was the part of her that had been missing for so long. The part she had been saving up for her angel Gabriel without ever knowing it. With a rush of euphoria, she came face to face with the overwhelming sensation that people called love or ecstasy or desire, and which only that self-same morning she had suffered the indignity of never having experienced.

Was her skin so ice-cold only in contrast to his

231

fever-ridden, fiery body? It was another way in which they complemented each other.

'We are one person,' he said, 'we cannot be divided.' And as he felt his love enfold him, he marvelled that he could once have thought that this miracle in which he was now enmeshed was an evil temptation against which he had been bound to fight for so many years. How could this holy experience ever have been considered original sin? This was a mystical phenomenon that had no place in the tangible world, certainly, but sin? His consciousness swam in and out of reality. One moment he was floating, the next he was unconscious, out of his corporeal body, and a part of the light that flooded the room.

'Oh my angel Gabriel,' Mary said. 'Can this really be the act that some consider unchaste, unvirtuous and obscene? How can that harsh, ugly description fit in with this beautiful, magnificent occasion of love?'

He lay spent and weak, and scarcely conscious. 'Beloved Mary, full of grace,' he said, with his eyes closed. 'Why do you call me Gabriel?'

She placed her cool cheek against his. 'Because you are my Crivelli angel.'

He opened his eyes and smiled. 'The painting,' he said, 'and you are my Crivelli Madonna.'

They drifted again into gentle, floating, non-existence, away from the world.

'Strange,' he said presently, 'because my name actually is Gabriel, but I was so shy of it as a child that I only told my second name when asked. My mother called me Gabriel, and my brother, in the short moments that I remember, used to call me Gel.'

He pronounced it Jel with a soft G, and Mary thought what an inconsequential conversation to be having amidst all this blessed escape from real life. 'My darling Jel,' she whispered to him, 'beloved Mr R. Cane – Jel – Gabriel, can you not take my life into your body, for if you cannot, then I will surely take your death into mine.'

232

'Do not talk so. You must live on.'

And they flickered softly, in and out of reality, sleep and delirium for an unmeasured period of time.

Later that day, Mary could not remember how she managed to be inexplicably in the kitchen, preparing the supper with Peg. There was only one clarity in her mind, and it was more like a vision than a memory. She realised that Peg was chattering, probably had been for some time, but that she had not heard anything of what she said.

'Miss, I'm having ever such a success with Joey Miss.' Peg's voice finally came through. 'I'm teaching him to talk Miss, and 'e's learning that fast Miss. You just 'ave to take it a bit slower Miss like Mr Barber does with me Miss, only even slower than that because he's older than me Miss so he takes a bit more time to understand like. But 'e's really starting to talk proper Miss and 'e's so grateful to me Miss, you wouldn't believe.'

The words began to penetrate, and Mary half emerged from the suspended animation of the previous sensational dream period.

'Talk? Joey talk? But how clever of you, Peg, to help him like that.' It flashed through her mind that she should have thought to do something about Joey's difficulty herself, instead of just taking it for granted. 'You are a good girl, Peg, and a very reliable one. I do not know what I should do without you now.' She felt an urge to pour out her own overpowering news to Peg there and then. To discuss, to explain and to hear reactions. In short, to share the tremendous joy, responsibility and pain that crowded in on her and weighed her down with its enormity.

But there could be no sharing here. Something so overwhelming could not be shared with others, it belonged to them alone.

In the days that followed, there were periods of reality interspersed with periods of bright ecstasy and time

233

passed quite unnoticed. Then, one sunny April morning the Crivelli angel suddenly died, without fuss, without pain, with a smile upon his face, and Mary Abrahams' heart and mind died suddenly with him.

She did not cry, she did not speak and she did not move. It was Peg, with the help of Mr Grebe who knew about these things, who arranged for the church service and the burial. Annie Abrahams was stricken with the disaster of having a consumptive die on her premises, and much more deeply with the sudden and complete withdrawal of her daughter, firstly from her and then from all life itself. Annie realised, reluctantly, and in spite of many misgivings, that she had been genuinely and deeply fond of this paragon of a daughter with whom she had been blessed. The shame, however, could not be overlooked, because it would seem that her daughter Mary had been in love with Richard Cane.

'Such a disgrace,' she wept to Mrs Grimsby, 'that a daughter of mine should so lose her self-control in such a useless infatuation. It is beyond belief, and I can only hope that she will waste no time in pulling herself together before the neighbours begin to talk.'

But days lengthened into weeks, and Mary did not pull herself together. Life seemed to have slipped out of her, and she could do nothing for herself. Annie, somewhat testily, took on the task of getting her up, washing and dressing her, and putting her to bed at night. It could be said that she gained some satisfaction – pleasure perhaps – in fulfilling the task. As though she felt all that she had foretold had come to pass and that Mary was now possibly repenting her folly.

Peg spent long periods trying to induce Mary to eat enough to keep alive, since Annie considered fasting to be a just penance. As Mary wilted, so Peg grew in stature and character, in order to fill the dreadful vacuum Mary left behind her.

'It's up to us, Joey,' she said, 'we got to hold on to things till she gets better, and you got to help me. I can't

234

do it all alone, not like she did, any road. You can do the rough work like the scrubbing and the vegetables and the polishing and that, and perhaps even go to market for me sometimes, so that I can look after our poor dear Miss Mary and see that her mother don't upset her. I got to bring the life back into her, or we'll lose her, sure as I stand here.'

It was only after six months of this struggle for all to survive, that certain facts became obvious. Annie Abrahams was unable to communicate with anyone about it, other than Dr Lucas, because of the terrible disgrace of the whole thing.

'Your daughter is most certainly with child, Mrs Abrahams,' he had said, and what was left of Annie's unhappy world collapsed about her in ruins.

'God had punished me enough,' she said, 'for whatever sin I must have inadvertently committed. I am humbled and humiliated and can take no more.'

Dr Lucas was soberly kind. 'Indeed, you cannot be expected to, dear Mrs Abrahams,' he said. 'The burden is far too great for anyone, let alone someone of your age and standing in society. I would suggest that you have Mary committed to an asylum for the insane, where they will care both for her and for the coming child in a way that you could not be expected to do. For she is, undoubtedly, of unsound mind, and I can see no hope of her recovery.'

It was the only way out, and Annie grasped it gratefully. But there would be difficulty in getting her there. In her present state, she would not venture outside of her own volition, and the idea of a removal by force was unbearable. It was said that they used strait jackets freely. Annie approached Peg who seemed to have some strange influence over her.

'Dr Lucas considers that Miss Mary needs some treatment in hospital in order to built up her strength, Peg,' she said. 'It has been arranged that she should enter the hospital next Wednesday week and I should like you to prepare her for this by assuring her that it is for her own good. You will also accompany her in the hackney carriage which I will hire for the purpose, so that she shall not be suspicious or obstinate about obeying Dr Lucas's instructions.'

Peg was distraught. 'We can't let her go there Joey. It's a wicked thing that she's doing to her daughter. Don't she know what goes on in them institutions?'

'I think – I think she –' Joey said, 'She's – she's a –' The new-found words failed him, but his distress showed in his face. 'You and me,' he said to Peg, 'You and me must . . .'

'Take her away,' Peg finished. 'Oh Joey, we must do that. We got to get her away somehow, before they come for her. I got some shillings put by, and that cart you built, we could get a donkey from one of the farms. Wouldn't cost but a few shillings.'

'Quick though,' Joey joined in.

'Ar, double quick we got to be, and quiet too. Fly by nights, that's what we got to be.'

It took them two days to make their secret arrangements.

'That daughter of old Mrs Whatsername 'oo works at Gardnor House, she married a farmer out Hatfield way, they'd put us up if'n we can get there. And we can sleep rough if'n we don't. The good Lord'll provide always, that I do know. 'E won't let anything bad happen to Miss Mary.'

So at two o'clock, one still morning, the donkey was harnessed to Joey's cart in the stable behind the house, Mary was wrapped in a rug and led silently through the back yard, to be settled on top of the very small bundles of belongings each had gathered together to take with them. The moon appeared fleetingly from behind the dark blue clouds as the small group stumbled its silent way up the twisting streets to the bare expanse of Hampstead Heath and on towards the star that hung in the north sky.

* * *

236

Annie Abrahams realised, when Aaron appeared on her doorstep shortly after Mary's disappearance, that it was not just coincidence. It was obviously the hand of God, and she grasped it gratefully. At any other time, she assured herself, she would have shut the door in his face, but strangely, when she saw him standing there on the step, a great flood of relief spread through her, and of course it was only right that he should bear part of the burden of grief and worry. Suppressed tears, finally released, seemed unstoppable.

Aaron, too, realised that the angry resentment he had built up against her on his way up the hill, collapsed and died when he saw her again. They found themselves, inexplicably and somewhat awkwardly, clasped in each other's arms and experiencing comfort from the embrace.

'Where is she?' Aaron asked, looking round the room. 'Where is she, Annie?'

That was when Annie knew for certain that this visit was no coincidence. Why, suddenly, did he want to know? He could not have heard that she had gone, could not possibly have known, because he had had no contact with the child since he had so wickedly bundled her out into the street, had he? And that was more than a year ago, so why this sudden interest? Unless of course God had sent him forth to take his share of responsibility.

'They took her away,' she sobbed. 'She was ill and I had the whole nursing of her all these months until the doctor advised that she must be taken into hospital for her own good.'

The whole, or not quite the whole story took an hour or more in the telling, because Annie skirted round the disgrace of the pregnancy without ever telling it, but intimating the wickedness of Richard Cane in his vain attempt to lead Mary astray, and of how he was greatly to blame for the unhappy state of her mind in these last few months. However, she added, the doctor confidently hoped she would improve with rest in hospital. 'All was arranged,' she moaned, 'in the best possible surround-ings she would have been, but they stole her from me, those wicked, ignorant servants stole her from me. My only daughter – they must be apprehended and brought to justice. I will not rest until . . .'

Aaron listened to her silently and with great pity. He found himself unwilling to tell of his contact with Mary since the original explosion of his life. The way that she had rescued him from despair and cared for him until he had recovered. How he was now able to approach his painting with renewed vigour and a complete change of mood. How he now spent his life with the poor of the neighbouring districts, with whom Mary had put him in touch; painting them, supporting them, sharing his earnings with them. How Mary had changed his life. This was all private. As was the fact that Peg had brought her to him on several occasions to try, unsuccessfully, to release her from her grief.

Instead, he unfolded a newspaper and pointed to a marked passage. 'God claimed her,' he said. 'She was too good for us.'

'The bodies of a young girl and a middle-aged man were recently discovered in a wood near Hatfield,' Annie read. 'The cause of death has not yet been ascer-tained. A complete set of a woman's clothing was also found nearby, but there was no trace of a third body.'

Annie clasped both hands over her mouth. 'It can't be, it can't be.' Aaron did not know what sin she had com-mitted; did not guess the disgrace. 'It was the devil,' she said, 'the devil took her. The shame of it all.' The tears had dried up with the shock of the news. 'But why should you think this – this story is anything to do with her?'

Aaron twisted his hands together. 'I don't know,' he said, 'but when I read it I somehow felt it must be her. I had this dreadful certainty that Mary had disappeared you see. Felt it in my bones suddenly, last week. Wednes-day, was it? Just as though I had lost a part of me; I knew it then. Was certain of it. She has been taken by God, you mark my words. She was too good, she wasn't meant to be here. I will find out who these two people were, I will see the authorities, but I already know the answer. Too good she was.'

He rocked to and fro on the chair in the front parlour which Mary had used as her own. Annie sat upright in the winged chair by the unlit fire and they both wept for the daughter they had lost, who had perhaps never been completely theirs.

Much later, as he was leaving, Aaron said, 'You cannot manage this place on your own; I will manage it for you and I will employ someone to work for you. And I will visit you regularly now, Annie, to see that you have everything you need.'

She would have wanted him to do that.

21

'She's been gone five hours,' Maggie's voice was high with anxiety. 'Something's happened to her, I know it has.'

All the members of the household were clustered in a restless group between kitchen, dining room and sitting room.

'We shouldn't have let her go,' Mim had tear streaks down her face. 'She looked dreadful when she left. I knew she was in a state, but I didn't sort of register when she said she was going out for a few minutes.'

'You're paranoid, the pair of you, for God's sake calm down.'

'But she was acting so oddly for the past few days.'

'She's been having on and off migraines.'

'You talk as if five hours was a lifetime. Can't see why you're fussing, she could have gone to a movie for heaven's sake.'

'Mary doesn't go to movies without telling us, and anyway, she wouldn't have, not if she'd had a headache. Added to which, she left this incredibly odd bit of writing open on her desk, look, it's under today's date, and seems as thought it's part of her diary, because it talks about her headaches. But then it goes on about someone called Richard being ill, and . . .' Maggie snapped the book shut in an agony of fear, and tried not to think of what she had read there.

'She seemed so depressed, and we didn't do a damn thing about it.'

'Oh Lord, do we have to dramatise everything?'

'Mim's right though, we're all so bound up in our own little miseries, we can't look outside at others.'

There was an explosion of embarrassed laughter. 'Oh please, do we *really* need the moral tone?'

Maggie rounded on them. 'Well why *not* for God's sake? We're all so anxious to laugh things off, aren't we? Do nothing but laugh, laugh, laugh, so that we don't have to be responsible for anything or face up to difficult situations. Just in case any of our friends could accuse us of being uncool enough to take life seriously.'

There was a very awkward silence, then Rollocks made a further attempt. 'I say I say, steady on old girl. Carry on like this and you'll have us all dashing out and joining overseas voluntary organisations if you're not very careful.'

No one laughed, and Ginny said, 'I do actually believe that working for some voluntary organisation would do us the world of good. I shall go and get all the literature tomorrow. You are so right about us Maggie.'

This was light relief, and everyone joined in the amusement, but it faded quickly enough and left them once again in the limbo of indecision and unhappiness.

'We can't very well ring the police,' Matt said. 'It's far too soon, they'd think we were hysterical.'

'Which I think we are – a bit,' said James. 'I mean to say, she's a grown girl, there's absolutely no reason why she shouldn't go off on her own if she wants to. Perhaps she's found a boy friend at last.' He smiled ingratiatingly, which infuriated both sisters. Looking at each other, they realised that there was no point in saying out loud what they both knew to be true – that Mary was in desperate trouble and distress. To admit to the psychic certainty, which they were both experiencing at the time, would have broken the group up in relieved, disbelieving mirth.

'Had we better start by ringing Clare and Sam?'

'I think that's the very last thing we should do. They'd

241

either get into a complete panic, or they'd consider us hysterical like everybody else does it seems. And she'd never go there.'

'So if you're so sure of that, where the hell do you think she would go?'

'I don't know, do I?'

They shifted and drifted aimlessly and unhappily, rearranging themselves in disconsolate uncertainty.

'Maggie and Mim obviously can feel some extra anxiety that we can't,' Jude said at last. 'I think we should ring the police just to alert them, and the hospitals, and some of us might go to the sort of places she particularly liked on the Heath, in spite of it being nearly dark.'

Maggie turned to him gratefully. 'Mim and I will go to Primrose Hill, she loved going there in the evening to see the city with its lights on. And then we'll go on to Parliament Hill after.'

'And Lou and I will come with you, and James, you could ring the police and the hospitals, and the rest of you could do the coffee houses and restaurants between you.' Whoever would have thought of Jude as an organiser? Maggie readjusted her existing character assessments to record the fact.

They galvanised themselves thankfully into action, with no laughter and no jokes, but with an anxious determination that few of them had felt before. They found the sensation curiously exhilarating, coupled as it was with the neglected warmth of looking at the outside and caring for it.

In the three days of intense searching and frightening suffering that followed, each one of them endured an experience that was alien and shocking. There was no trace, no sign, no clue concerning the girl who had once been a part of their lives, and the tragedy forced them all on to a different level of existence. The police added her name and photograph to their lists of missing persons, and were non-committal and professional. 'Don't worry too much,' they said kindly. 'You have no idea how many young persons go missing for a time and then turn up again, safe and sound.'

Sam and Clare were told the morning after the first abortive search parties had returned, empty-handed and dejected. Their lives at once became enmeshed in grief and guilt, which brought them together as nothing else had ever done.

But after the eternity of anxiety, which was in reality only three days, Mary walked through the front door into their midst, dirty, bedraggled, and half dead from exposure.

'I – just – went out – for a few moments. I had to rescue her you see, so I brought her back with me.' She started to cry. 'But the other two – I couldn't – I couldn't – God took them. He'll look after them.' The life seemed to slip out of her, and she collapsed, like a bundle of rags, on to the floor.

It took several days before she emerged from her semi-conscious, torpid state into a life of any sort. Sam and Clare wanted to put her into a nursing home straight away, but the sisters could not allow her to go.

'She'll die if she's taken away from us.'

'She has to be here with us – really, she has to be here, she told us.'

'How can she have told you? She hasn't said anything at all yet.'

'Not actual words, no, but – well, she's – well, given us to understand.'

'She'll be all right if you leave her to us.'

'All right? What do you mean by all right? How do you know? You're not doctors, how can you possibly know if she'll be all right?'

'I insist on a doctor.'

'A doctor won't be any use.'

And indeed, he was not. Mary reacted to his presence with a paroxysm of fear, and clung to her sisters. The doctor prescribed some drugs for her, and strongly advised that she be taken into the London Clinic straight away.

Whether this advice penetrated Mary's conscious mind was difficult to assess, but from the next day, she began her slow climb back to where she once had been.

'Don't let them put me away,' were the first words she said, after which she started to stammer out a long, sometimes incoherent and always confused account of what might, or might not have happened to her during those lost three days. 'What did she mean – I brought her back with me?' Maggie and Mim listened to the jumbled words that streamed out of her mouth but which seemed to make little sense. She talked of angels and primroses and sunlight and the blessed angel Gabriel, who was dying and who was being borne up to heaven in a donkey cart. Joey and Peg sat on each side of God our father which art in heaven hallowed be thy name, she said, and her mother was forgiven because she knew not what she did. Often, a smile would creep slowly across her face and she would sigh deeply and say quite loudly and clearly: 'My soul doth magnify the Lord and my spirit doth rejoice in God my saviour. I am with child by the Holy Ghost,' and sink back into sleep.

'Poor darling,' Mim said. 'She thinks she's the Virgin Mary. God, Maggie, do you think she's really gone bonkers? Or is it just a breakdown? Or is she delirious?'

'I don't know. How can we possibly tell? We shall just have to wait and see. Matt and I think she must have had some ghastly experience that's temporarily sent her round the bend.'

'We've got to get her back.'

'Of course we'll get her back.'

'But no drugs and no doctors.'

'Not at the minute. And I don't think we ought to tell anyone about the dotty things she's saying because if they know, they might insist on her going into a loony bin. She's bound to get better if we can help her.'

And Mary did begin, very slowly and very steadily, to improve. She started to eat and be clear in her mind for part of the day, but lapsed occasionally into some fantastic account of what was obviously a figment of her disordered imagination. As she got stronger, Maggie and Mim tried to encourage her to recount as much as she could remember of those three lost days, however fanciful the accounts might be.

'Three days?' Mary stared round at them. 'But it was six months since he died.' Tears coursed down her cheeks, and she turned into her pillow and cried softly.

'Who died, darling?'

'Gabriel died. My blessed Gabriel died.'

Mim hugged her. 'No, no, Em love, Gabrielle didn't die. Don't you remember? You and I brought her back to life soon after she was born. Don't you remember?'

'And incidentally got me going again at the same time,' Maggie added.

Mary stared at them both and forgot why she was crying. The memory of holding Gabrielle in her arms took over, and she smiled. 'So we did,' she said.

It was not until late summer that her mind seemed to clear completely, apart, that is, from the lost three days. These she could not remember at all, but she had at least ceased to fantasise. There was no confusion any more, just an absolute blackout of memory. But by this time, it was also obvious that Mary was pregnant.

When they realised this, Maggie and Mim talked together with Matt.

'So that's what happened. God, how awful.'

'She must have been raped, and then blocked out all memory of it. How perfectly ghastly.'

'Should we take her to the Tavistock or somewhere, to get it out of her system?'

'We ought to tell the police.'

'Oh no – we can't do that, it would be too cruel for her to be forced to remember it all.'

'Do more harm than good, surely.'

'But suppose it only goes underground for a bit. It might come out later in some awful way, like her not being ever able to accept any sort of sexual relations with anybody.'

There was a moment's silence, as they all thought about Mary's previous apparent sexlessness and wondered whether or not to mention it. Matt said, finally, 'There wasn't much evidence of her having any leanings that way anyway.'

'That's not a very nice thing to say about anyone,' Mim said huffily.

'Don't be stupid,' Maggie said. 'We all know Mary wasn't sexy. There's no shame in that is there? Some people are and some people aren't, that's all. But she was very young and obviously not completely developed.'

'Whatever the state of Mary's sex life was or was not,' Matt said, 'I think we might as well leave things as they are and hope for the best. It does look as though she is going to recover completely, except for having a blank about those three days. And if what we think happened, did happen, then perhaps that's just as well.'

So they sat back, cautiously, to see what the next step might be, though the intense anxiety that had possessed them since Mary's disappearance receded with every day. Mim was disturbed. 'We can't just forget that it happened, and carry on as normal,' she said, 'We ought to *do* something.'

'Nothing we can do at the moment,' Matt said. 'As long as we look after her and see that she's not unhappy.'

'She's certainly not unhappy,' Maggie said. 'I've never seen her in such a wonderful mood. Positively glowing.'

'All pregnant women glow,' Mim said.

'Not when they've been raped by an unknown.'

'But she doesn't know that.'

'I would have expected some sort anxiety, I must say,

she seems to think that the future will be nothing but roses all the way. It's slightly irresponsible if you ask me.'

'Don't be churlish darling. Mary has probably been through hell, we should be grateful that she seems unaffected by the experience.'

Was it because of the shock of reality which had entered their lives that the mood of the whole group seemed to change from that time? Maggie began to feel, after a while, the need to break away from the close companionship of communal life, and the Lavender Cottage mob started to peer out into the nineteen seventies, and think about taking tentative steps into the unknown.

'Can you believe,' Mim shrieked one morning. 'I got that job with the RSC at Stratford, and so did Tony, and he's got a cottage near there so we can share. Oh isn't it neat!'

'Who's Tony?'

'You know, he's that fantastic actor who was in Upstairs and Downstairs.'

'Oh that fantastic actor.'

'You're not the only success,' Lou said. 'I'm thinking of going to the States with some of the Lindsay Kemp group.'

'And I'm either going to divorce him and make him pay me alimony, or I may steal the money to go with him,' Jude said.

'I wish you'd pissoff, darling, there are sure to be far more attractive types than you in the States.'

'Matt and I might be thinking of setting up somewhere on our own,' Maggie said, 'though of course we'd be taking Mary and John with us. We've seen this fantastic derelict cottage-type residence in Holloway.'

'Holloway? What kind of a place is that?'

'It's up and coming.'

'That's what you said to me last night,' Lou said, and there was a burst of the old-style laughter.

'You're so disgusting,' Penny said. 'I don't know how

I've munuged to live with you all this time. I think Rollocks and I are going to move in with Mummy and Duddy for a bit and then get somewhere in the country.'

There was general hilarity at this statement, but when it died down, a sense of sad unease settled in as everyone collected their thoughts together, towards the idea of moving out of the closed community into something which could quite likely be a great deal less secure, less funny, and where responsibility might attempt to catch up with them.

'I don't much like the idea of just trailing off into the future like this,' Jude said, 'just as though all this had never been. As though it didn't *mean* anything to any of us.'

Rollocks sank his chin into his chest and hunched his shoulders in self-conscious discomfort. 'Which of course it did? I only ask in case I'm missing out on something.'

'You certainly are,' said Penny, 'you exclude yourself from most of the human qualities.'

'Like sentimental reunions and meaningful relationships with these disgusting people with whom you find it so difficult to live?'

Penny turned her back on him.

'I think it's a wonderful idea,' Ginny said. 'I've had a super time over the last year or so with all of you. We just mustn't lose touch.'

'I don't somehow think that any of us will lose touch,' Mary said.

'We shall unless we make a special effort,' Maggie said, 'and is it worth the special effort I ask myself.'

'Of course it's worth the effort,' said Mim. 'Let's make a pact.'

'And sign it in blood,' said John. 'You cut your wrist and get a chicken feather and sharpen it and dip it in the blood and . . .'

'Bags use red ink instead,' said Lou.

'I am somehow quite sure,' Mary said, 'that the twelve

of us are going to get together again, sometime in the future.'

'And there, after all, speaks the oracle.'

'So let's say Fagin's or Farquharson's or the Coffee Cup on January 1st 1980 even if it's thundering lightninging or raining,' said Lou.

'You are about the most embarrassing set or people I know,' Rollocks said.

'But you love us really,' Lou insisted.

22

It was at this time that Sam Stein stepped in. Both he and Clare had thankfully accepted the truth that Maggie and Mim were far more able to help Mary in her troubles than they were. Clare hid her guilt in an almost complete opting out of the situation. Having made her insistence that the doctor should be called, and having accepted the failure of this approach, she shrugged proverbial shoulders and tried to put the disaster out of her mind. She had failed, others might succeed; there was obviously nothing more she could do. Her very presence was unnecessary. She pushed the guilt and the sorrow below the surface of her life, and carried on living.

After the anxiety of Mary's disappearance had brought with it the unexpected closeness to his ex-wife, Sam found the re-emergence of his daughter gave rise to an embarrassing sense of anti-climax. He backed away from the whole thing with immoderate haste. 'I told them she'd turn up,' he told his business partner over lunch some time later. 'I somehow never really believed there was all this need for panic.' And he truly forgot the anguish which he and Clare had gone through during those three lost days. It had all been a mistake, and therefore something to be erased from the mind.

'Turned up, right as rain,' he said. 'A sort of amnesia, the doctor said. Nothing to worry about. Pretty well recovered now. Sweet girl, she is, you must meet her sometime. Give her a break from that sordid little squat they live in, along with all those drop-outs.'

'What caused the amnesia?' Joseph Zimmerman appeared really much too unassuming to be the successful businessman that he actually was. He did not look efficient, he did not look aggressive, his clothes and his manner were casual, but for all this, he had built up a considerable empire in the furniture trade in which Sam dealt with the advertising and public relations.

'Who knows what causes things like that?' Sam did not want to be taken back into the confusing and time-wasting realms of supposition and about what led up to a crisis. Things were on an even keel now, and should be taken through from there.

'What about next weekend?' he said. 'I'll get her down to stay for a bit and you can come and meet her.' Poor old Joe had recently lost his wife and had no kids. Young company would do him good. Not a very social type, too quiet for his own good. He and Mary could cheer each other up. Sam lit a cigar, well satisfied that with this simple gesture he could benefit them both. Kill two birds with one stone in fact. There was the nagging uncertainty, hidden away at the back of his mind, that he possibly had opted out of his responsibility a little, where Mary was concerned.

He called at Lavender Cottage that evening to make amends, and was flattered by the welcome he received. He suddenly felt like a father, and was surprised at the strength of the sensation, which he had never really experienced before. Was it because he had reached a period in his life that was slightly stagnant, he wondered.

'Well hallo my little ducks,' he said when Mim and Mary both came to the door, which was in any case wide open to the street. 'Don't you care about being invaded or burgled or anything like that?'

'Oh Pa, how good to see you.' They both hugged him at the same time, causing a confusion of arms and kisses. 'We don't have anything worth stealing,' Mim said, and Mary added, 'And we like being invaded. Maggie!' she

251

called up the stairs, 'Sam's here,' and there was immediate activity all over the house. Doors opened and a crowd appeared from all corners to view the new phenomenon of Sam the Father.

Sam's satisfaction grew at being the centre of a curious group, who seemed to consider him without particular animosity even though he could, presumably, have been termed an enemy alien. He actually had a brief feeling of belonging, which rather shocked him.

'I had the idea of asking Mary to come and visit me,' he said. 'Seeing as how she's not been too well of late, I thought some country air would do her the world of good. She could also give my new house her blessing.' He sensed a movement of awkwardness on remembering that none of them had seen the house, and looked round the room rather vaguely. 'I'd have you all down,' he said, immediately regretting the turn of phrase, because of the large number of people in the room who might have considered themselves included in the invitation, 'only you might not all fit in that easily.'

'We fold up quite small,' Lou said helpfully.

'And we're practically no trouble,' said Jude.

'But you're homosexual,' Rollocks said, 'so that puts you right out of the running.'

'I don't see why,' Lou argued. 'We're ever so legal, after all.'

Sam's smile began to look forced, and Mary rushed to his rescue, 'I would love to come and stay with you,' she said, 'when can I come?' She had the sudden, unexpected desire to walk off with Sam straight away, there and then. 'Now? immediately? I have very little to bring.' It was perhaps less a desire to stay with Sam, than a wish to be away from the all-enveloping crowd of the present. She wanted to feel solitude and quiet, so that she could begin to allow her own thoughts space and time to expand either backwards or forwards in time. 'Will you take me down with you now?' she asked.

It was not until that moment that Sam noticed his

252

daughter was pregnant, and he almost let out the gasp of surprise that he felt. 'Of course,' he said mechanically, and Mary ran from the room.

'Will somebody tell me what's going on?' he said explosively when she was out of earshot. 'Doesn't anyone think it necessary to inform the grandparents any more?'

Maggie spoke quickly and under her breath. 'We were going to tell you, but we hardly ever see you, and it's not a thing you can hand out breezily on the telephone.' Her voice dropped to a whisper. 'We think she was raped during those three days you see, only she doesn't remember anything, and in her less lucid moments – which are very rare now – she is inclined to say rather odd things.' There was a short pause. 'Probably – sort of – excusing the whole thing I suppose. I mean she says things like God gave her the baby, or the Holy Ghost or something. Virgin Mary and all that stuff.'

Sam was literally speechless, which was as well, because Mary returned with a Union Jack carrier bag, slightly overflowing. 'There, I'm ready,' she said, beaming her pleasure. 'Not that I'm suggesting we leave straight away. We could have a cup of tea perhaps?'

'Sam would like more than a cup of tea, I'm sure,' Maggie said rather sourly. She could not help feeling slightly nettled at Mary's enthusiastic response to the invitation, and was annoyed at her own pettiness. 'We have some gin, and I think some vodka.'

'Vodka,' Sam said, his smile now looking permanently stretched. Along with most of the world, he could not consider such things happening within his own family, least of all to Mary. He was appalled at the thought of spending one to two hours alone in a car with his ravished, pregnant daughter, without having any idea how to cope with her possibly deranged reaction.

He need not have worried. After the first few minutes, Mary kept up a mostly unrelated stream of conversation all the way down to Goring-on-Thames, precisely because she knew of his fear. 'You don't have to worry about me, Pa,' she said, as they crawled through London towards the A40. 'Whatever they told you about me, it's only what they *think*. They don't know what happened during those three days any more than I do at the moment. But I think one day I will remember it all properly. Even now, I am quite sure that it was something good that happened, not something bad. One day I will tell everyone, but not yet, not now. I'm still a bit confused, so you and I won't talk about it, all right?'

'Your choice my pet, just so long as you're not unhappy.' He felt a certain relief. 'But anything I can do, you know I'm always there. I won't interfere, but you only have to ask.'

'I'm anything but unhappy now,' Mary said. 'At first I was a bit afraid, but not any more, and everything gets better and better every day. A sort of fulfilment thing – can't explain so I won't try, and I promise to call on you for help if I should ever need it even though I don't think I am going to need it. Now tell me about the new house. Has Clare seen it? Will anyone else be there?'

She found the unhurried, uncluttered atmosphere of the large, luxurious house on the banks of the river unashamedly comforting. Sam had recently broken up with his last lady, so that there was only a friendly, housekeeping couple to contend with, and they were only vaguely and politely interested in an unexpected daughter of their employer. Sam came and went in between business commitments, and there was even a small rowing boat to make her isolation more complete. The situation was idyllic.

Joseph Zimmerman was asked to lunch the Sunday after she got there.

'Rather a sad man,' Sam told her before he came. 'A bit anti-social after the death of his wife, so I'm not asking anyone else.'

Mary was relieved to know that it was not to be a party. The idea of people starting to intrude on the new

254

solitude she envisaged did not appeal. A business friend of Sam's would not need her attention.

But of course things turned out differently. After lunch, Sam fell into a deep sleep in the garden, where they were drinking coffee and brandy, and Mary felt herself obliged to make polite conversation to the rather dull-looking middle aged man sitting beside her.

'Can you row?' she asked him rather desperately.

'As well as the next man,' he said. 'As long as the next man doesn't happen to be a rowing blue.'

'You are a restful person,' she said later, as he rowed her inexpertly up the river. 'I don't have to make an effort to talk to you, and that's very nice, because I am so tired of making efforts.'

'What sort of efforts do you have to make?'

'Efforts to get better, efforts to remember, to convince my sisters that I'm not mad, efforts to keep a secret.'

'Quite a lot of efforts. But you certainly don't need to make them with me. You can even tell me your secret if you want to. I don't have anyone I could ever tell secrets to, so I'm boringly safe.'

Mary paused to consider. She sensed an unusual bond that seemed to have developed between herself and Joseph Zimmerman, and wondered what it could possibly be.

'I've had a most wonderfully strange experience,' she said, 'but I can't quite remember what it was.'

'That sounds very promising,' Joseph Zimmerman said. 'Perhaps I can help you to remember.'

But how could he? Mary thought. So why the sense of certainty that he could? Be realistic. It was just not on.

'I seem to have become a different person,' she said. 'Sometimes I don't quite recognise myself. When I think back, I remember myself a weak, indecisive sort of person who had no self-confidence. But now –' She stopped and turned towards him, smiling. Of course he could help. 'Now there are times when I feel as though I could

255

conquer the world. I am quite someone else,' she said, 'who has a fiery spirit inside her.'

Unsure what she was waiting for, Mary stayed on, relaxing uneasily in the still atmosphere of that hot September. There was a solitary silence surrounding her days that emptied her mind of irrelevances, and when in her boat, the absence of earth beneath her feet enhanced the sensation of floating outside reality.

It was during one of these golden periods of stillness, when she was alone in the boat, that she first heard the voice.

'Well Mary,' it said, 'I hope you realise your good fortune and your responsibility.'

She did not have to answer, of course, because a presence that could make itself heard, could naturally read thoughts.

What does it mean, good fortune? she thought, needing some clearer indication.

'I mean your baby, Mary. Has the penny not dropped yet?'

The baby gave a kick inside her and turned itself around.

Well not really, she thought. She knew somehow that the whole thing was a colossal stroke of good fortune, and that she was being specially favoured in some way; that the normal expectancy dreams of pregnancy were enhanced a hundredfold in her case, but why this should be the case, she had not yet worked out. All something to do with those lost three days.

'But I've given you so many clues,' said the voice, 'I thought you would have picked it up by now. In fact you seemed to have understood it at one point, until you had this psychological forgetting.'

'Perhaps I didn't want to face up to the responsibilities,' Mary said, remembering with the very back of her mind something that she still could not contemplate bringing forward.

'Understandable,' the voice agreed, and there was a moment's silence as a robin warbled and there was the quiet plop of a fish jumping. Mary watched the ripple rings widening, with her heart beating painfully because of what was about to be revealed, which she knew already.

'You know really what it's all about, don't you?' the voice continued. 'The carol puts it very nicely I think, and I'm so fond of the tune.' A heavenly choir immediately started up:

'The angel Gabriel from Heaven came
His wings of drifted snow, his eyes as flame.
All hail, said he, thou lowly maiden Mary,
Most highly favoured lady, Gloria.

For known a blessed mother thou shalt be,
All generations laud and honour thee.
Thy son shall be Emmanuel, by seers foretold,
Most highly favoured lady, Gloria.

Mary joined in the third verse, sitting there, alone in a rowing boat in the middle of the river:

Then gentle Mary meekly bowed her head,
To me be as it pleaseth God, she said,
My soul shall laud and magnify his holy name,
Most highly favoured lady, Gloria.'

There was a sound of clapping in the air, or was it in the heavens? 'Oh well done,' said the voice, 'well done indeed. You sing so beautifully, really delightful that was. So there you have the picture.'

'But you can't mean –' Mary gasped. 'I mean why me, of all people?'

'An obvious choice,' the voice said. 'Gentle, loving, meek, innocent, virginal.'

'But –'

'But me no buts.'

'You said that to me before,' said Mary.

'That was several moments ago.'

'Several moments ago?'

'Several moments or a hundred years. What's time between friends?'

'I've never had to take responsibility. I'm not capable.'

'Rubbish, girl, Mary Abrahams had all the qualities, except she was lacking on virginity.'

'But I'm Mary Stein.'

'Mary Abrahams and Mary Stein, together with Maggie and Mim Stein are one and the same, haven't you understood that?'

'No,' said Mary huffily. 'It's all so far fetched and ridiculous and I don't believe it. I mean, what is this? Are you actually saying that my baby's going to be the Saviour of the world and be called Jesus or something?'

There was a sudden rustle among the leaves of the golden trees. She could have sworn they were laughing, and looked up at them angrily. Even the voice sounded amused.

'No, innocent one, things don't usually repeat themselves. You will have a girl, and you will call her Emmanuelle.'

'I was sure it was going to be a boy.' Mary felt decidedly let down. 'But oddly enough, I had already decided to call him Emmanuel.'

'I know,' said the voice.

'I suppose you know everything.' Mary said rather sharply.

'Well in a way I do,' said the voice, 'but there is a certain amount of free choice. No point otherwise.'

'Absolutely no point,' Mary agreed.

The voice took on a slightly different tone. 'Three sisters will bring forth three girl children,' it intoned, 'Gabrielle, Emmanuelle and Seraphine, and this trinity will be thrice blessed, and of this trinity Emmanuelle shall be called the daughter of the Highest.'

Mary shivered, and became cold and very afraid. She looked round her and saw that the light was beginning to fade and that a large orange moon hung overhead.

But of course none of this was true. All in her mind which was still not as stable as it might be. She picked up the oars purposefully and started to row towards the opposite bank.

'That Joseph Zimmerman,' the voice called after her, sounding much more homely this time, 'he's a really good man you know. You should take him into your confidence.'

'Is he another of your coincidental arrangements?'

'I thought he might be a help and support to you, but it's your choice, my dear.'

Joseph was walking down through the garden as she manoeuvred the boat into the bank, and she had to admit to a glow of pleasure at seeing him there. But it was all too pat, she didn't have to go along with the arrangement. There was such a thing as free will.

'I came to ask you to take dinner with me at the pub,' he said. 'Will you come, and we can talk about remembering strange experiences and what they mean, if you would like to.'

'I would love to,' said Mary, feeling relieved, and anxious to share her problems. 'There is a great deal about which I would like your advice. For instance, if you hear voices it means you're schizo doesn't it?' There was no harm in telling all to a stranger, because it didn't really matter that he might think her mad. It was important to get the reaction of an ordinary man in the street.

'So some people say,' he said. 'But being schizophrenic needn't be all bad. Look at Joan of Arc.'

But as she walked up the garden beside him, the enormity of the whole thing suddenly struck her like a deluge of icy water. 'Oh Joe,' she said, catching at his hand. 'I am truly in a fix and I don't know which way to turn.'

He put his arm round her shoulders as they walked towards the house. 'We'll find a way,' he said, 'I'm sure we'll find a way.'

23

Mary stayed on with her father, remembering everything slowly, with the help of Joe and the river, and the quietness of the silent September. It was not until the days shortened and the night air crisped that she felt the necessity to return to everyday living.

'I think I ought to make it forty days and forty nights,' she said to Joe, 'just to fit in with all the biblical references.'

'What the seers foretell,' Joe laughed, 'but the symbolism is all so hopelessly mixed in your case. A lot of red herrings I would call them.'

'Mixed allegories rather than mixed metaphors. Just to be sure we don't take things too seriously. To be certain we can look back and laugh if it doesn't come off. So that we can say to ourselves that it was only a joke and we didn't really mean it.'

'Perhaps.'

'Should I tell the others?'

'Only those directly concerned, just to prepare them.'

'Maggie and Mim you mean? So strange that I don't need their support any more. It's almost as though I have to support them now. Couldn't do without you though.'

They sat, isolated, in the boat, among the mists, the mellow fruitfulness and the wailful choirs of gnats.

'It isn't really true, is it?' Mary said.

'Shouldn't think so for a minute,' he replied.

When Mary made the break from the poetic unreality

and arrived at Lavender Cottage without prior warning, she found that the others were all in the process of some adjustments and transmigrations. She was made very welcome, almost as though they had considered her lost to them.

'Lost lamb returns to the fold,' Rollocks called out as she entered the open front door. 'What about serving up the fatted calf?'

'Darling!' There was a shriek from Mim as she charged into the hall and clasped Mary to her. 'You rat,' she said. 'Why ever didn't you tell us you were coming?'

'If she'd known you were coming, she'd have baked a cake,' Lou said. 'And if you'd been four days later you would have missed us. Just imagine that, because we're off to California in the morning.'

'New York next week,' Jude corrected. He hugged Mary. 'It's so good to see you again. Without you, the cottage has not been the same.'

Mary noticed, with shock, genuine feeling in his voice. She kissed them both, still locked in Mim's embrace, and became the centre of the excited, noisy mass which she found herself enjoying greatly.

'Did you really miss me?' she said. 'I was being such a drag, I thought you must all be delighted to be rid of me for a bit.'

'You look great,' Maggie said. 'I've never seen you looking so well, but why didn't you tell us you were coming? We'd have arranged a party or something.'

'I didn't really know until last night,' Mary said. 'It's taken me all this time to sort myself out, and only yesterday did the whole thing resolve itself and fall into place. Took me quite by surprise actually.'

'You must tell all,' Maggie said.

Everyone moved into the sitting room and ranged themselves in the age old way on cushions and chairs and sofas, wherever there was space. Mary viewed them all affectionately, delighted to be in their midst again, and in the house that had been the scene of so much of her life.

'We're going to get a little house,' John said. 'Maggie and Matt and Gabrielle and me are going to buy a house and there'll be room for you there, but not for Pete because he's got a job in Clapham and Ginny and James and Lou and Jude are going to America and Rollocks and Penny are going to live with her Mum and Dad and Mim is going to Stratford with a man called Tony to act in Shakespeare and you're coming with us and some American people are going to live here and pay us a lot of money so we are going to be very rich.'

'Not a bad précis of the situation,' Maggie said. 'But it's still all in the wind. What do you think of the idea? We couldn't imagine selling this place but thought we might make a bit of money out of it which would help us to pay off a mortgage. Would you hate to live with us in Holloway? You could get a place on your own later if you felt like it, after you've had the baby I mean, though we'd love having you and the baby living with us if you wanted to.'

'I think it's a wonderful idea,' Mary said. 'But as it happens, I have got a few plans of my own. Much as I'd love to live with you all, I've had a – well, a sort of offer myself.'

'Offer? What sort of offer?'

'Someone wants to marry me.' She started to laugh, and the whole group joined in.

'*Marry* you? But who?'

'How *great*! Can I come to the wedding?'

'Can I be bridesmaid?' This was Lou, and Ginny, of course, clasped both her hands and said, 'I'm so *glad* for you Mary. What a wonderful man he must be,' which made for more laughter.

'Things which could have been better expressed,' Rollocks said.

Ginny looked at him angrily. 'What have I said?' she asked.

During these various reactions, both Maggie and Mim had remained stunned and silent, and Mary now turned towards them. 'I wasn't going to tell you until I believed it myself, but last night we both realised – we both knew what we had to do.'

'But who is it?' The sisters spoke together, still suffering profound shock. They had not been prepared for this. It amazed them that Mary could have taken such a step without either of them suspecting anything.

'He's a friend of father's. I met him down there.'

'But why didn't you tell us?' They both felt anger and resentment at this sudden, secret life that they knew nothing of. They felt betrayed.

'I just didn't know. I told you, I've been going through a sort of rebirth. I didn't want to talk about it until I knew what it was all about.'

There was a slightly hostile silence, and the rest of the group, except for John, who by this time had the television on, began to melt away tactfully to allow the family to sort out its problems without interference.

'Well,' Mim affected a bright smile. 'At least you can tell us now.'

Mary looked from one to the other. Her own smile was full of warmth, and an understanding of their displeasure. 'Not until you stop being cross,' she said. 'You don't have to feel responsible for me any more. I suppose I've grown up at last.' She hugged them both. 'It's not that we're drifting apart or becoming separated or anything like that. We're still a complete unit, the three of us, and we always shall be, but in the last few years, since we've been at Lavender Cottage in fact, we've become individuals, and therefore not so totally dependent on each other as we used to be. Don't you see that? For all her practicality, Maggie wasn't really a very balanced character on her own, nor was Mim, and I certainly wasn't.'

Mim made a face. 'So now we're all beautifully well-balanced and boring.'

'Probably.'

'All right, so we're not upset by your infuriating secrecy. Get on and tell us.'

'His name's Joe Zimmerman.'

'Nice, down-to-earth Yiddish name.'

'Mary Zimmerman – not bad I suppose, if you like that kind of thing. Go on.'

'He's quite a bit older than me, forty-five in fact,' she said, and then carried on, rather too quickly, before they could comment. 'His first wife died a year or so ago, and they didn't have any children, and so he's terribly excited about the baby.'

They looked at her, unbelievingly. 'Are you sure? Sounds too good to be true.'

'He's the sweetest, kindest man that you could possibly imagine.'

'They all are to begin with.'

'Specially when they want something. Is he penniless and expecting to live off your money?'

'Can you imagine any of Pa's friends being penniless?' Mary give a giggle. 'As a matter of fact, he's incredibly rich and has this colossal farm and stables in Berkshire *and* a string of race horses.' She collapsed into laughter. 'I just can't get used to the idea of being so rich, but it will be nice to be able to give lots away to good causes,' she said.

'So let's turn the last question round. Are you, in your new role as an independent individual, changed beyond all recognition, intending to marry him for *his* money?'

They were all laughing by this time. 'You're crazy,' Mary said. 'I am completely in love.'

'And about time too,' Mim said. 'But as it's your first experience of the phenomenon, I don't think you ought to marry him, because calf love doesn't last, you know, and anyway, who marries anyone these days? It's all so unnecessary, isn't it?' She paused for a moment's thought. 'I don't know though, with all that money, you ought to get things tied up properly at the start. You'd be mad not to.'

'Trouble is,' Maggie said, 'he really does sound too good to be true. I mean, an old man with far too much

264

money who wants to marry a girl who's pregnant by somebody else. He *can't* be any good. There aren't such people. And if he's just doing it out of kindness, that's no good either.'

'He's probably kinky and only likes schoolgirls.'

Mary smiled at them. 'We love each other,' she said, 'and we always shall. I know I can't convince you of that, and I can't really explain it to you adequately, but we are quite, quite certain that this is the right thing for both of us. It's something we have to do. It's ordained.'

Both sisters looked at her sharply, with some anxiety. Looking back at them, Mary's heart sank as she considered just what to tell them. Was it really necessary to tell them at all? But she owed it to them to let them know, she supposed. The knowledge would take time to penetrate, so the sooner she told them, the better.

'You see, I've been chosen,' she said, and blushed.

There was a confused silence, and then Maggie said, 'Well good for you, pet. Joe's obviously got impeccable taste.'

'I mean I've been chosen by *God*.'

The silence became embarrassingly prolonged. Maggie and Mim shot sidelong, despairing glances at each other. Was this a relapse? Just when they thought she had finally recovered? It was too depressing to bear thinking about.

'What has he chosen you for, darling?' Mim said it carefully and slowly, and Mary laughed at her studied caution, but then her heart went out to her sister. How could she be expected to understand or believe when she didn't really believe it herself?

'I know it sounds crazy, but ... ' she took a deep breath and placed her hands over her stomach, 'but it's been revealed to me that this baby is God's baby, saviour of the world sort of thing, and that Gabrielle, and Mim's baby, when she has one, are all somehow involved.'

Maggie was rigid with shock. 'Does Joe know about this? Have you talked to him about it?'

'Of course I have. We've talked of practically nothing else. He's as unsure as I am what to believe, but he doesn't think I'm *mad* – not in the medical sense, anyway – but he's so wonderfully understanding, and he doesn't think it *couldn't* be true, he's just open minded about it and hopes I'm right.'

There was another long drawn out stunned silence.

'I know you all think I was raped,' Mary said finally, 'and then just shut it out of my mind by forgetting. But that's not what happened at all.'

'You *do* remember?'

Mary put her hands to her head, as though trying to compress small, individual portions of her brain into a comprehensible whole. 'Not exactly, not in an actual sense, because it was something like a dream, only much more than a dream. It was an experience, like a . . . like a . . . well, a visitation I suppose; and it was all absolutely wonderful. Something I was watching and yet a part of – you know how you do that in dreams.'

Mim opened her mouth to say something, but could think of nothing adequate.

'But you seemed so . . . somehow odd and tragic when you came back,' Maggie said. 'Stunned, sort of. Do you remember that part? Why were you so sad?'

Mary sat down on the floor, and for a moment they were afraid she had retreated from them again, because the radiance slipped away, and she sat, still and withdrawn, until the silence became unbearable, but at the same time unbreakable. Maggie felt a fearful despair, in case she had inadvertently undone all the agonisingly slow improvements they had all been at such pains to build up.

'So much grief,' Mary said suddenly, and tears ran down her cheeks. 'The joy and the ecstasy were somehow all mixed up with despair, sorrow and death.'

She saw a still, shrouded figure; the face was white, like the sheet that had cocooned the body, and her eyes were blinded with a new flood of tears. 'Oh the death, the death of my heart, the death of my soul and at the same time the light of the world was there and I was in the centre of it and yet outside it, because my death was also my birth and my reincarnation.'

'Oh God,' Maggie thought. 'What have I done? She's flipped completely. She obviously hasn't really recovered at all. I should never have asked her if she remembered. These hallucinations are the result of a hopelessly unbalanced mind. My sister is insane.' She also started to cry, turning her head away so that the crying should be hidden. Mim had her face buried in a cushion in an attempt to quell her own fear.

'I had to rescue someone, you see,' Mary said. 'Actually I had to rescue myself so that the story could carry on. But in doing that, I became someone else. I became myself, in fact.'

There remained no doubt in either of her sisters' minds: Mary was mad, and would probably never recover completely.

The intensity of the emotion all round her seemed to penetrate the unearthly atmosphere that had wrapped itself round Mary during the past few moments. She appeared suddenly to see her sisters again, and at once reverted to the joy, rather than the sorrow and mystery of the situation.

'Don't be such idiots,' she said. 'It really isn't a disaster, I keep telling you, and I'm not out of my mind, whatever you may think. It's just that something wonderful has happened to me, and I want to share it with you, just you two and Joe, that's all. I'm not going to tell anyone else because they wouldn't understand and they'd probably give me valium and lock me up; but I had to tell you because you're really a part of me, and you are involved in the whole thing.'

Mim and Maggie struggled with their panic and dashed tears away in their attempt to appear normal and at ease. Humour her; go along with what she says;

she must not suspect they considered her statements to be anything exceptional.

'There was grief, you see,' Mary switched as suddenly to a sad stillness. 'Terrible, blinding grief at the loss and the death, but the sensation of ecstasy was so mingled with the sorrow that I find it impossible to separate the two. I don't expect you to understand, because it wasn't an earthly feeling at all.' She paused. 'It was such an immense sensation that it blotted out my whole life for a time. I didn't remember anything about it after those wonderful, incredible moments until much, much later, when I was staying with Sam and I met Joe. He helped me to remember.' She took hold of her sisters' hands. 'You don't have to worry about me, nor about what I've told you. Joe can cope with me and he wants to. I know I shall be happy with him because he's all part of the miracle you see. You can just forget the whole thing for the time being until it starts to happen, really you can.'

Maggie and Mim left their hands in Mary's and felt acutely embarrassed. It was a disaster.

Later that night, Maggie, Mim and Matt whispered together in the dark privacy of Mim's bedroom.

'She's stark, staring bonkers,' Mim said.

'It's religious mania,' Maggie said. 'What on earth shall we do about her?'

'She's just not completely out of the wood yet, that's all,' Matt's voice belied his certainty. 'We've got to give her more time.'

'But she sounds so sane.'

'They usually do.'

'And what about this Joe bloke? She says she's told him everything and that he understands. Do you think he's crazy too?'

'Doesn't appear to be where business is concerned.'

'Poor darling little Em,' Mim said.

'We should try to get her to see a psychiatrist at the Tavistock,' Matt said.

'And I think we ought to talk to Joe at least.'

'But no one else.'

'Absolutely no one else, not even Sam and Clare unless they say something first.'

'I'm sure she'll get over it in time.'

They emerged, rather stealthily, from the secrecy of their surreptitious plans, and found the house strangely silent. Mary was sitting, quite alone, on the floor of the sitting room. Each sister felt her own degree of sheepish guilt about discussing Mary behind her back. Had she heard? Would she feel hurt? Would she start to mistrust? Maggie and Mim felt deep grief that the loving sister trinity might possibly be in the process of dissolution.

Matt faded out of the room, quietly, and Maggie and Mim sat down on either side of Mary, unsure what to expect. Mary took their hands again and smiled at them.

'Don't worry,' she said, 'You really don't have to. Everything is going to be all right, I promise you. Everything is going to be wonderful.'

Her smile grew, and her outstandingly blue eyes suddenly appeared dramatically large and dominant. Her gaze had something that seemed almost hypnotic and overpowering about it. Her loose, blue maternity dress draped itself over her swelling body and spilled in folds on to the floor where she sat upon the heaped cushions.

Maggie and Mim stared in surprise at the individual so suddenly transformed into an almost unrecognisable stranger. Was this truly their little sister, so lately dependent upon them both? So sweet, so silly and so vulnerable? Was this really just one member of the family trio? One point in the triangle?

John's small treble voice could be heard upstairs at that moment, practising to Pete's recorder accompaniment: 'Hail Mary, full of grace,' he sang.

THE END

The Governess
Patricia Angadi

This is a sophisticated book, so confident in intention and execution that the long shadows of THE TURN OF THE SCREW do not dim its effectiveness
VICTORIA GLENDINNING, SUNDAY TIMES

How should Mable Herring ('Herry'), governess and heroine of this intriguing first novel, be regarded? Is she a saint or a devil? Did she manage, against considerable odds, to hold the Lane-Baker family together for many years, or was she the instrument of its destruction?

Herry is engaged as governess by Eleanor Lane-Baker in the summer of 1918, and her appointment is itself the conclusion of a battle between Eleanor and her husband, Edward. The couple have six children and for his growing, pleasant, middle-class family Miss Herring, so calm and competent, seems the ideal companion. Yet from the start, Eleanor has her misgivings. She has the uneasy feeling that she engaged Miss Herring against her better judgement because of some inexplicable power.

But is it really this which causes the destruction of the family, and is it based on reality or a distortion?

'I had to read on, mainly because Mrs Angadi has such an acute knowledge of the habits and foibles of youngsters *en familie.*'
DAILY TELEGRAPH

0 552 99201 1

BLACK SWAN

The Done Thing
Patricia Angadi

'Angadi's writing is filled with acute observations of
English mores under strain. The period and setting makes
the novel doubly interesting'
TIMES LITERARY SUPPLEMENT

'Miss Jones, you do know, do you not, that Mr Hiremath's
religion allows him to take more than one wife?' Heather
Hamilton Jones is asked by an anxious Registrar when she
marries the charming, ebullient and irresistible Mohendra;
for in the 1940s it was certainly not the done thing for a
girl with such a solidly middle-class upbringing to marry an
unknown Indian, however beautiful, brilliant and
fascinating. But Heather is so overwhelmed by Mohendra
and by the freedom he represents that nothing her shocked
parents or bigoted brothers can say will deflect her.

'Refreshingly traditional in its style – coherent,
unashamedly readable – the marriage of a conventionally
bred upper-middle-class English girl to a mercurial Indian
intellectual, a marriage contracted in the war-time London
of the 1940s when such unions were rarer than today, and
in Heather's world of governesses and nannies, tennis and
formal dances with programmes, not at all "the done
thing". Thought-provoking entertainment'
BRITISH BOOK NEWS

'Mrs Angadi has a vivid and descriptive style of writing
and this portrait of a marriage seen over the years in all its
various aspects is compelling to read'
OVER 21

'Handled with freshness and authority'
SUNDAY TIMES

'A most attractive book. Patricia Angadi writes with
enormous verve'
FINANCIAL TIMES

0 552 99248 8

BLACK SWAN

A SELECTED LIST OF
OTHER BLACK SWAN TITLES

☐	99198 8	THE HOUSE OF THE SPIRITS	Isabel Allende	£3.95
☐	99313 1	OF LOVE AND SHADOWS	Isabel Allende	£3.95
☐	99248 8	THE DONE THING	Patricia Angadi	£4.95
☐	99201 1	THE GOVERNESS	Patricia Angadi	£3.95
☐	99185 6	THE DESPERADOES	Stan Barstow	£3.95
☐	99193 7	A RAGING CALM	Stan Barstow	£4.95
☐	99186 4	A KIND OF LOVING	Stan Barstow	£3.99
☐	99189 9	WATCHERS ON THE SHORE	Stan Barstow	£3.99
☐	99187 2	THE RIGHT TRUE END	Stan Barstow	£3.99
☐	99321 2	B MOVIE	Stan Barstow	£3.95
☐	99159 7	THE GLAD EYE AND OTHER STORIES	Stan Barstow	£3.50
☐	99176 7	JOBY	Stan Barstow	£2.95
☐	99075 2	QUEEN LUCIA	E.F. Benson	£3.95
☐	99076 0	LUCIA IN LONDON	E.F. Benson	£3.99
☐	99083 3	MISS MAPP	E.F. Benson	£3.95
☐	99084 1	MAPP AND LUCIA	E.F. Benson	£3.95
☐	99087 6	LUCIA'S PROGRESS	E.F. Benson	£3.99
☐	99088 4	TROUBLE FOR LUCIA	E.F. Benson	£3.95
☐	99202 X	LUCIA IN WARTIME	Tom Holt	£3.50
☐	99281 X	LUCIA IN TRIUMPHANT	Tom Holt	£3.99
☐	99228 3	A FINE EXCESS	Jane Ellison	£3.95
☐	99257 7	THE KILLJOY	Anne Fine	£3.95
☐	99130 9	NOAH'S ARK	Barbara Trapido	£2.95
☐	99056 6	BROTHER OF THE MORE FAMOUS JACK	Barbara Trapido	£3.95
☐	99117 1	MRS POOTER'S DIARY	Keith Waterhouse	£3.95
☐	99210 0	HARNESSING PEACOCKS	Mary Wesley	£3.99
☐	99126 0	THE CAMOMILE LAWN	Mary Wesley	£3.99
☐	99082 5	JUMPING THE QUEUE	Mary Wesley	£3.50
☐	99258 5	THE VACILLATIONS OF POPPY CAREW	Mary Wesley	£3.99
☐	99304 2	NOT THAT SORT OF GIRL	Mary Wesley	£3.99